Everyone, regardless of their feelir
and clapped. The dancers bowed. Augusta ......,
not before glancing my way with what looked to me like a
cruel smile. The music changed to "Orchids in the Moonlight."
Daniel held out his gloved hand for me.

I strode to him, seeing nothing but Daniel. Old wounds reopened. My pulse raced as I recalled his affair with Rhonda. I
took my position in his arms and muttered, "So, how often
were you...uh...*waltzing* with Augusta behind my back?"

He looked aghast, then quickly readjusted his expression
for the onlookers with a fake smile. He said, "Exactly the
mood for a tango."

"You think?"

"This wasn't exactly planned, Georgiana. Dixie couldn't
come to half the practice sessions. I'm happy, however, despite your mood, if it goaded you into dancing in public."

Hyper-aware, I felt the beat of his heart as we performed
what was essentially a rough sex act to music, in public. "You
didn't answer me about how much time you spent with Augusta."

He twirled me out, then reeled me in. I sneered at him,
digging my index fingernail along his cheek but not deep
enough to draw blood. I heard every musical note over the
voice in my head screaming, *bastard, bastard, bastard.*

He entreated, "Augusta was kind enough to fill in for Dixie
Metcalf. It was the only way I knew to make you show these
gals what you could do on the dance floor. We practiced waltz
steps a couple of times. *Nothing else.*"

The music ended. "Liar." My eyes raked his face more
sharply than my nail had.

His eyes pleaded, but I gave no mercy. The ovation
brought me to the present. I tried to remove my hand en-
closed in Daniel's, but he would not relinquish it. Stuck together, we bowed as I bestowed upon the BILL members a
stare ten times colder than Augusta's had been.

Ripping my hand from Daniel's, I stalked to my chair,
grabbed my purse, and started to leave the room. I was too
hurt and angry to cry. Humiliated in public, again.

Alarmed at the turn of events, Lourdes looked over at
Janet and signed a slicing move against her neck. She
mouthed, "End it."

Janet dashed behind the screen and turned off the music.

I tracked toward the double-door entryway like a train, but Lourdes ran after me. "Don't be angry. Please, Georgiana, listen. Dixie couldn't come today. There's nothing between Daniel and Augusta." She blurted, "It's not like her and Mendez." Lourdes' hands flew to her mouth. "God, forget I said that."

I stopped and took a much-needed breath. "Interesting. Homicide just crossed my own mind. Maybe Mrs. Mendez once felt the same way."

Lourdes went pale.

Another BILL member meowed. "Watch out. Rumor has it Augusta's affairs start in the men's card room then move to the bedroom. Maybe this time, she stopped off on the dance floor."

"Shut up," Lourdes snapped. "Drink your wine and keep those comments to yourself. Besides, the men's card room is off limits to women, just as ours is to men."

I searched Lourdes' face. "Yes, that's true, isn't it?" I grabbed the lifeline of a shaky truth.

"Sure it is. Now, you go over there and make up with your husband who only did us a favor."

Before I acted on Lourdes' suggestion, the social director rushed in, practically knocking us aside. A uniformed police officer followed.

Sharon scanned the room and zoomed toward Becca Bernstein, indicating Mrs. Bernstein should follow her behind the screen. Standing just outside the screen, the officer said something.

Becca came out from the screened area, went white, and swayed.

Daniel, the only other man present, rushed over in their direction. "What's wrong?" He brought over a chair and the officer helped Becca into it.

Sharon wrung her hands.

"No, you're wrong. It's a mistake." Becca wailed in decibels that would put a commercial airliner's jet engine to shame. "Benny would have called me if anything was wrong. He always carries his cell phone when he jogs. My Benny's not dead, I tell you. He can't be. Certainly not from any god-damned heart attack."

MERRY ACRES WIDOWS WALTZ

Nan D. Arnold

Whimsical Publications, LLC

Florida

Merry Acres Widows Waltz is a work of fiction. Names, characters, and incidents are the products of the author's imagination and are either fictitious or are used fictitiously. Any resemblance to actual events or persons, living or dead, is entirely coincidental.

To purchase the authorized electronic edition of *Merry Acres Widows Waltz*, visit www.whimsicalpublications.com

Cover art by Traci Markou
Editing by Brieanna Robertson

Published in the United States by
Whimsical Publications, LLC
Florida

ISBN-13: 978-1-936167-41-8

Printed in the United States of America

ACKNOWLEDGEMENTS

To Jeanie and Jan

PROLOGUE

Something was wrong.

"Son of a—! A flat tire." Manny Mendez cursed his luck.

His shortcut through Mandalay had been ill conceived. Stalled in this defunct residential development, little more than a spiffy brick entrance wall and overgrown esplanade, he sat in his car on the lone paved road that sliced through sandy soil lots covered in charred slash pine and palmettos. The latter, victims of lightning strikes helped along by last year's drought.

Though deserted, it was still probably safer to change a tire here than if he'd taken the longer, direct route to I-95 from his house using busy Kanner Road.

Didn't matter. He blew out an exasperated breath and gazed upon the expanding sunrise. It was early yet and he'd allowed time for traffic. Besides, he was meeting friends for breakfast in Boca, so it was no big deal if he was late.

He opened his glove compartment and fished for the key to disengage his tire rims. Presently, he heaved his five-foot-nine frame, amply fleshed, out of the sedan. Too bad he'd closed on the sale of his auto dealership weeks before; otherwise, one quick call would summon someone with a demo. He wasn't complaining. His had been a Japanese import shop and he'd sold before the brake pedal woes hit.

As usual, Manny had come out ahead of the game.

He'd cleared his golf clubs out of the trunk and lifted out the tire and necessary accessories to change the flat one when another car pulled up.

He recognized the woman alighting from a BMW. Judging

from her scowl, he doubted she'd forgotten their last encounter or the reason for it. She sallied over, arms crossed in a defensive posture.

Nope, she hadn't forgotten.

Odd anybody else would drive through what Manny considered his own private shortcut. Only his wife Pilar knew he'd taken this route today and she was abuzz about some upcoming social do at the club. Curious. His wife seldom attended such functions, usually busy with their children and grandchildren. Or shopping.

Occupied with the chore at hand, Manny braced for some quip about bad karma or a screaming match. He studied the tire punctured by an ugly three-inch nail, which he'd probably picked up on the drive through Mandalay. The place radiated bad luck. He wouldn't drive through here again no matter how much time he saved.

His visitor had yet to say a word so he initiated conversation. "Hey." He positioned the jack, curious about her dressy attire. "On your way to church or something? Why the gloves?"

"Woke up in a June Cleaver frame of mind."

Always a glib remark, one of the reasons he was glad they'd parted company. He grunted, positioning the jack. "Hand me the jack handle, would you?" Her shoe tip came in view as she pushed the tool an inch closer to him. *Designer* shoes, of course.

"This thing?"

"Yeah."

"Happy to oblige."

CHAPTER ONE

*Days later, in the clubhouse of the Barrier Island Golf &
Country Club*

I quake like an activated fault line whenever I speak to
any group larger than three, so why then, was I standing
here waiting on twelve strangers who would check out my
social invention, the Barrier Isles Ladies of Leisure Club? And
me.
What if nobody shows up?
Frankly, I was surprised at the number of women who responded to my blurb in the club newsletter Daniel had goaded
me into placing. They'd sounded enthusiastic about my lunch-
bunch idea, at least during telephone conversations. All had
prepaid for today's luncheon, so there should be a fair turn-
out.
Pacing an annex off the club's dining room, I stared out
wide, twelve-foot high windows overlooking a man-made
lake. It was almost one o'clock according to my Movado. The
watch was an ABC gift—meaning Anniversary, Birthday and
Christmas gift—from Daniel during happier times in our marriage. Outside, the lake, like most retention ponds throughout
Merry Acres, resembled a bead of jasper spilled from a broken string.
Two choices stared me in the face: run away or get this
show on the road.

Merry Acres, a planned community in south Florida, catered to the over-fifty crowd. After Daniel and I looked over several communities in the area, I pressured him to buy here. Why? I can't say exactly, but this place sort of called to me.

Two other couples left their table as I entered the dining room. A few golfers were working off their food minimums as well. From experience with Daniel, I suspected they were comparing score cards, reliving every drive, putt, and waterhole horror story of the day. We greeted each other casually while I walked over to the area reserved for my group.

Georgiana, what in the world were you thinking?

As women in social settings are wont to do, we'd draw conclusions and make judgments today. I wondered what they'd think of me. I pulled items from a satchel and placed them on the baker's rack near an entry door to the private dining area.

Sitting down at the center table, I drummed my fingers. The hair coloring I'd selected was off one shade and had been left on too long. I should have colored my hair weeks before, not last night. This product covered the grays all right, but the dark brown aged me beyond my fifty years.

Presently, a woman in a white pin-tucked shirt and black twill pants approached. "Hello, Mrs. Duncan." She looked at a clipboard and we went over a limited selection of menu items.

"It all sounds wonderful." My mouth was awfully dry. "May I have some water?"

She poured ice water from a pitcher, frosted from condensation, into an empty glass and set it down before me.

"Thanks."

She smiled in return and left.

Minutes later, two women paused at the entry to this area.

"Hello." I put on my best social maven smile. "Are you here for the Barrier Isles Ladies of Leisure luncheon?"

They entered and the taller of the two said in a voice as commanding as her appearance, "You bet. Barrier Isles Ladies of Leisure. B-I-L-L. I like it. I like it."

"Sit anywhere." I disliked meet-and-greets, but they were a necessary evil. "Please initial the guest list next and jot your name on the blank card stock. Toss it into the straw hat on the baker's rack."

A trim, well-dressed woman with platinum hair and strong features in a wrinkled face drawled, "Why? Will there be a prize drawin'?"

"No. This is a working club. Hostess duties rotate to each member so no one is weighed down with the full-time responsibility." Better get that settled right off the bat. I was *not* getting saddled with this job every time we met, even if I did initiate the thing.

"That's fair, I suppose." The woman with the southern accent turned back to the doorway.

Huh? Was she measuring the distance for a fast break? If so, she changed her mind because she eased into the chair beside me. "I'm Dixie Metcalf. You're—? Sorry, darlin', memory fails."

"Georgiana, Mrs. Daniel Duncan." Okay, what next? "Lovely dress." It was, too. A pale green georgette number that implied fifties retro-chic. Only a pill box hat and wrist-length gloves were missing, although she wore the era's requisite pearls and a unique brooch.

"Thank you." Her eyes wandered over me, but I felt confident my blue suit with a peplum jacket passed muster. "Your ensemble sets off your hazel eyes." She leaned closer. "That's Augusta St. James who came in with me. She writes a column in the *Merry Acres Gazette*. Look!" She clucked. "She's checking out the guest register. Augusta's the sort has to know everybody's business. Don't you, Augusta?"

"Don't I what?" Augusta asked with amplified vigor.

"Act as our resident busybody."

"I'm merely curious," she replied.

Augusta would stand out anywhere for her height alone. The beige shirtwaist dress she wore exposed gym-taut arms and a trim waist set off with a belt. Probably the athletic type. Bare, leathery-tan legs bespoke of time on the tennis court or the golf course.

She stared back at me, her head tilting slightly. "I know." She snapped her fingers. "You bought on Carnoustie Way." She looked down on one of the table tops and ran her fingertip across the cloth. "Say, you made a good buy."

"Credit for that goes to my husband's sound negotiation." What a joke. Remodeling and unforeseen repairs would slash any profit we might someday realize. Still, it was I who demanded we move to Merry Acres.

Dixie reached over and patted my hand. "Goodness, cold as ice. Warm heart, I suspect."

One reason I avoided church was my cold hands. Yet, I felt a connection when her hand touched mine, or thought I did. Something niggled at me. Oh gosh, had I met her and forgotten the occasion? That was crazy. Until recently, the move had consumed all my time.

Dixie nodded toward Augusta, fingering cheery yellow mums in the small vase on her table, brighter for their contrast to the white linen backdrop. "We're both single. I'm widowed myself. Fact is, most of us 'round here are." Her delightful giggle had a girlish quality. "You know about that legend, don't you?"

"No."

"You haven't heard about that? Well, I'll fill you in. All this land was owned by one family for generations. They operated a trading post way, way back. The last family member had hold of it was a woman, Meredith Montgomery. Meredith and her husband tried a citrus grove, but that failed. Then, they tried some commercial crop or other. Tomatoes? Nothing better than Florida tomatoes in winter, you know. That is, unless it's corn. That didn't work out either. Years went on and Mrs. Montgomery's heart was set on keeping the land in her family. The couple was childless, you see. Her husband thought otherwise—"

"Dixie loves that foolishness. Where is everybody?" demanded the gray-bobbed Augusta.

I answered, "On their way, I hope."

Dixie huffed. "I'll finish my story later, darlin'." She gave Augusta a sour look. "When our conversation isn't apt to be rudely interrupted. Augusta has a point, however. It's twenty past one and I'm famished."

With no answer for the others' tardiness, I remarked on Dixie's jewelry. "Interesting pin."

"Isn't it?" Dixie giggled again. "It's hard to read, but teeny, tiny rubies create three lower case letter *a's*. Chester, my late husband, gave it to me. He called me his Triple-A baby."

"How sweet." I recalled Daniel's love offerings when first we met, most sold off to cover debts.

"Ches sold bonds on Wall Street in his younger days. Triple-A is the gold standard for bonds."

Before I could comment, the woman who'd served me water strode in with wine. "Chardonnay, ladies. First glass on the house for you early birds."

"Obliged." Augusta took a seat. "I'll fill in at this table. If we get a fourth, I'll break out a card deck."

Dixie snipped, "Not today, we are not here for cards." She looked at me with a self-satisfied grin.

I basked in her kind eyes. They were a startling blue, the sort colored contacts provided.

Dixie said, "Augusta writes a column in the *Merry Acres Gazette*."

Hadn't she already said that?

"What's your background?" Augusta asked. "You look young to retire."

"Daniel retired a year ago. When we relocated from Florida's west coast, he wanted me to keep him company." The truth? I wanted to keep an eye on him. "Before that, I was the office manager for his insurance agency." A scab the size of China, etched on my heart after Daniel's affair, threatened to tear loose.

"I'm still working," Augusta said. "Part-time for the benefits." She rolled her eyes. "Certainly not for the salary. I'll be eligible for Medicare a couple years hence." She smirked. "That is, if Congress doesn't push back the starting age as they did with social security."

"It's my turn," I said, "to say that you look much younger."

"Thanks. Dixie's a retired dancer." Augusta playfully waggled a finger at Dixie as if in "gotcha" for Dixie's earlier exposé on Augusta. "She danced on stage in The Big Apple, too, in her salad days. A dance school teacher before that."

I teased Dixie. "I thought you entered the room with Loretta Young-like flair."

"Thank you."

Augusta chortled. "You should see her after a stiff martini. Then she's The Mambo Queen."

Dixie uttered another sweet, lighthearted giggle. Before she could strike back with a bold rejoinder, a gaggle of gals sallied into the room and she turned her attention to them. "Hey, y'all."

"Greetings, Dixie," one responded.

"Well, glory be, the town crier is among us. Hello, Augusta," another woman said before she nodded at me.

I urged them to sign the guest book and complete a card before tossing it in the hat. "At some point, we'll need to create a directory of members."

More women arrived.

Cliques formed at the door then broke like braces of exotic birds as each woman took her turn and signed in. A woman in the crowd asked, "No name tags?"

"No." *Big mistake.* "Hi, I'm Georgiana Duncan."

First names chorused back then vanished like burst bubbles before I could attach mental markers.

Everyone eventually settled into faux-bamboo folding chairs and wait staff bustled about pouring water and taking drink orders.

"Isn't this wonderful?" Dixie encouraged.

Emboldened by Dixie's support, I stood. "You have me at a disadvantage. I spoke with most of you over the phone, but haven't met you until today."

In response, there were nods and smiles, wholehearted and otherwise.

One vacant chair caught my attention. "I know some of you enjoy cards."

Augusta gave a thumbs-up reply.

Who hadn't kept her word about coming today? I wondered, and rambled on, "Some of you practically live on the links." A last minute personal crisis could befall anyone. "As for me, I've no memory for cards, or patience for golf. Even the treadmill in the club's fitness room makes me feel like a gerbil on a wheel."

Everyone smiled at this and I relaxed with the ice breaker joke out of the way.

"Anyway, I know how precious your time is and appreciate your coming."

Pleasant reactions came from the assortment of colorfully arrayed women. They looked liked foil wrapped candy pieces. I wondered if the majority were hard or soft-center types. Overall, my lifetime experience with women was checkered, starting shortly after birth.

Augusta brayed, "Don't sweat it, Georgie. You'll know us all before dessert." She twisted to face one of the women seated on either side of her and started talking.

Georgie? I detested that nickname, but let it slide.

"Fishing for that column," Dixie whispered.

"Could be," I agreed.

A stout woman with brown, curly, chin-length hair stood up at the next table. She slapped a napkin at droplets on black pants. "Thank goodness it's only water. Will this group be a weekly lunch thing?"

"Something like that," I said. How should I know? I was ad-libbing.

Augusta said, "Sounds good to me, only don't request we hold meetings in members' homes. I haven't cleaned since global cooling."

Several laughed.

"I see it as get-togethers open to whatever chairwoman of the week envisions."

Expectant looks drilled into me. One member said, "Some of us leave for our summer homes. That will seriously crimp membership numbers."

"Oh? We live here all year." Oops, did my brow furrow just then? That would make deeper creases at my forehead and I was afraid of Botox. "I'd wanted to meet women for shopping, lunch dates, and so forth."

The woman who'd checked the menu with me stood in the doorway awaiting the command to serve the entree. Though one chair remained empty, I nodded a go ahead. "Anybody know our missing attendee?"

Everyone looked at the empty chair.

"I'll check the register."

"Good idea, Georgie." Augusta signaled for another glass of wine.

At least the Ladies of Leisure now stood at a dazzling dozen rather than an unlucky thirteen. One name on the list lacked a corresponding initial beside it. "Anyone know Pilar Mendez?" I went back to my seat.

An attractive Latina nearer my age than the others spoke up. "Hi, I'm Lourdes Valdes. Only Mendez I know around here owned Mendez Motors, on Useless One. She referred to the name locals assigned U. S. Highway One, the main drag through the county. "It's his wife, Pilar."

A blonde woman, younger than most of us by a decade, wearing what looked to me like a designer sundress and bolero jacket, chirped, "You know, I've seen Mr. Mendez around the club, but I seldom see his wife."

"I've noticed that, too," Dixie said. "Who told me he retired?"

"I bet you read it in the *Gazette.*"

Dixie chortled. "Selling subscriptions, too, Augusta?"

"Whatever it takes." Augusta waved her hand airily. "I'm buckin' for a raise."

Meals were served. Near time for coffee and dessert, the social manager for the golf club marched in wearing a crisp dress and starchier expression. From her posture, I expected unpleasant news.

Augusta read the signs too. "What's up, Sharon? Someone double park under the porte cochere?"

I wasn't disappointed. When she delivered her news in a hoarse whisper, I couldn't strangle a response. "Oh no!" My reaction drew attention like mosquitoes to exposed skin at twilight.

"Foul play's suspected, that's all I know," Sharon said loud enough for those close by to hear.

Dixie exclaimed, "Murder, you mean?"

I took a breath, and announced, "Apparently, Mrs. Mendez's husband was murdered."

A hush fell. The thud of Augusta St. James' chair hitting the low-pile commercial carpet broke the silence when she made a beeline for the retreating social director.

I overheard someone say, "Who would do that, and why?"

"Bad service?" somebody else said.

Still someone else said, "Perhaps a romantic trade-in gone sour?"

"That's ugly gossip," Dixie reproached.

"But motivational," Augusta said, halfway out the door.

At some point, servers hurried in with dessert, but I knew from the group's antsy mannerisms that the news about Mr. Mendez had essentially terminated the gathering. I quickly spoke up. "Somebody pass the hat to me so we can find out next week's hostess." The first card I drew was blank. I drew two more, they were also blank. I shuffled through them. "They're all blank!"

"Poor taste," Dixie mumbled.

Indeed, dear, but so is yours.

Dixie said, "Since snow birds will soon fly the nest, one of you ought to step up."

"Volunteers?" I asked tentatively, wondering if I should grab a napkin to dab the egg on my face.

Silence.

Yep, hard-center types just like the aunt who raised me.

Dixie said, "I'll oversee the next meeting, but let's meet every two or three weeks. Same time and the same place, if I can arrange it. Is that okay with y'all?"

Coiffed heads bobbed affirmatively.

"Thanks for the bailout, Dixie." I rose. "This concludes the first meeting of the Barrier Isles Ladies of Leisure." Sprinkling ice drops in my closing, I said curtly, "Thank you all for coming."

Members fled, chattering as they went. I'd bet fifty bucks the topic was the untimely demise of Mr. Mendez. A few approached to say they enjoyed meeting me and looked forward to future luncheons. Others confirmed imminent departure for cooler climes.

"News about Mr. Mendez provided quite a finale for the B-I-L-L," the thirty-something blonde said. "I'll act as treasurer next time if you like."

"Thanks, there's not much to do at this point. I'll refund Mrs. Mendez's check. Is that Lilly Pulitzer you're wearing?" I asked.

She nodded. "Uh-huh."

"Pretty." So were her shoes. "Sorry, what's your name, again?" I fished for my car key in the black satchel, pushing aside the straw hat that held the blank cards nobody had filled out, and a small metal money box I'd brought in case anyone showed up who hadn't mailed their dues beforehand.

"I'm Susie Esterhause, Mrs. Karl Esterhause. You've probably seen Karl at the clubhouse pool, his second home."

Dixie covered her mouth with a liver-spotted hand sporting a salon manicure. "Susie is one of our few married ladies." She turned to Susie and teased, "Can the BILL trust you with money? You're at the Merry Acres mall more than I."

"Just window shopping."

"Oh? Every time I see you, you're wearing something new, vibrant, and stylish."

"Not really." A blush stained Susie's neck. "I haven't heard many positives about Manny Mendez. Still, the man just retires, and wham, he's dead. I bet retirement weighed on him. You know how men are in our society. You are what you do. Obsessing over it, he apparently grew careless."

Dixie retorted, "In his case, something stronger than retirement weighed in."

Susie said, "There won't be many tears for him unless they're the alligator variety."

Curious, I asked, "What do you mean?"

Susie and Dixie exchanged startled glances.

"Nothing," Susie said, accepting the cash box.

Dixie languidly applied a fresh coat of lipstick. "Poor Mrs. Mendez." She replaced the tube in a palm-sized purse, then gently tugged at the guest book, which I released to her care. "I'll take this with me."

"See you in two weeks," Susie tossed back, the metal box banging against her hip.

"See ya." I rolled up the hat and addressed Dixie. "I don't know Mrs. Mendez and the circumstances are grim, but I'd like to show her we're thinking of her. Maybe we could call on her together? Take her a casserole or something."

"Sounds like a plan." Dixie patted my arm and, again, some unspoken connection made me feel as if I knew her. "Call me." With a smile, she acknowledged another woman, the one who'd brought up summer homes. Dixie said, "Here's my ride home."

They moved off toward the powder room and I stood alone raking my memory over where I could have met or seen Dixie before today.

I overheard Dixie say, "A murder. Isn't it terrible?"

Summer Home snipped, "Maybe he got what he deserved."

Obviously, Mr. Mendez hadn't a reservoir of good will among these women. Still, the awful news had dampened my BILL inaugural. "A bad start," I mumbled, especially since not a single woman bothered to fill out a card to determine the next chairwoman.

That still rankled.

All my life, I had made friends at work. Finding myself a workhorse put prematurely to grass, even temporarily, put me at loose ends. My plan to stay home for a year rather than drive south to the next county where the jobs were was perhaps rash. Thus far, any gains in working out problems with Daniel were negligible, but I'd only half-heartedly participated. I'd promised to give our marriage a second chance and meant it at the time.

Outside in the parking lot, I unlocked Daniel's blue-and-white vintage Corvette.

Unlike the previous week, when a cool snap plunged nascent April temperatures to the low sixties, today's mercury skimmed eighty, and the humidity had risen with it, encouraging me to remove my jacket. Remembering milk for Daniel's daily cereal, I dashed into the Merry Mart, a convenience store within the gated community.

After leaving the market, located less than a mile from home, I drove along landscaped winding roads. Transplanted palms waved their fronds at me. Wood storks honked complaints, chastising golfers for turning the birds' former scrub pine playground into manicured fairways. Egrets pecked in lush fairway grass for insects while my thoughts gravitated to Mendez and the peculiar responses to his death. The legend of Meredith Montgomery that Dixie had alluded to floated in, and then out of mind when I opened our garage door.

The SUV parked inside indicated my husband was home from his nine-hole game with our next-door neighbor.

Daniel came out with a half-eaten sandwich in his hand. A speck of mustard dabbed the corner of his mouth. "How'd it go?"

I climbed out of the car and wiped away the mustard with a fingertip as he thrust out his cheek for a kiss. I obliged with a brief lip smack on his cheek. "Okay, except the affair was hijacked."

"Hijacked?" The smile in his brown eyes vanished into an expression of confusion.

My return gaze couldn't match the warmth in his. Truthfully, my grudge-holding nature was stymieing our reconciliation. "The social director pranced in to announce Mrs. Mendez couldn't make the meeting because her husband died today, murdered, no less." I pulled off my sunglasses.

"Murdered?"

"Yep. Mr. Mendez ran a local auto dealership." I twirled my Ray-Bans. "Lots of cynical comments were bandied about, like bad service." I leaned into the car tossing my shades onto the center console to avoid Daniel's eyes, adding, "Hints of a less-than-monogamous married life, too."

Daniel took another bite of sandwich and chewed and chewed. Twenty times or more. "That's too bad."

"Yeah." I'd once found his masticating obsession endearing. Now it annoyed me but, unlike me, he never suffered digestive upsets. I pulled out the stuff piled in the passenger seat.

The aging process had been kind to my six foot tall, 68-year-old husband. Then again, Daniel took every nutritional supplement he read or heard about. This, combined with great genes, resulted in glowing good health as well as a hefty credit card balance. Occasionally, his back gave him fits, but golf could be blamed for that.

Daniel took the grocery bags, the satchel, and my purse, setting them on the Vette's hood before putting his arm around my shoulders.

His hands traveled up and kneaded my neck.

Could his fingertips feel the tension there? The malaise that snuck up whenever he touched me? "Better move the milk, the hood's still warm," I warned.

He placed the bags on the hood of the SUV. "Any playmate possibilities?"

"A couple." I breathed in the beachy smell of his suntan lotion. "Everybody scattered at the end, jabbering about Mendez, naturally. Not knowing Mr. or Mrs. Mendez, it's hard to relate on a personal level." I moved beyond his reach. "Many married members, unfortunately, are seasonal residents who will leave soon. However, I clicked with a refined southern type who's a tad forgetful. Then, there's a columnist for the *Merry Acres Gazette*. She's...interesting. Most year-rounders are widows. Busy ones."

He polished off his lunch and dusted his hands together. "Widows, huh?"

"Darn. I just thought of something."

"What's that?"

"Mrs. Mendez moved from the meager married side of the BILL roster to the plentiful widow side."

"So long as you don't, dear."

"Merry Acres is a regular Mecca for widows." I reached for the milk. My stomach knotted. If I scrutinized the heart of our marriage for love, trust, and romance, the usual qualities in a successful union, I might as well be a widow.

Daniel blocked the access to the back door. "Widowhood is not a problem for us. I'm in fine fettle." He hummed "Blue Skies" and offered me his hand.

We box-stepped around an abbreviated space in the cramped garage.

Yes siree, Daniel could be charming. I pulled away. "It's hot in here and I want to change."

"Aw, come on." Daniel picked up the tune again and we danced to his off-key serenade, sidestepping bags of potting soil, a dorm-sized fridge, and enough golfing equipment to open a pro shop, not to mention the cars. The cart garage, awaiting a golf cart one day, was crammed with boxes and furniture that hadn't made the first cut in the decorating lottery.

Daniel dropped me into an unexpected deep dip. "Whoa," I said. "You're frisky."

He pulled me up abruptly. "Uh-oh." He released me and grimaced. "The old lumbar."

"Fine fettle, eh?" I rubbed his lower back with obligatory strokes that lacked the authoritative tenderness of true affection. "Come along, Mr. Astaire. Methinks you need an ice pack."

"By golly, Merry Acres is deadly. To think, nearly done in while dancing in my own garage."

I gave him a sardonic smile as I gathered up the bags. "Hardly ballroom conditions, dear." I taunted further, "You know what they say?"

"Most accidents occur around the house? Due, I'm sure, to tiresome 'honey-do' chores."

"No." I opened the backdoor entry off the garage and stepped inside, holding the door open for Daniel. "Retirement kills."

CHAPTER
TWO

A week later, the mood inside 112 Carnoustie Way matched the thunder and lightning outside.

"Daniel," I huffed, "can't you find your own pants?"

My husband, wrapped in a towel as damp as I'd probably made his hopes for a pleasant afternoon with me, stood in the doorway to our kitchen looking forlorn. He moved closer and leaned over me to wash his hands at the sink where I was scrubbing a large Idaho potato.

"Can't you see I'm busy at the sink? Honestly, Howard Hughes' reputation for obsessive hand washing is nothing compared to yours. Ever consider the powder room sink? It's close by."

Daniel sighed.

"What? Is Lord Chamberlain channeling the rules of appeasement to you?" I affected a snide tone with a British accent. "'Poor Daniel,' he must tell you, 'how gingerly one must tread on the egg shells of domestic diplomacy.'"

Daniel's lips thinned further. "I'll check the dirty clothes hamper in the laundry room for the pants. I'll even wash them, but, remember, I haven't the same regard for lights and darks as you have." His size ten flip flops slapped along the tile floor as he headed down a hallway.

"Whatever," I called after him. Vexed, I scrubbed vigorously enough to peel the spud with nothing sharper than the brush in my hand. I rinsed and dried the vegetable, then, with gusto, pierced it with a fork.

Neither lost clothes nor Daniel's hygiene-happy ways had brought on this snit. Almost a year and several sessions with a marriage counselor later, I was still slogging through betrayal's aftermath. Instinctive, playful intimacy remained wounded behind the enemy lines of a private war, possibly mortally so. Did I love Daniel enough to right things or was fear of an unknown future motivating me to stay? Probably both, maybe neither. We weren't rolling in dough. The job market was tight, especially for anyone over fifty. This was selfish, shallow thinking, I knew, but I was nothing if not practical.

Refocusing on meal planning, I figured I'd stuff the baked potatoes with bacon and leftovers. Chicken was thawing in the fridge for supper, the same thing we ate most nights. How should I prepare it tonight?

"I'll get it," I cried, when the phone rang. "Probably a contractor calling to say he can't come tomorrow because more rain is expected, or an invasion from outer space, or some other excuse." I snatched the receiver from the cordless phone, expecting to duel with one of the three contractors working on our house.

"Hey, Georgiana, it's Dixie."

"Hi." Nearby, the chirp from a computer chip announced the oven had preheated to 400 degrees and stood ready to accept my potato. "Nice to hear from you." My unchecked sarcasm hopefully implied "finally." Not all women were like that two-timing family friend, Rhonda, or my runaway mother, and neglectful relatives. Or, Aunt Irene who'd fobbed me off on child welfare services first chance. But I gave every new woman I met a test of sorts.

"Georgiana, honey, I regret not returning your call earlier," Dixie said. "My arthritis flared up, one of the nastier consequences of a career in dance. I called my family doctor in Georgia who suggested I see an orthopedic specialist. 'Course, earliest I could get in for an appointment as a new patient is two or three weeks. Might as well wait till I visit Georgia and see my regular physician for my annual checkup. I'll just gobble aspirin in the meantime."

"I'm sorry." So, Dixie had a legitimate reason for forgetting me. "You're going to Georgia? When?"

"Don't worry, darlin', I'll hang around long enough to chair the next BILL meeting. I'll be back and forth to visit after that."

"Good." I would not budge on the rotating chairwoman idea. "I called you about visiting Mrs. Mendez. I sent her a sympathy card and returned her check, but wondered if you still thought a visit was a good idea."

"Not really. I sent her a personal note." Dixie chuckled. "Mama always said there were two kinds of cards, greeting cards and breeding cards. The latter meaning a personal note. She insisted we write out our sentiments on good quality, plain paper. Anyway, I'm cold on a visit."

After the mini Daughter-of-the-Confederacy lecture, I said flatly, "All right."

"What would we say, Georgiana? Dealing with a husband's death is trying, but under these circumstances? I can't imagine."

"I was going to offer her assistance with insurance matters since I have experience in that field, if she wanted it."

"How thoughtful. Incidentally, as we're speaking of Mr. Mendez, Augusta's buttering up her contacts at the police department with bakery goods." She cackled. "Told me her prying has yet to yield a single nugget about the murder. At least, nothing Augusta considers share-worthy. Knowing her, that would be his name, birth date, and possibly the killer's social security number."

"His? Have you heard it's a man?"

"No, but do you know many women runnin' around wielding tire irons? Neither here nor there. How are you getting along?"

"Tire iron? I hadn't heard that."

"It was in the papers."

"Oh, I must have missed it. By the way, I'd like to hear about Meredith Montgomery's legend. Right now, however, I'm in the middle of preparing lunch and Daniel's loose in the laundry room. I better check on him."

Dixie purred, "I won't keep you, then. Don't forget our pledge to get together for a shopping spree and so forth. I'll tell you all about Merry then. Call me, darlin'."

"Or you can call me."

"Time flies and I must finalize plans for the next BILL meeting. Bye-bye, honey."

"Bye-bye."

Still out of sorts, I relived conversations at the BILL meeting when I'd ambled around the tables making small talk before lunch. "What school did you attend?" Most quizzers, college grads, hardly expected my junior college response. "Clubs?" None, except church. Daniel and I came from different faith traditions, but neither of us attended regularly. "Any children?" None, unless I counted Daniel's, both adults who were distant, geographically and emotionally.

I mentored a girl in an after school program for at-risk children in our west coast community. The tween appreciated the fact my family hardly matched *The Brady Bunch* variety. Similar possibilities might exist outside Merry Acres. Since there were no schools within the community, or need for them, I might call the county school superintendent.

I popped the potato in the oven and strolled into the laundry room where Daniel hovered over two piles of clothes, a heap of towels and a clump of shirts, pants, underclothes, and my short, silk house robe. "Here they are." He triumphantly pulled his khaki, pleat-front trousers from the middle pile. "Was that call for me?"

"No, for me. Dixie Metcalf reneged on a condolence visit to Mrs. Mendez. She's probably right, although it steams me that she says one thing and does another. Her excuse for not calling sooner is a valid one. She's older, you know. I'd say seventyish and suffers the aches and pains attendant a former dance career."

Daniel pursed his lips. "I can relate." He bent his knees and rested a forearm on his knee to steady himself against another back strain. "You've only just met these women. Relationships take time."

"Time," I scoffed. "I have plenty of that. Between grocery shopping, cooking—more than I ever did when I worked—and keeping contractors on time, and within our budget, I haven't a second to spare."

Daniel continued loading the washer. "Metcalf. Metcalf. Somebody mentioned a Chester Metcalf once. Our realty agent? Whoever it was said Metcalf made big bucks on Wall Street and backed the developer of this place. Is your friend related?"

"His widow. Her husband was a bond trader."

"Explains the money. Can your silk robe go in with these on the warm, permanent press cycle?"

"I'll hand wash that." I caressed the robe before tossing it back in the hamper. "Sorry I verbally assaulted you."

Daniel adjusted the cycle setting and held the blue plastic detergent bottle an arm's length away to aid in reading its label. He carefully measured, pouring the capful of soap into the washer. "Sure."

I should do something, say something, but pride hurried me back to the kitchen. There, I chopped onions. My eyes watered, but onion fumes weren't the only cause.

Daniel sidled next to me in a few minutes. "It's all right, my hard-fragile flower." He kissed the back of my neck. "I had my middle age crazy phase, too."

Which one? "Those minor repairs multiply like algae on the back, north-facing fence. I never catch up." I grabbed a package of turkey bacon from the pricy, profile style, stainless-steel fridge and looped two strips of meat onto a fat-saving microwave bacon cooker.

While the potato cooked, I'd call the cabinet maker about the master bathroom vanity installation, two weeks overdue.

"Let's go out tonight."

"Wonderful idea." My lips brushed his cheek. It wasn't much of a kiss, but the closest thing I could offer as an apology for yet another eruption of entrenched rage. "Where?"

He grinned sheepishly. "We've got a way to go yet on the club's food minimum."

I'd prefer something exotic like the Punjab Palace, Mae Chen's, or The Athenian Garden, but Daniel's taste took a back seat to good service and an extensive selection of single malt scotch.

"That settles that," I said, "since it's paid for." Bills were mounting at an alarming rate. "Treasury interest nudged up this week, but the increments failed to arouse much enthusiasm."

"You were right, dear." He sounded defensive. "We should have rented."

"It's not your fault, Daniel. I insisted we move here. True, we bought at the wrong time, but nothing was available for lease that appealed to both of us. We could have rented in another area, but Merry Acres appealed to me. And it was a good price at the time. Who knew the market would slide even more."

"I'll call the contractor. You sit down and read the paper,

but there's not much in it."

"Anything on the Mendez murder?"

"Teensy blurb in the local section reads: 'Investigation continues; no new leads.'"

"What old leads have we read about?"

"None I know of. No scuttlebutt in the men's card room either, other than he was quite the ladies' man. The buzz is Mendez bedded a quarter of the female club members at some point, married and otherwise, and several ladies in Merry Acres proper who weren't members. Could have been an irate husband or jilted lover who dispatched him to the great beyond."

"I guess the snarky comments bandied about at the BILL luncheon were based on fact."

"I'd forgotten. Go, sit, and relax."

"Thanks." I recalled those fish-eyed exchanges between Dixie and Susie Esterhause when I'd asked what they meant about feigned tears for Mendez. Maybe one of them had been a former romantic interest of the car dealer. Nah. They might know others who were, though. I opened a Coke and leafed through the *Merry Acres Gazette*.

I moved from the front page to the local section and read over the brief article Daniel had mentioned on the Mendez homicide. This section shared space with the lifestyle portion of the paper and, for the heck of it, I looked over the calendar of events. Nothing there interested me.

Skipping gardening tips, since our exorbitant monthly homeowner's fee included yard care, I zoomed in on Augusta's column. It detailed the trials of maintaining femininity post-fifty, "the new forty" in every boomer's mind, if not in fact.

Readers would never guess Augusta's age from the with-it slants and dead-on slang-of-the-moment peppering her prose. In fact, should they meet her, they might mistake her for someone a good ten years younger.

The printed words revealed a softer, sexier side to the woman than my first impression. Perhaps my Augusta would accompany me on a call to Mrs. Mendez. No harm in asking. I reached for a folder and consulted my BILL notes and found the columnist's home number.

"Hello." I heard an abrupt recording in Augusta's hurried voice encouraging the caller to leave a message on an answering machine. "This is Georgiana Duncan." I paused and thought I'd simply leave my number, requesting a call back. But I changed course. "I plan to visit Mrs. Mendez. Call me if you'd like to go, too. I know you're a working woman and time is limited. If you can't join me for the condolence visit, call me sometime and we'll just chat." I decided against leaving my cell number, choosing instead our home number, and hung up.

Augusta St. James had many facets to her personality apparently, and wasn't simply the brash woman I'd witnessed at the first BILL meeting. I chuckled. Augusta would definitely call back. The magic words, "visiting Mrs. Mendez" ensured it. Curious Augusta would never decline such an opportunity.

Depending on how talkative the columnist might be about what she'd found out about the murder, I might have lucked into a ringside seat at the unfolding events of a Merry Acres mystery.

CHAPTER THREE

A couple of days later, I settled the matter about who would drive to the Mendez house. "You know the area better than I, Augusta. I'll drive next time."

Augusta's six-year-old burgundy Camry, crammed with phone books, clipboards, scratch pads, raincoats, umbrellas, paperbacks, and a makeup case, purred along. The driver's seat practically kissed the back bench seat and still Augusta's knees pointed skyward. Today, Augusta presented a somber column of slate: gray hair, gray tunic, and gray pants. Silver jewelry echoed the monotone.

Picking at some hairs to frame my face, I hoped they simultaneously lessened the severity of the quick and easy pulled-back do and softened my strong, half-Greek features. Adjusting my fanny in the bucket seat, I fought for floor space. My size-seven ballerina flats pushed against Augusta's chrome-colored makeup case. "Have you always been a writer?"

"Heavens, no. I'm a retired teacher. The pension offers a safety net for my hobby, writing." She flicked her finger toward the case. "If that bothers you, toss it in the back."

The woman never missed a thing. "A column is hardly hobby writing."

"For the pittance?" Augusta threw her head back and cackled. "Believe me, Georgie. It's hobby writing. However, it keeps me off the streets and out of the shopping centers. Not that I'm a fashionista. My size limits me to a tailored look."

"Stately."

"Stately? That's double-speak for"—she cleared her throat theatrically—"'big-boned women,' as mother says."

"Is she still alive?"

"Oh yeah. Dames in my family are just getting started when they hit sixty. We're long lived."

"You get along with your mother?"

"Sure do. We're cut from the same cloth." She looked my way. "Guess you figure in the majority, huh? So many women don't see eye to eye with their mothers." She shook her head. "Sad."

I hitched my shoulders. "I wouldn't know. I was raised by an aunt." I didn't comment further, hoping the driver would pick up vibes that I did not want to expand further on the subject.

"Speaking of cloth," Augusta said, "when I can find them, I buy classics. I buy quality—they never wear out. These pleated-front, summer-weight wool pants, for instance; they're twenty years old, if a day." She honked at a silver-haired gentleman who moved into our lane without a signal.

I braced when Augusta sped around him.

"Watch it, buster." Augusta regained her composure and continued our conversation without missing a beat. "Lucky girl, you're skinny enough you can change your look with the vagaries of the fashion season."

"If I was a clothes horse, maybe." Couldn't help but appreciate Augusta's perceptive change of topic away from my spotty family relations. "I'm not tall enough for bold looks a tall woman such as you can wear."

Augusta said, "My weakness is designer shoes, which ain't easy to find in my size, let me tell you. If it came to my mortgage payment and a new pair of Ferragamos, I'd have to bunk at a mission."

I played with my locket. Inside was a snip of water-soaked cotton ball tinged with a drop of Joy perfume. I preferred strong, exotic blends, but to keep Daniel's persnickety sinuses happy, I diluted my perfume with water. "Frankly, I adore dramatic clothes and colors, but my average height and inner critic insist on neutrals."

Augusta nodded. "Inner critic? Ah, yes, those pesky inner voices that damn us all in the wee hours. You're built tall, however, swan neck, long arms and legs."

"Um, reasonably long legs." A gene from mother's side, I assumed, since Aunt Irene was tall. No one mentioned dear old dad. Maybe there were so many men in mother's life, nobody knew his identity. Aunt Irene seldom talked much about anything except what interested her and that was not me. Her resentment, however, told me plenty.

I tugged at a knee-length, black rayon-blend skirt. Partnering it was a faux two-piece top consisting of an ivory tank piped in black with attached black, shrug-style jacket. "Here's the address. Wow, gorgeous home."

"Should be. Mendez made a mint as the only car dealer in the town proper, not to mention his satellite used-car lot, and the wrench jockeys at his auto repairs stable." She parked one house down as several cars were parked in the front of the Mendez house and more filled the driveway.

"Full house looks like."

Augusta peered over the rim of cat-eye-framed sunglasses. "Stand back and appreciate my outgoing nature." She pushed the sliding sunshades back up the bridge of her nose. "What I mean is, you're no extrovert."

"True." Everybody at the BILL luncheon had probably gathered that, I thought, reaching through the opening between the bucket seats to retrieve a platter in the back seat. It held finger sandwiches I'd prepared. A paperback caught my eye, or rather, the flash of its orangy red cover did. It made me think of one of one of my favorite drinks, one Daniel had introduced me to, a mimosa: champagne and orange juice tinged with cranberry juice.

How good one would taste right now. But then, even bottled water would be welcome. I lifted the sandwiches, glad the metallic platter was still cool thanks to plastic ice packs surrounding it in the special carrier I'd placed them in. That also protected it from buffeting by extraneous matter scattered in Augusta's back seat, flying about like space junk at every fast-jerk lane change and heart-thumping brake for traffic lights. Miraculously, the food remained neatly arranged and wasn't smashed flat.

"Bet you were an only child," she said.

"Yes. And you?"

"I came from a flock of five. I learned early to speak up and speak loudly." She gave me a smile. "You bought food.

It's only fair I handle the small talk. Don't worry. I'll be the epitome of decorum."

Now was not the time for her to show her investigative side, but I was hoping once we entered the Mendez sanctuary, she might unearth something about the murder and tell me later.

We sauntered up a manicured walk bordered by exotic landscape grasses in varying heights and colors. A concrete block structure painted a muted terra-cotta color loomed before them. It featured heavy-handed Moorish flourishes like an entry through a small courtyard set off by wrought iron gates.

"I met Mrs. Mendez once," Augusta said. "I was at the cashier's booth at the dealership shop paying for some car repair when Mendez breezed by."

"Yeah?"

"He and the Mrs. exchanged words in Spanish, heated words, if the inflection meant anything." She gave me a knowing look. "I gathered he needed a quick diversion, so I said a quick hello, mentioning I wrote for the *Gazette* and how we appreciated his advertising. Blah, blah, blah. Turned out, my handy presence derailed further argument and he tossed me a financial bone via a discount on the repair charge."

"Ah, the privileges of celebrity."

"You think? People imagine I have pull with the advertising department. I don't dissuade them from that false impression. Still, a free coffee here, a discount on dinner there, offsets my paltry salary."

The entry was barred by heavy, dark double doors brandishing serious hardware. They reminded me of tales from Arabian trade days when a man's door announced more than an entry; it indicated wealth and stature. The more ornate and formidable, the more implication that treasure lay inside. I rang the bell. "Do you suppose Scheherazade will open the door?"

Augusta wiggled thick brows. "Personally, I'm hoping for a jinn. Guys my height interested in, ahem, mature ladies are few and far between. So what if a guy's a few centuries old with purple-tinged skin, packs a scimitar, and hangs out in a bottle?"

I couldn't help but smile.

Almost a minute passed.

"I assume Mrs. Mendez knows we're coming?"

"Yes," I said. "I called yesterday to confirm she was receiving visitors today."

"Huh? Maybe we should try, 'Open sesame.'"

Chuckling, I promptly turned stone-faced when a young girl with eyes as black as her hair stared at me through a wide crack in the door. "*Abuela*," she cried, swinging on the door. "Some more ladies."

Chattering ensued. Squeals exploded from several children before scuffling erupted. Someone came to the door, admonishing them in Spanish. I recognized Lourdes Valdez from the first BILL meeting.

"Hi, Georgiana. I'm on my way out after dropping off some guava pastries." She looked at my tray. "More food? How considerate. Not that Pilar needs so much as a biscuit crumb. That kitchen is loaded. Food prepared by her help, friends and neighbors, as well as club members expressing our sympathies. *Dios mio*. There's enough for a third world country in there."

"Good to see you again." I smiled. "Is Mrs. Mendez well? Reasonably well?"

Lourdes shrugged. "Her grandchildren are taking time from school to be near her. They fill the void when her daughters run errands." She edged past us.

"Hello, Lourdes," Augusta said.

Lourdes' dark eyes flashed. I read more there than mere recognition. Mrs. Valdez flicked her dark, shoulder-length hair, as if suddenly annoyed. "Pilar's pretty tired," she said pointedly, staring intently in the upward direction of Augusta's sunglasses. "I suggest a *brief* visit."

Lourdes' Jimmy Choos clicked away. "She likes me," Augusta said under her breath. "I can tell."

"What was that attitude about?" I wondered if Augusta and Mrs. Mendez were better acquainted than Augusta let on. And not companionably so. Maybe Augusta and the late Mr. Mendez were better acquainted than Mrs. Mendez would have preferred.

"Who knows?" Augusta removed her sunglasses. She tucked them into a massive mock-crock hobo bag. "Probably needs a shot of estrogen."

"Don't we all?" I fanned my face with one hand.

"Guess we're going to stand in this courtyard all day. Good thing you brought food. We can eat lunch right here."

"If I don't get these pimento cheese, tuna, and egg salad finger sandwiches in the fridge, salmonella poisoning might land the widow in the hospital."

Eventually, a uniformed maid came to the door. "Señora Mendez regret cannot receive now." Her eyes darted from me to Augusta. "She appreciate visit."

Flabbergasted, I croaked, "We understand." I held out the tray. "Please, give this to her."

"Si, Señora." Her wide-eyed expression confirmed Lourdes' commentary on the food stuffs mounting inside. "Gracias." The door shut.

"You did call yesterday."

"Yes, Augusta. I talked directly to Mrs. Mendez."

"Did you mention I would come along?"

"Not exactly. I told her I'd be with someone from the BILL," I said. "What difference would it make who came with me?"

"None I can think of."

Considering Lourdes' reaction and the maid's brush off, I wasn't sure. "Well, heck. I wanted to see inside an Arabian palace."

Augusta *tsk*ed. "Me, too." She sighed deeply in exaggerated disappointment. "All right, I admit I hoped a tidbit about the murder might, you know, fall from somebody's lips."

"Augusta."

"I wasn't going to ask outright; just listen, very carefully."

"Pilar never came to the door. How did she know you were with me?"

"Lourdes probably saw me when the little girl opened the door and spread the word. I don't speak Spanish, but that's my guess."

"I suppose your occupation caused all this angst."

Augusta crossed her hands over her breasts, dissembling innocence. "What? The only thing my son-of-a-witch editor allows me to write is that dinky column. Oh, if they're short, I can cover current events: fashion shows, cat-in-tree stories, that sort of thing. My interest isn't professional, Georgiana. Really, it's not. I'm merely curious like anybody else in Merry Acres."

"Uh-huh." I remembered Dixie's comment about Augusta's trips to the local police station, with pastries in hand. "We'll chalk this up to grief. We caught Mrs. Mendez in the anger phase. Since we aren't going to be offered one of my sandwiches, let's go someplace and eat lunch."

"I bet you eat three thousand calories a day and never gain a pound, right?"

"Guilty. Although my metabolism slowed in my late forties, but yeah, pretty much."

"I hate you."

"Yeah, sometimes I hate me, too."

"Hey, Georgie, lighten up."

"Sorry."

"Know what's wrong with you? You're having a glycemic melt down. There's a Greek place nearby that serves fab pastries. If you don't have a sweet tooth, there's lamb shank, to die for spanakopita, and a passable gyro. You like exotic?"

"You mean The Athenian Garden?"

"Aw, you've been there already."

"No, and I really want to go."

"That settles it. Stick with me kid and I'll broaden your waistline." She pulled down her shades and grinned wickedly. "Your horizons, too, while I'm at it. We'll get your mind off whatever's deviling you."

This woman's perception was too close for comfort. Augusta read people well. Daniel once told me gamblers learned to read minute facial signals, particularly those around their opponent's eyes. Maybe newspaper columnists picked up the same ability to read "tells" when interviewing subjects.

"You read, don't you? I mean other than my column—that goes without saying. Everybody in Merry Acres reads that."

"I love to read, when I have time."

"Wonderful. You haven't succumbed to e-readers, have you? I ask because there's a used book store across the street from The Athenian that stocks a well-rounded inventory. We can browse after we eat. Perhaps there's a used bridge procedural in the stacks. Cards"—Augusta pointed at her temple—"keep the mind in good, working order. Wish I could force Dixie into a weekly bridge game. It'd keep her sharp."

"Forget it. I hate card play of any kind."

"Okay, okay, it was just a thought."

Augusta folded up the cardboard and foil sun shield advertising the *Gazette* she'd braced earlier on the car's dashboard and flung it in her back seat with the other stuff. I noticed that paperback with the pretty cover on the back seat floorboard. "What are you currently reading?"

"Tea leaves for a column idea."

"I love to carry a book to read while standing in line at the bank, or eating in my car after grabbing a quick fast-food snack. Books are great company."

"Phew," Augusta said. "It's toasty in here despite the valiant effort of my promotional protector—an office freebie."

We buckled up.

As we drove along, I experienced something missing in my life for a while, cheer. Augusta acted like a tonic. "Fill me in on that legend Dixie was telling me about. I never heard the rest of it."

"That? If you insist, I'll tell you later, over lunch."

"Yay." Maybe some beneficent being had pointed me to Merry Acres after all. I looked forward to Greek food. It brought back memories of my childhood, some good and some bad.

≡ ≡ ≡

Two weeks earlier at the first BILL luncheon, Dixie had looked straight into the face of a secret, a dark one. Staring at a photograph tucked away in her seldom-read Bible, she saw Philip's square jaw, the shape of his eyes, the way his lips curved. Didn't the Good Book say the truth would set you free?

Yes, the features and height of Georgiana Duncan mocked her plan of secrecy. Dixie's original nose with its slight bump on the bridge, professionally altered, her olive skin, lightened with chemical peels, stared back at her, too. Dixie had nearly keeled over from heart failure that day, but kept it together.

Today, heart trouble wasn't the reason she reached for a nearby prescription bottle. A capsule, the latest advance from big pharma, kept the creep of memory loss at bay. It was too little, too late, unfortunately. Short term memory slipped more each day. Ironically, details from fifty years ago registered as fresh as if they'd happened minutes before. Like Philip's face. The family resemblance in Georgiana was remarkable.

Dixie consoled herself that her old eyes had played tricks.

Still, Georgiana Duncan looked so much like Philip she'd nearly left instantly, but since she no longer drove, that wasn't possible. If she'd asked Augusta to take her straight home, there'd have been questions.

One thing was certain, Dixie dared not spend more time with Georgiana until she confirmed her suspicions and knew all the facts. That was why she'd canceled the Mendez visit.

Dixie picked up a Jitterbug, a white cell with large black buttons for better contrast. She dialed a number programmed into this phone and no other.

"Carlotta? Yes, it's Dixie. I want you to contact that detective agency in Atlanta the foundation sometimes uses. I want them to find out everything they can about a woman I met recently. They may need to hire help in Florida. Tarpon Springs, Florida. The woman's name is Georgiana Duncan. Her maiden name may or may not be Panagiotopoulos. Her date of birth might be November third, nineteen-fifty-nine."

The woman, who'd answered in a lilting Caribbean accented voice, replied, "Is she threatening you in any way, Mrs. Metcalf?"

"No, darlin', nothing like that. It's something I can't share. Hold the information for me. I'll read it when I visit. I know you'll keep this strictly confidential, won't you?"

"Of course. I'll handle the matter personally as soon as we hang up."

The last thing Dixie needed was to provide ammunition to Chester's nieces or nephews for another attempt to wrest control of the Metcalf Foundation from her. "Thank you. Bye, now."

"Goodbye, Mrs. Metcalf."

If her chickens had come home to roost, Dixie puzzled over the ramifications to an aging woman with a wobbly mind, one who'd done what she thought was best. What could Dixie do to avert fallout? What means could she employ to protect herself? Legal, illegal, or both?

≡ ≡ ≡

The Athenian Garden would not win a five-star plaque from any restaurant rating agency. The décor was standard mom-and-pop establishment. There was, naturally, here and there, a framed picture of an ancient Greek god. Cheerful ocher-colored, sponge-painted walls warmed the small space while a rendering of the Parthenon hung on the wall near the cash register.

The place was packed even though it was, by then, late afternoon. Bentwood chairs flanked chrome tables covered with white cloths. Four booths rounded out the seating. All were filled with diners.

Nick Papagalos greeted Augusta and crammed us into a small table for two. The table was no pleasure for one Augusta's size, nor was the cushion-free chair especially comfortable, as my bottom attested, but the table boasted a nifty menu of American and Greek specialties.

My heart twisted when I considered ordering dolmas. Grape leaves reminded me of childhood. Greek cooking was one of the few pleasant memories in mine. Instead, I ordered spanakopita, or spinach pie as some called it, while Augusta settled for a Greek salad.

The food appeared promptly. Between bites of leafy spinach baked with gobs of feta cheese sandwiched between layers of flaky phyllo dough, I prompted Augusta about the legend.

"Dixie loves that old saw probably 'cause Chester was related to the Montgomerys. I don't know exactly how, a fifth cousin thrice removed or some such. That's why he backed Merry Acres. I think the man knew Florida real estate was a gold mine. Yeah, yeah. We're in a downturn, but it always comes back. Hello? Snowstorms anybody?"

"Well, we have hurricanes."

"Every now and then. Snowstorms are regular." Her salad was prepared Athenian-style with potato salad incorporated into the greens, loaded with olives, feta cheese, and tomatoes.

"You certainly can build suspense, Augusta. Have you ever considered writing mysteries? In the meantime, tell me that myth, would you?"

Augusta laughed and signaled Nick. "How about Greek coffee and baklava over here, when you get a chance."

"One baklava only." I looked at him and shook my head ruefully. "Calories."

Augusta shrugged. "Make that one baklava, on my tab, but bring two forks. I don't need a whole one either." Once he left, Augusta finished her iced tea and leaned back.

"The legend?"

"Keep your heels on, I'm getting into proper oral dramatic form," Augusta teased. She fluffed her hair. "We are in a Greek establishment, after all. You know, of course, the Greeks originated the three-act structure." She crossed her arms and leaned forward on the table. "You know from Dixie a childless couple owned the land, right? Mrs. Montgomery wanted to keep the acreage in her family after she and her husband passed on. Mr. Montgomery, on the other hand, wanted to sell the land to an unrelated third party and use the proceeds to move them to greener pastures. Guess what?"

"I don't know."

"He met with an accident. Speculation was ol' Merry arranged it. Some say her spirit—" Augusta lowered her voice and added an eerie "woooo" sound effect to her wiggling fingers, but said nothing more.

I played along. "I'm hooked. Merry's spirit what?"

"Haunts Merry Acres."

"Very interesting."

"It gets better. Mrs. Merry Montgomery"—Augusta drew out her next word—"s-u-p-p-o-s-e-d-l-y"—and then she leaned back in her chair, waited a couple of beats and said, "seeks out her own kind. Women betrayed in some fashion: cheating husbands, lying lovers, victims of some you-done-me-wrong scenario or other."

"Yep, you should definitely write mysteries." The words "cheating husband" stuck in my craw. I pushed away my plate, but little food remained.

Augusta flagged down a harried waitress. "Check, please. Nick's adding minor charges for dessert and coffee, which I hope we get in our lifetime. Some of us work for slave drivers who stand by the office time clock.

"Where was I?" Augusta played with the strands of silver at her neck. "I remember. Furthermore, some say whenever a man dies in Merry Acres, it's Merry who causes it. Natural or not." She made a face. "Hooey."

"Well, the community is a widow magnet."

"C'mon. That's merely the demographic."

Nick appeared and made a show of ripping up Augusta's tab.

"Thanks," Augusta said.

He signaled with his hand. "No problem."

"Wait," I protested. "I'll pay for mine."

He looked at Augusta who shook her head at him. "Not this time." He removed our plates and the waitress served the coffees and lone dessert.

I cut off one small ceremonial bite of the sweet, but sweet thoughts were not on my mind since the word betrayal had entered the conversation. "So, what are you working on for your column?"

"Shush. Don't ask. The creative well is dry and a deadline is looming."

I put a half spoonful of sugar into the demitasse and stirred. "You'll come up with something." The hot, black coffee, five times stronger than espresso, was invigorating. "Maybe you should print the legend. On the other hand, with the Mendez murder, readers wouldn't take kindly to such a piece now."

"Bingo. Besides, it's old news."

"You're right. I hadn't thought of that."

"Otherwise, my hands would be tickling the keyboard with some rendition of the legend after I left here." Augusta finished the baklava and her coffee. "Let's visit the bookstore."

I surreptitiously stuck a ten dollar bill under the dessert plate.

We walked across the street, entered Barb's Book Nook, and meandered around the store, made purchases, and talked about our selections. We bantered about banalities like the weather as Augusta drove us to the ol' Duncan homestead on Carnoustie Way in Merry Acres.

"Thanks, I really enjoyed it."

"Except for not making it inside the Mendez home, I did, too." Augusta waved. "Keep in touch," she said before she roared off.

I thought about what she'd said and more about what sly Augusta hadn't said. Like what, if anything, she knew about the Mendez murder.

≡ ≡ ≡

Susie and Karl traded barbs on their walk to the pool.

"I thought you'd reformed."

"So, I slipped up," Karl said.

Susie clenched her jaw. Earlier today, the woman assigned to them by their weekly cleaning service had handed her a photo she'd found in Karl's pants pocket while sorting laundry and asked innocently if the pretty young girl in the skimpy bathing suit was a member of their family.

"How old is this one, Karl? Twelve?"

"She's sixteen."

"She says." Susie, twenty years younger than Karl, was staring forty in the face, too old, apparently, to hold her husband's wandering eye. She'd once been the girl in the bathing suit in Karl's life. Susie had been sexually wise for her age back then and talked Karl into marriage at eighteen. Pregnancy helped. That and her father's strong-arm tactics by demanding a paternity test. Karl raced to his physician for a vasectomy months after their marriage. The arrival of a son and marriage had tempered Karl's lustful ways until this year when Karl Jr. graduated from college in Miami.

"Look, what's your complaint? I don't play around in Merry Acres, or this county. Miami is a world away."

"Statutory rape, anyone? How long before one of your little hotties cries foul? Headlines would look great splashed across the front pages of the *Miami Herald*. Karl Jr. would love that. Or, the *Merry Acres Gazette*. I'd so enjoy that, Karl, as would your mother."

"You worry too much. Only person who knew about my...uh...hobby was Mendez. He can't tell anybody now." He gave his wife a sordid wink. "Not that his skirts were clean."

"His conquests were well over twenty-one."

"Way over."

Susie didn't respond. Instead, she took in the scenery along the walking path as Karl droned on. They weren't far from the tennis courts. She heard balls ricochet off rackets and bounce on hard surfaces. A cluster of condos hid the area from her sight. She wondered if residents enjoyed the brightly lighted courts at night and the sounds of play and repartee during the day. She momentarily envisioned Karl's head as a tennis ball and her hand as a racquet. She smiled at the impact of her perfect lob.

She dropped behind Karl to allow a biker to pass on the trail. Susie wondered if Manny Mendez had told anybody about Karl's adventures before he died.

"To most folks, I'm just visiting my son and ran into some friendly company at the beach in the bargain. I'm discreet. Karl Jr. knows nothing if that's worrying you."

"I see. So, I shouldn't care about some cute young thing going postal because you dumped her? Say she doesn't suspect you're lying to her while playing a very rich field. What if she takes pictures on the latest model camera phone Daddy bought her and downloads your illegal romp on Facebook, YouTube or MySpace?"

"In that case, I hope she gets my best angle."

Susie bit her lip.

At the pool area, they tossed their things into two unoccupied chairs under an umbrella shaded table. Few today sought out rays in the waning days of April.

Karl ignored her and headed for the diving board. The high dive.

Tanned and toned, sixty-year-old Karl's body jackknifed and broke the water with the form of an Olympian. He slipped into the water with minimal splash. His precision, Susie granted, was as sharp as the emotional blade of his predatory instincts for underage girls. Images of his physical gymnastics with some nubile young thing sliced and diced her esteem.

Her heart was way over him.

Susie sucked it up, refusing to let him see her angst. She beamed at him and waved. Her narcissistic hubby demanded approval. No one was visually worshiping him from the pool's edge so he basked in her adoration, unaware it was as heartfelt as Karl's sustained interest in his newest pretty prey.

Susie's smile hid a growing hatred. She'd love to cut him as he'd cut her. Trouble was, an odd dynamic in her personality made her love him all the more for his abuse. Or had. Today, that photo had pushed a hot button inside her. Fear of exposure and scandal rose like bile.

Aware Karl was still looking her way, Susie rubbed oil on her skin as he watched. She languidly slid her hand up and down her arms. She slipped her hand inside the blue triangle covering one breast and pinched her nipple, blowing him a naughty kiss. She'd get him one of these days.

She noticed a young Hispanic pool attendant picking up stray towels. She called him over.

"Yes, Mrs. Esterhause?"

"Could you rub oil on my back, please?"

He looked uneasy.

"Karl," Susie called. "You don't mind if this nice young man rubs suntan lotion on my back, do you?"

Karl shrugged. "Wouldn't want you to burn, sweetheart."
"See, he doesn't care."

The young man slathered her back and hurried away. Before the show was over, Karl turned away from them and started his afternoon laps.

Thoughts of revenge danced in Susie's head. Maybe she'd suggest Karl take her to Miami with him. For a threesome. Only, she'd alert the cops beforehand. She sighed. That was only a pipe dream. She had her son's reputation to protect, and her own.

Still, there must be some way to punish Karl other than maxing out their credit cards.

≡ ≡ ≡

I drove by the library and signed up for a card and then checked out a couple of biographies for Daniel and a mystery for me. Then, with cavalier abandon, I offered to help out four hours once a week. Additional outside activities, as well as the BILL, might eradicate lingering ghosts of Daniel's infidelity and squelch worry about Daniel's ongoing gambling habit.

Remodeling wasn't the only reason money was tight for us. Daniel, a regular bettor at the race tracks—dog and horse—when we lived on the west coast, had sworn off. We'd sold stocks and hawked most of the jewelry he'd given me to dig our way out of a financial hole. The remaining emotional crater was another story.

Life in Merry Acres progressed apace.

Prone to bridge burning, I wondered if, for once, I could build and maintain a few. Maybe there was something to Meredith Montgomery's legend. An emotionally injured woman, I had been drawn someplace where I could fit in.

What did that portend for Daniel?

CHAPTER FOUR

The final Friday in April found me and other BILL members milling about the clubhouse dining room. It was the afternoon of the group's second luncheon and Dixie had yet to appear. One of the women said she'd run into Dixie who was "off to Georgia for a spell" but due back last week. No other rumors where Dixie might be.

I held my breath, fearing someone would volunteer me for the job of hosting this thing.

Finally, Dixie appeared, fashionably late. The acting chairwoman wore a daffodil-yellow chemise, her hair and makeup a tad slapdash. With her was an attractive woman who sat quietly in the back. A companion? A nurse? Rumors flew. Dixie didn't elaborate and introduced her as a family friend named Gloria.

"All right, y'all, settle down." Dixie banged a gavel. "We are not reading minutes or anything like that. Not that anybody took any last time. We're just here to eat, drink, and be merry."

Everybody clapped.

"How's that for an agenda?" She stared off a moment, absently rubbing her thumb against her fingertips. An unhealthy pause followed before she caught herself. "I know. I'll ask everybody what they love about our lovely community, Merry Acres."

There were some groans.

Dixie, more composed now, shook her finger at the crowd of women. "Naughty, naughty. Who'll go first?"

"I'll go," Augusta said.

Dixie said, "Bless your heart." She looked sincere at first and then said with an impish grin, "As if we could stop her."

That brought laughter.

Augusta didn't mind. She stood and faced the other members. "I love the weather. And the fact there's a murder mystery in our midst doesn't hurt."

Dixie *tsk*ed. "We can do better, can't we? Who's next?"

Janet Jessell, the woman who had spilled water on her pants at the first meeting, turned in her seat. "I am not standing up. Sorry. It took me too long to slouch down in my seat and get comfortable. I love the friendships I've formed. It's a large, planned community with a small-town feel."

Augusta said, "How much did the Chamber of Commerce pay for that promo?"

Susie Esterhause, decked out in another designer outfit, said, "I second what Janet said, but as with most small towns, sometimes"—she looked straight at Augusta—"people intrude on one's privacy. Anyway, I have news, girls. Karl is bribing me to swim laps with him. I've freed him of quite a few dollars, too. Pretty soon, I'll have enough money to spend a week in Maine this summer, solo. And, rest assured, no water sports are on the agenda once I get there. What with all the snorkeling and diving we did last year in the Keys and swimming laps this year, I won't deign to put one toe in the water. Too cold anyway."

"Woo hoo," a few called out.

"Go, girl," said someone else across the room.

Susie put her clasped hands over her head and pumped them in playful reply. "Gotta say, my hubby's prodding is not only advantageous financially." She rubbed her thumb against four fingers. "It's forced me to exercise like a dervish to brave public displays in the skimpier and skimpier bathing suits he insists I wear. That means eating right, too, and foregoing carbs." She mimicked a boo-hoo and said, "Carbs, my favorite of the four food groups, next to sugar." Before she sat back down, she said, "Back to you, Dixie."

Dixie's attention again wandered a minute. "Who's next?"

A woman of average height with dark hair streaked with a slash of gray at her left temple slowly stood. The makeup on her moon face was as flawless as her coiffeur, but her form was over-ample. "I'm Becca Bernstein, if we haven't met." Her voice wavered a bit. "I love get-togethers like this." Becca took a sip of water. "Just give me a sec, okay. This reminds me of oral reports in school and speech class in college, which I hated."

I nodded agreement, dreading my own turn to speak up.

A few women chorused encouragements.

"I love the convenience of the place," Becca said. "A handy on-site market for staples and a nearby shopping mall, even if Lulabelle's is the anchor store. I don't know about you, but I wish they'd build a Bloomingdale's nearby so we wouldn't have to drive to the next county south to shop."

Dixie, more like her old self, chided, "I love Lulabelle's. My frock"—she stood and twirled around, but wobbled at the last and then grabbed the chair back—"oops. My dress is from that very shop."

"Mine, too." Susie chimed in.

Becca said, "If I wore your sizes, I'd love Lulabelle's too."

Several women grinned sympathetically.

Augusta said, "Becca is the best cook in the community for anybody who doesn't know it. That's a hint, Becca. When are you and Ben having your next party?"

Becca blushed. "Not for a while. You know Benny's working on that book of his, about life after bypass surgery, and he insists I include heart-smart recipes." She made a face. "Low fat ones."

Augusta groaned.

"Exactly. So, I've been busy with that. Benny's dragging me to the fitness center, too, and along our walking trails as well. Oy. That's okay, but the result, as you see, is minimal."

Everybody laughed.

Becca shook her head. "While I'm glad Ben's health has improved, I miss my laidback lifestyle, meaning cooking, eating, and lying in our outside hammock." She looked sly. "But, on a positive note, my youngest daughter and her husband are expecting our fifth grandchild in a few weeks."

Dixie clapped. "Congratulations. Ben is a real hottie in those walking shorts. He's lost at least twenty pounds since last year. I swear, your man lives on the walking trails."

Becca looked puzzled. "Are you walking now, Dixie?"

"Me? No, honey, I see him while driving around, or rather,

while some kind friend motors me here and yon. Who's next? Don't be bashful. Lourdes?"

She rose. "Carlos wants to return to Miami, some business deal flying cargo to South America has piqued his interest. So, I don't know how much longer I'll be with you. Before I forget to tell you, Pilar Mendez sends her thanks to all who dropped by and sent her cards. She really appreciates the community's concern."

Augusta said, "Has she heard anything about the culprit who killed her husband?"

Dixie chided. "Behave. Next?"

Boredom with this gambit set in so Dixie signaled the wait staff, hovering near the door. "Before we dine, let's have our drawin' to see who Fate chooses for the next chairwoman." She made a show of waltzing to the baker's rack, and drew a card. She drew out the suspense with a dramatically slow return, waving at some and touching the shoulders of other women here and there before reaching the lectern and announcing, "Susie Esterhause."

"Rigged," Susie said. "Okay. Two weeks from today. Who will handle the money then?"

Lourdes said, "I'll do it."

"That's settled," Dixie said. "Therefore, I officially end our meeting so we can enjoy our meal. Those who want to stay and visit afterward, feel free."

Thrilled the show-and-tell ended before I had to say something like, "Oh, I've had a swell time corralling contractors and trading barbs with Daniel," I savored the oriental salad with mandarin orange bits, chicken chunks, and crispy fried noodles on top. So far, the BILL had netted me several phone chats but only one lunch date, the one with Augusta the day of the aborted condolence call to Mrs. Mendez.

After lunch, we women milled around and gabbed. "Hey, Dixie," I said. "Thanks for hosting the day's affair."

"Oh, Lourdes, honey, we're so sorry to hear you might be leaving us. It's nice of you to take on the treasury duties."

"Dixie?" I tried not to look shocked. "I'm not Lourdes. I'm Georgiana."

"Oh, that's right." She giggled and gently knocked her knuckles against her head. "What is wrong with me?"

Augusta broke away from a conversation and hurried over. Ruffling like a wet hen, she frowned at me before signaling the woman introduced to all as Dixie's family friend to come over. Gloria gently intruded and walked away with her arm around Dixie's shoulders. Augusta's stern expression emphasized her words. "She had a senior moment, okay?"

"All right, I didn't mean to hurt her feelings. I was surprised, that's all."

We went our separate ways and continued with the social hour.

When Augusta caught up with me in the parking lot after the meeting, she explained. "Dixie's memory falters now and then. She doesn't drive anymore because of it. She checked out some neurophysiologist in Georgia. She's got a place there, you know, and visits frequently. Has family there, she says. In the meantime, Georgie, just go with the flow."

"Got it."

"Hey, I have some spare time next week. Are you ready for more adventures in dining? Mae Chen's or maybe Indian?"

"I'll check Daniel's calendar and strong-arm him to stay off the links and out of the card room one day so he can wait around for that sorry so-and-so contactor we hired. I'll call you."

"Sounds good."

"What's up with the Mendez murder? The crime reporter at the paper drop any hints your way?"

"No, damn him." Augusta chuckled. "But he wouldn't. He knows I've been asking around on my own." She gave me a wry smile. "I haven't yet found an opportunity to question Pilar."

Fat chance she'd open the door to you if the last visit was any indication of her feelings.

As if she'd read my mind, her tone grew stringent. "I talked to a guy at the auto dealership, however. As well as a couple of cops I know. Nothing...yet."

"I look forward to reading your scoop in the *Gazette*."

"Bye, then. I'm off to dream up something for my column. I hope my muse bursts forth when I boot up that antique I call a computer. Otherwise, I'm up to cover the opening of Dave's Dive Shop. That, according to my editor, means diving instructions, too."

"Sounds intriguing."

"You think? Me in a granny one-piece strapped with tanks, my face hidden by a diver's mask, looking like *The Creature*

From the Black Lagoon, while some Baywatch type, à la Susie Esterhause, instructs me on the finer points of exploring a chlorine-laden kiddie pool?" She made an ugly frown. "My editor's such a sweetheart. He's pushing me to quit, but"—she chuckled—"I ain't gonna."

"Here's a thought. If you want to see the interior of the Mendez's Arabian palace, I overheard Lourdes chatting with someone after lunch. Mrs. Mendez listed her house for sale a couple of weeks ago. Go see the place and write about it."

Augusta's eyes widened. "You sound like an editor. Wanna come?"

"I can't—remodeling chores. Talk to you soon."

"See ya."

≡ ≡ ≡

Over dinner with Daniel a few days later, I mentioned my suggestion to Augusta and regret over it. "What if Augusta uses the ploy as an opening to interview the widow, you know, looking for leads on the murder?"

"Mrs. Mendez is a big girl. She'll nip that in the bud if she's even at home. Remember when we sold our place? Realty agents want owners out of the house whenever prospective buyers come by."

"I hope so."

A week later, Daniel came home with news. "The Mendez place sold to some offshore owner at a fire sale price, or that was the buzz in the card room. Furthermore, the sale resulted from that article by your columnist friend. Some tourist visiting the area picked up the *Gazette*, read the piece, faxed it to a friend who faxed it to a friend of a friend and, bingo, the place sold."

My chest felt as if someone had dropped a bowling ball on it.

"Why so glum? You should ask for a commission."

"When I first read the column, I'd been so relieved there was no allusion to the murder, I didn't think of the ramifications for Mrs. Mendez. Like taking a financial loss."

"Forget it. Augusta's column admirably presented the blend of exotic detail and comfy home environment she apparently gleaned from the showing. Mrs. Mendez was probably grateful for the publicity. You know the realty agent was. This is a tough market."

Still, I remembered how happy I was when we sold our place. In a raging market, we could have waited for other offers and made a lot more money, but we took the first offer. Our loss had been another's gain.

Was Mrs. Mendez leaving the area upon closing? That would mean she wasn't a suspect in the murder, wouldn't it? Police insisted persons of interest remain accessible at all times. At least on TV.

After dinner and KP duty, I said, "I've got some minor housekeeping to do. I'll join you in front on the television in fifteen minutes or so."

Daniel was settling in front of his new plasma television in the den when there was a knock on the front door. Our doorbell was still broken and the so-called handy man had yet to show up to repair it despite repeated calls.

This prompted me to call out from the master bedroom area. "Can you get that, please?"

"Okay." His tone was hardly enthusiastic when he shifted out of the recliner. "Great timing," he grumbled, putting down his bowl of popcorn, but not before he took one more swig from his long neck bottle of beer.

The knocking grew stronger.

"Coming," he groused.

≡ ≡ ≡

He opened the door to a king-sized woman who beamed at him from their threshold. "Hey, you must be Georgie's hubby. Daniel, isn't it? I'm Augusta St. James." She held out a beribboned box. "I apologize for not calling first and I won't stay long. I just came by with a thank you gift for your wife."

"How thoughtful. Please, come in. Follow me to the kitchen, won't you? I'll get Georgiana. Oh, we enjoy your column, by the way."

"Thanks. I received positive responses about my piece on the Mendez house. The realty agent gave me a little something, and I even got a nice note from the widow. I wanted to thank Georgie for her idea. I like to give credit where it's due and a phone call wouldn't work in this case."

"Have a seat." Daniel moved some newspapers from a rattan arm chair. He noticed Augusta didn't take the hint. She

walked around the room checking out their bookcases, peek-
ing over her eyeglasses to take in photos and books.

"Georgie didn't mention how attractive you are."

He paused, not sure how to respond. "Uh, thanks. All
compliments are gratefully accepted."

≡ ≡ ≡

I heard Daniel's comment as I came in to the den. "Hey,
there." I smoothed my hair and tugged at the T-shirt over my
Capri pants. "I guess you two introduced yourselves."

"Yep. You're holding out on us BILL dames. You should
bring Daniel around sometime. He's easy on the eyes."

Taken aback, I looked at her and then to Daniel, gauging
his response. Rhonda, my west coast nemesis, had been a few
years older than I. "Let's move to another room, all right?
Daniel wants to watch his golf tournament. He bet on Phil
Mickelson. A *small* bet, right, dear?"

Daniel ignored me and looked at the guest. "Popcorn?"

Augusta declined with a head shake and looked at the
televised event. "Your guy's plus three and the first-place
player is only up one. No sweat. How many holes remain to
play?"

Daniel's mouth was set in a grim line. "Only one, a three-
shot hole. I can probably kiss my bet goodbye unless he aces
it for a playoff."

"Ew. Other man could choke though. Doubtful, but if anyone could put some mojo on an opponent, Phil could. I mean,
I'd hate to be in a playoff with him, wouldn't you?"

I didn't like the dismay evident in Daniel's posture. Could I
trust his word this was only a ten dollar bet? "What's that?" I
pointed to the box on the table.

"Something for you." She handed it to me. "I was telling
Daniel about my good fortune with your idea on the Mendez
house."

Hoping she wasn't a Trojan horse about to attack my marriage, I opened the box. "You really shouldn't have, but thank
you."

"Well, do you like it?"

"This is incredible. Look, Daniel, a candle."

Studying the tournament, he said without looking, "Yes,
nice."

I shrugged, embarrassed.

Augusta grinned good naturedly in response. "I'm sure he's seen candles."

"The taupe color is an exact match for our bathroom walls," I prattled on. "What's the circumference, six, eight inches? The black iron holder will look great on the ledge of the roman tub. Thanks so much."

"Glad you like it. Actually, it's practical. You never know what storm season will bring. Although, on the ledge of a roman tub"—she glanced slyly at me—"it can impart a little...romantic ambiance."

I ignored the innuendo.

Augusta got up as if to leave then sauntered back to the den. She picked up a deck of cards from the end table where Daniel sat. "Spiffy design." She shoved them at me. "See?"

An hourglass in the foreground of an orange disk. "I suppose." If I never saw another deck of cards in this lifetime, I'd be thrilled. So far, Daniel hadn't gambled away our home. "Where'd you get these, dear?"

He barely glanced at the cards. "Card room, someone left them."

Augusta asked, "What do the images mean, Daniel?"

Impatiently, he said, "Haven't a clue. Some promotional gimmick, a Florida theme, time in the sun or something like that. Take them. I buy card decks by the gross. One caveat, if whoever left 'em wants them back, you must return them to me."

"Fair enough. Thanks." Augusta lifted her brows and scrunched up her mouth, as if to acknowledge Daniel's tacit request for quiet. "Alrighty then. I'll shove off. Nice meeting you, Daniel."

He absently waved in her direction.

I took comfort in his preoccupation with the televised golf match but wondered about Augusta's unseemly comments. Was it just Augusta's pushy nature or was this turning into another potential threat to our marriage?

Hustling Augusta through the living room to the door, I said, "If your schedule is clear, Wednesday would be good for lunch." Better to employ the adage keep your friends close and possible enemies closer. "I have to be at the library no later than one-thirty though, my day to volunteer."

"Perfect. Chinese? Indian?" She said loud enough for

Daniel to hear, "You want to bring Daniel along?"

"Can't," Daniel responded loudly. Then, as if to terminate his interest in the visit once and for all, tossed out a pronounced, "Bye."

I relaxed. I wanted someone with whom to share girl talk. Daniel would hinder that and until I knew Augusta's motives better, I'd keep Daniel on a tight leash. "Sorry, Augusta, no two-for-one this time."

"Another time, then. So long."

Augusta drove away. Something about that card deck design floated into my mind. Hadn't I seen that logo somewhere? Back in the den, I asked, "What's your impression of Augusta St. James?"

"Shy little thing, isn't she?" On the TV screen, the other player held up a trophy. Daniel grabbed a fistful of popcorn and shoved it into his mouth. His eyes glowered.

So, Daniel had lost the bet.

Piqued, I very nearly mentioned Rhonda, the object of his affair, a slightly older, statuesque bottle-brown-brunette, and how Augusta fit the same mold, but bit my tongue. Instinct told me I'd better stop looking for trouble where none lay. "She's assertive. That's probably a good trait considering her current profession."

Daniel's come back, filtered through prolonged chewing, was indecipherable.

I fingered the candle. "Nice gift."

Daniel washed down another couple of popcorn kernels with his beer. "She has an eye for beauty."

I chortled. "Are you referring to the candle, or her comment about you?"

Daniel hunched his shoulders and gave a silly grin and pop-eyed expression. "Both?"

Cradling the gift against me, I reached over him to see if he'd left even one piece of popcorn, wondering if it would spoil his appetite for dinner. "Sorry you can't join us for lunch."

He eyed me. "I wouldn't want to intrude."

"Right answer."

Setting the gift down, I joined him for an hour's worth of television viewing, the time limit I could stand for the action thriller he'd chosen. I read a bit while he continued to watch, mesmerized. Was his mind on the plot or that bet?

"I'll test-drive the new tub." I went back to the master

bathroom with the new accent piece in hand. A good, long soak in the new tub was just what the doctor ordered.

After lighting the candle, I engaged the dimmer switch to lower the brightness of the lights over the vanity. Pouring bath salts into the rising water, I added a capful of scented bubble bath for froth and fragrance.

Soon, hot water worked its magic. My neck muscles relaxed against an inflatable pillow I'd purchased that buffered my head from the tub's edge. An aromatic blend of jasmine and honeysuckle bubbles softened my skin and pleased my nose, working in concert with Augusta's jasmine-scented candle. I grew drowsy.

"Mind if I join you?"

Awakened, I answered, "Sorry, I was dreaming." *Yes, I do mind.* He was making an effort, therefore, so should I. A momentary flash of his slow dancing with Rhonda at a club dance, his passionate kiss with Rhonda under the mistletoe in our foyer when they thought no one was around, slashed my conscious thought.

Augusta's teasing had conjured these memories.

For an instant I wished he'd slip on the step up to the tub. One fatal fall and I, too, would go from the married to the widowed column of the BILL.

Hateful, hateful, hateful. "Watch your step, Daniel." I blew out the candle flame. "Come on in. The water's cooled off, however. I'm ready to dry off anyway."

"I'd better not, since you'll be getting out. There's no point wrenching my back getting in and out of that wading pool you're soaking in."

Good. "Don't forget the adjustable wall jets in the shower. They'll feel wonderful on your back."

Daniel looked sad. "I remember when you used to rub my back."

Me, too. "Tell you what. I'll give you a back rub when you get out of the shower."

His expression told me he knew my game. His words confirmed it. "Sure, if you're still awake."

Under his intense scrutiny, I climbed out. He handed me one of the new, freshly laundered, still warm-from-the-dryer, thick, beige, Egyptian cotton towels. A splurge, but the feel of the warm cotton against my skin made the cost worthwhile.

Daniel watched as I dried myself. Afterward, he removed

his robe and brandished his erection. A glance at the candle made me wonder if Augusta's remark about romance had also encouraged Daniel's ardor.

We moved into the bedroom and I lay naked on the bed.

"You're still so beautiful, Georgiana." His hands roved over me.

"Thank you." Gravity had acquainted itself with my body, as I well knew. My fingers returned Daniel's favor, and I stroked his chest, playing with gray hairs there. He was fit for his age, but for the first time, some belly fat hugged his middle.

We kissed. As a good wife, I accommodated my husband's needs. I neither resisted nor matched his lust, but allowed my body to follow the familiar forms of marital passion. Could Daniel ever fully meet my sexual needs, or more to the point, could I ever again allow him to?

Nor could I say why my libido was mired in emotional quicksand. Anger certainly, but physiological changes, too, played their part. A time to embrace, a time to refrain from embracing. Perhaps this was the path marriage took from this point on. Neither hot, nor cold, but lukewarm.

The next day, after breakfast, we rode bikes, pedaling along in companionable silence broken by bits of conventional conversation. In the distance I saw the pro shop. Outside it, carts lined up like modern prairie schooners, waiting to ferry players over the links. Later, players would hit the club's grill room, gobble down a calorie-laden lunch, then hurry back to play. Others might buy a sandwich or snack from the roving refreshment carts prowling the course between eleven and two. Or eat at home, like Daniel, after an early nine-hole game.

The greenskeeper kept the course in tip-top shape. The fairways were freshly mowed and the scent of grass wafted through the air. We commented on the birds, the golfers, the weather, the house, the repairs, and the state of the world in general.

As was his custom, Daniel rode on to the clubhouse fitness room for his daily workout while I turned for home.

There, I made a phone call to the handyman who promised he'd be out in the afternoon. I readjusted my schedule on the off chance he was telling the truth this time. Daniel returned a couple hours later, showered, dressed, and ate the soup I prepared from leftovers for lunch.

"See you later, dear."

"Bye." I watched Daniel trek through a path worn in the backyard that linked the property to our neighbor's yard. The years had been good to Daniel except for his recent back ailment and penchant for snacking. Daniel was energetic. Spry, some would say.

Daniel reached the neighbor's driveway. Every other day, he hopped a ride to the club on our neighbor's golf cart. Daniel remained undecided about purchasing one. The garage, cramped as it was, meant I wasn't encouraging him to buy one.

Watching him disappear from view, I wondered what had happened to the Daniel I'd married? That man would never have hurt me for a brief ego boost such as an affair provided. Yet, wasn't that exactly what I'd seemed to his first wife?

Rhonda had been approximately the same age and had possessed similar physical attributes, educational degrees, and social accomplishments as Daniel's first wife. When news spread of Daniel's attraction to Rhonda, I imagined the vindication his first wife felt.

Later on that day, I cleaned chicken for dinner and marinated it for the grill. After that, I looked over bills but wasn't in the mood to fire up the computer and write checks. Augusta would be working, so there was no point calling her.

I relented and telephoned Dixie. "Hey there, are you free? Thought I'd invite you to meet for coffee and window shopping at the Merry Acres Mall. I have to be home by four, however. Our handyman says he'll be here to fix our doorbell and give us an estimate for some other odds and ends."

"Sure, darlin'. Let's meet at Mojito Joes, say in an hour? There's a sale on at..." She sighed in exasperation. "...my favorite dress shop."

"Want me to pick you up?"

"No. I'll make arrangements."

"See you there." Dixie's pause was possibly owing to a momentary mental blank on the shop's name: Lulabelle's. After dressing in suitable clothes, I left Daniel a note telling him I'd be back by four o'clock for the appointment with the handyman. If by chance I was detained, he'd have to readjust his schedule today, even if that meant forgoing cards. I snickered at killing two birds with one stone, a social outing for me and thwarting Daniel's gambling habit.

I arrived first. The local watering hole stood near the mall in a free-standing building. The place served in-house roasted coffees and soft drinks in addition to wine, liquor, and snacks. I ordered one of their flavored iced teas. Some time passed and I accepted the first refill but declined a second. When an hour zipped by, I reached for my cell and punched in Dixie's number. Irritated at first, I was obligated to find out what the matter was. What if she'd decided to drive herself and had an accident? Or her car had broken down?

When Dixie casually greeted me on the second ring, I was shocked. "Dixie? What happened? You were to meet me at Mojito Joes."

"Today?" Dixie's distress sounded sincere. "I thought it was...tomorrow. I'm so sorry. You recall I no longer drive. Shoot, Gloria is marketing. I'll call a cab. Will that be all right?"

"I can't wait, Dixie. A repairman is coming, I hope. It's okay, really." Right. "We'll do it again another time." I could hardly rail at Dixie. When I thought about it, Dixie was lucky in a way. At least her memory couldn't ambush her as mine did.

Back at home, I wrote out a deposit slip. Still restless, after driving to the bank then home to pay waiting bills, I called a west coast friend. We'd been coworkers at Daniel's office, but she wasn't home. I picked up the BILL directory one of the members had created on her home computer with the help of a teenage grandchild, and chatted with some of the members.

Becca bemoaned Ben's manuscript demands.

"He's got an agent interested now and, ever since, that infernal book has overtaken their lives. Ben writes every spare moment. In the process, he pushes himself. He doesn't look good, he gets winded too easily on the walking trails, and the man's driving me crazy for more recipes."

"Having an agent is exciting. You like to cook, though."

"Cooking isn't fun anymore; it's work," Becca said. "All I really want to do is play with my visiting grandchildren and squeeze in a visit with our pregnant daughter, but no, can't go, on account of that darned book."

"I'm a golfing widow myself." *Not that I mind the time alone.* "Well, keep your chin up. See you at the next BILL meeting."

When we hung up, I called Susie Esterhause.

"Hi, Georgiana. Do you scrapbook? Our group meets at

my place once a week. We have a blast. Everybody tries to outdo the next gal with some unique creative touch. Of course, the real winner is Ted's Craft Shop in the mall. We're meeting now, in fact. Come on over."

"Thanks for the invitation but I don't scrapbook." *What pictures would I include?* I snidely internalized. *Look, here's a dandy shot of Daniel's daughter at our Thanksgiving table looking like she just bit into a cranberry. Or how about this one? Daniel making eyes at Rhonda when he thought I wasn't looking. Let's enclose that one in a big, red foil heart, shall we?* "I think you parents and grandparents have that hobby cornered."

"Oh, I forgot. You don't have kids of your own. Sorry."

"That's all right. I'm not the mommy type."

"Augusta might use scrapbooking for a column one day," Susie said. "We played tennis earlier today and got to talking. She's always trying to dream up something for that column, you know. Anyway, she came by, took my picture, as well as shots of my scrapbook," Susie bragged. "I might make the paper one day."

"Fantastic."

"Well, I better go. Good talking to you."

We hung up so Susie could return to her scrapbookers.

Perhaps Karl's swimming habit was his way of staying out of his wife's hair. I'd learned from hearsay that Karl, an Olympic finalist decades ago, gamely jumped in the clubhouse pool, rain or shine. Winter hardly mattered. There weren't many days too cold to swim in our part of Florida. Summer, too, Karl rose early to avoid kids home from school or visiting their grandparents who frolicked in the club's pool.

Perhaps I'd avail myself of the pool's charms more frequently. Daniel eschewed swimming, but I enjoyed splashing around after a light lunch in the grill room or a sandwich eaten poolside.

There was the summery smell of chlorine and the colorful awnings that shaded the take-out side window of the grill room. The lounging chairs were usually dotted with vibrant beach towels brought from home by those swimmers not using towels provided by the club's pool or spa staff. Daniel said the recently constructed spa, open to the public, was a money maker and a real convenience for members of Barrier Isles.

How different my life was from my childhood and early

adult life. For that, I was grateful. Marriage had brought about the boon but I wondered how it was some women kept the hearth fires burning decade after decade? Or, did they?

Merry Acres widows were lucky. They weren't widowed mothers slaving in sweat shops. They weren't living hand-to-mouth among disease-carrying flies and squalor in some third world country run into the ground by some idiot dictator who'd dispatched their spouses to the next life by some brutal means or another.

Way too self-absorbed. I'd check local schools about mentorship tomorrow.

I felt a guilt pang barge into my do-gooder thoughts. Could Daniel and I surmount the doubt and suspicions bogging down our union? Why did I stay? I knew why, partly because I didn't want to spend my later years alone. I had no illusions about dating prospects at middle life. Money, too, played a factor. Callous perhaps, but I'd worked hard for what we had and was, at least, a good financial partner to Daniel.

Besides, we had precious few assets to divide. After settling his gambling debts, we were nearly broke. Selling this home in this market would be difficult, with no guarantee there'd be a profit after paying off the mortgage and realtor's fee—not after factoring in remodeling and repair costs.

Better to make the best of things. To settle. But hadn't I always?

Change was up to me. Daniel loved to dance. Although I could take or leave ballroom dancing, I'd encourage the activity with lessons. No more widow-in-waiting for me. If I couldn't breach this emotional divide, at least I'd know I tried.

Near seven, Daniel returned from card play and I greeted him with a kiss, a sincere one.

"To what do I owe that token of affection? I know. The handyman showed up."

I shook my head. "Of course not, but I had a good day regardless. Guess what? We're taking dancing lessons."

"What?"

"I've called a studio and arranged it. It's not far from the Merry Acres Mall. There was a choice of Tuesday or Thursday nights from seven to nine, and a four week schedule for Latin, smooth, or rhythm, whatever that means. I chose the Thursday time slot, and Latin dances since I know you like those best of all, though you do a mean waltz."

He looked quizzical. "That's okay with me."

"Good, now get out there and grill our dinner, mister." I led him by the hand to the fridge and handed him the marinated chicken pieces. Humming in the kitchen, I finished making the macaroni salad. He frowned at the salad bowl.

"I know you hate pasta so there's fresh veggies to grill and a baked potato for you."

Still holding the platter of fowl, he looked confused. "Wife, I wish you'd see a doctor about your mood swings. You're acting really odd, considering."

Considering? "Shoo, it's getting late. Skeeters come out at dusk. Daylight savings extends brightness, but we don't need a case of West Nile virus even if this isn't maximum bite season." I spun him sideways and aimed him outside. "March."

I doctored canned baked beans with crisp fried turkey bacon, modest clumps of brown sugar, ketchup and mustard, adding a kiss of Tabasco, then set the table before taking Daniel a beer.

Standing in the outside kitchen area, one of the main draws of the house, I watched him fuss over the grill. "So, what's new at the clubhouse?" I took a long sip, then gave the bottle to him. "Here."

"Thanks." He stood in a fog of smoke.

"I guess you won't need more DEET with that surrounding smoke cloud."

He rubbed the chilled beer bottle across his forehead then drank. "Maybe some fresh clothes since smoke damage is ruining these. I still haven't mastered this grill." Daniel waved away smoke and turned down the temperature a few degrees. "Of course, I could read the directions. And I will, someday." The grill smoldered while he checked a wire basket holding sliced vegetables and the potato on the grill shelf above the briquettes. "You haven't heard about Karl Esterhause?"

"What about him?"

"No wonder you're so cheerful. You don't know."

"Don't know what, Daniel?" I grew annoyed.

"Karl Esterhause died."

"Uh-uh! I talked to Susie before five. We chatted a few minutes on the phone. She had people over there working on a group scrapbook project at the time and we couldn't talk long."

"All I know is Karl never showed up for cards. Someone

called his house. I'm not sure exactly when, but sometime this afternoon, Karl Esterhause drowned while recovering golf balls in one of the lakes."

CHAPTER FIVE

When the news registered, I repeated, "Dead?"

"Yes, dead."

"But the Esterhauses are well-heeled, at least from appearances. Karl hardly needs"—I looked at Daniel and then corrected my words—"*needed* to harvest lost balls. He didn't even play golf, did he?"

Daniel shook his head. "I don't get it either. Hey, signs are posted. Everybody knows how dangerous the hobby is. Alligators, for one thing. Then, there are snakes to consider, not mentioning run off from fertilizer. So the guy liked to swim. Why choose a toxic pond? I haven't heard any details."

"They have a college-age son who lives further south. I suppose he'll drive up to help Susie make arrangements. She's pretty chummy with her immediate neighbors, too, but I'll call on her tomorrow. Maybe I'll go over for a little while. Want to come?"

Daniel shook his head. "Nah. I didn't know Karl that well. And, that handyman might actually show to fix the doorbell one of these days."

Disquieted, I paced around an outdoor wicker rocker, a chaise, and two wrought iron tables. Eating outside tonight was out of the question, even if the lingering smoke would keep bugs at bay. This time of year there weren't that many compared to the swarms that would accompany the fast-approaching soggy, humid, summer months. "Will there be an autopsy?"

"Yeah, I guess."

Absently, I pulled dead leaves from a climbing vine of clematis, but it made me think of Karl. Instead, I trained my eyes on lush green leaves covering most of the bush. According to the realty agent who sold us this place, it seldom bloomed because the vine lacked sufficient sunshine due to the northeast exposure.

After hearing about Karl Esterhause, I could use some sunshine myself. "I'll call Augusta later and maybe Dixie, though she's undependable. Not that she can help it." Dixie could appear so with-it, I wondered if her "senior-moment" episodes weren't a convenient excuse to escape appointments she'd rather not honor.

Daniel piled the food on a platter and brought it inside where I served it at our eat-in kitchen table. Even though the thigh was my favorite piece of meat, I let him take the second one and settled on the wings, which I also loved, leaving the breast for chicken salad later. After munching, I remarked, "That BILL group I started has expanded its widows list by two in only weeks."

"Egad, I'm an endangered species," Daniel said. "Not that I plan on treasure hunting in the bogs of Merry Acres for golf balls."

"Wise thinking." I ate as if starved. "Odd, don't you think, that I'm so hungry Under the circumstances, you'd think I'd forego food. Not that we were close to the Esterhauses."

Daniel shrugged. "It's a knee-jerk reaction from your subconscious. Karl won't ever eat again. You're eating for two, so to speak. Three, if you count Manny Mendez. Officials still haven't zeroed in on whoever knocked him off either."

"No, but it's not the same thing. Mendez's death was a homicide. Karl's was accidental, wasn't it?"

He put down a chicken leg and wiped his mouth before sipping beer. "True."

After dinner, I made coffee in a French press and poured a dram of coffee-flavored liqueur into our cups. "This will further mellow our moods and serve as dessert."

Daniel lifted his cup. "To Karl."

We clicked our cups together. When we finished the coffee, we adhered to our evening routine. Daniel cleared the table, scraped the plates, and took out the trash while I rinsed and loaded the dishwasher.

Later, I proceeded to the den where Daniel, ensconced in his recliner, perused the television listings. This was essentially his room and I'd decorated it in navy and tan. I settled into a rattan wing chair and put my feet up on a matching plaid ottoman, setting a glass of ice water on the side table.

We negotiated. Daniel was good in that regard, I knew, but I never pushed things by grabbing the remote. That was his domain exclusively. I once mused about organizing a women's group to combat the problem, calling it WAR—Women Against Remote Control—but decided I'd organized my last group thing with the BILL.

Tonight, our disparate tastes ended with an action thriller, compliments of our satellite dish.

When the phone rang, I nearly cheered. "Hey, Augusta. Yes, Daniel told me. Unbelievable."

Daniel's face signaled irritation at the interruption so I took the cordless receiver to another room, along with my glass of water.

"I'm going over there tomorrow." I sat down in the living room on a seldom used, hump-back sofa. This area was furnished with jewel tones and the windows were covered by plantation shutters that I noticed could use strokes from a dust cloth.

Before I could even ask, Augusta cut off my planned invitation for her to join me when visiting Susie Esterhause.

"Sorry, I can't go with you to see Susie tomorrow. I've got a deadline and brain freeze on subject matter."

In addition to water, I swallowed disappointment. "Susie mentioned you were over there talking about scrapbooking. Why don't you use that?"

"I was, but once again, Merry Montgomery's curse nixes my column."

"Why?"

"Think about it. It'd be tacky to write a column displaying photos showing a beaming woman attesting to happier times while she's in mourning, don't you think? I'm tired, dearie. I must go. I want to take a nice, hot shower and put on my jammies, then crash. With luck, my subconscious will spit out something translatable into a thousand words of copy tomorrow morning. I'll call you soon about lunch someplace weird or exotic. Hello to your hubby."

"Bye." I returned to the den and watched a little more of the movie, but having missed too many crucial scenes, grew antsy. My mind kept skipping to Susie Esterhause. "If you don't mind, I'm going to call some people."

"Sure." Daniel shoved a pretzel into his mouth.

First, I left a message on the librarian's private line explaining my errand of mercy the next day so I couldn't be counted on for my four hours. Something niggled. It wasn't like Augusta to miss out on an opportunity to grill a recent widow for details about a death. I reckoned she wasn't interested in this case since the cause of death was natural.

Wondering if Dixie had heard the news, I called, but immediately hung up. Let the Merry Acres tom-toms relay the sad news to her. If I asked Dixie to accompany me to Susie's house, could I depend on her? No.

I ambled back to the den. "I'm going to read before turning out the light."

Daniel grunted, his attention on the movie.

I pecked him on the forehead, realizing Susie Esterhause would never kiss her husband again.

One never knew what transpired behind bedroom doors or, for that matter, when Death would call.

Would Susie consider widowhood a curse or a blessing?

≡ ≡ ≡

Two weeks later, Dixie Metcalf staggered toward the bathroom of the rented house on the golf course. She'd sold her home and taken the place after returning from a brief trip to Atlanta to clear the few personal items from the house before the closing. Janet Jessell would pick her up and they'd visit Susie Esterhause. She'd better dress.

Fortunately, Gloria, Dixie's nurse, not only kept Dixie's mind from permanently wandering off, she helped Dixie apply her makeup.

How sad. She couldn't even make up her face anymore.

Dixie thanked her lucky stars she'd recently completed a skin peel session with that ultra expensive dermatologist in Atlanta. His technique couldn't erase sagging skin or deep lines, but that wasn't the purpose. Altering her skin tone was. No one would guess a woman of Greek descent faced the mirror, especially after she popped in her blue contacts.

Turned out Dixie's suspicions had proved true. Georgiana Duncan was a true blend of her parents. What did this grown daughter know or not know?

Fear forced Dixie to continue her ruse, rather than confronting Georgiana and stating their true relationship. For that matter, why continue to present a cosmetically anglicized face to the world? The answer: habit. Chester had met and married a fair woman. Ethnicity would have hardly furthered her cause back then. Chester's family had had enough qualms about her sketchy social background as it was.

Dixie's mind skipped to the early years with Ches. She liked the past and felt comfortable there. Wait. Who was she thinking about before that? Something unpleasant, wasn't it? Chester's family? Yes, but another, more distressing. Who?

Oh yes, Georgiana.

The progression of Dixie's memory loss meant a continued barrier to friendship with Georgiana. She couldn't take a chance that the lies between them would slip out.

Staring at her reflection, Dixie doubted she could ever justify her actions to Georgiana. She barely understood them herself when she thought of the audacity she'd showed when she made those life-altering decisions. So long ago. She closed her eyes and ambled among the players of her past.

≡ ≡ ≡

Olympia, as Dixie was then known, refused to contact Philip when she missed her period, weeks after their moonlit rendezvous. He'd left and never contacted her. Not once. He'd given her an address beforehand and promised to write, but the address was invalid. His deception was as dreamy as moonlight. His lies as soft as the Florida sand on which they'd strolled.

Much later, Olympia again saw the young man of privilege. He was visiting Tarpon Springs on another holiday from his expensive military boarding school.

Her heart leapt, then plummeted. Philip was with another girl, a smartly dressed blonde who sported an engagement ring. How distinctly it glittered in the sunlight near the sponge docks, a beacon to stay away. The pair laughed and walked hand-in-hand before disappearing into a quaint restaurant. The very place where she and Philip first met while she waited on him. Thankfully, she'd had the day off when he'd returned with the new girl.

The shock. That, she remembered, and the gut-gnawing fear once she learned of her pregnancy. She'd found a listing for a home that helped pregnant girls give their babies up for adoption. Then financial concerns shut down the home. The girls were turned out. With help from a church group that also paid her hospital bills, Dixie found work as a domestic. After Georgiana, named for Olympia's deceased father, was born, Olympia couldn't give her up. She tried to work things out, but live-in positions for domestics with children were nowhere to be found.

She was too proud and too afraid to ask help from her mother.

When she and her baby ended up at a mission in the run-down section of Ft. Lauderdale where they were offered meals and a bed for a few nights, Olympia knew things must change. That's when she made the pact with her sister, Irene, to raise Georgiana. Irene agreed, exacting a steep price. Olympia must never reveal her true relation to her daughter.

Olympia had gone to Atlanta.

Irene told their ailing mother Olympia had run away to New York. When quizzed about the baby Irene was raising, she'd fabricated a tale. The child was the daughter of a friend who had lived in South Florida but died in a freak accident, the result from a fall into an elevator shaft under repair. She had no husband and no family and presciently begged Irene's promise that, should anything ever happen to her, Irene would look after the child.

Irene had given her word. What could she do?

Or so Irene relayed to Olympia in a rare tête-à-tête years after the fact. This conversation took place from a pay phone in New York, far from Tarpon Springs in every way possible.

Irene had bragged her bluff worked among family be-cause, unlike Olympia, Irene possessed neither the tempera-ment nor physical attributes to attract a husband, so everyone pretended Fate had intervened and smiled upon Irene in a way. Irene never disabused them of the lie.

All despaired of ever again hearing from flighty Olympia, but Irene covered that well, too. She invented successes in Olympia's life that she passed on to family members. To them it seemed natural Olympia wouldn't contact them directly.

She'd always been ashamed they weren't rich or famous. They believed the lies of her success, too, because Olympia had always been lucky.

Until Philip.

Fate, however, had turned benevolent once more when Olympia moved to Atlanta.

The young woman saw an ad in the *Atlanta Constitution* for dancing lessons. Olympia loved to dance and grew good enough to attract attention from local dance instructors who trained her to teach and then she auditioned for theater folks. She changed her name. Olympia Panagiotopoulos, with its multi syllables and impossible spelling, was no more.

She chose the name Angela Aurora for its connotations of angels and light, a guiding light. Audette, she plucked from the air, with help from a nearby phone book.

Angela succeeded beyond the wildest dreams of a young, Greek American woman who once innocently believed the moonlit lies of a selfish man.

Luck held when she moved to New York City where she enjoyed success as a dancer in a few minor Broadway shows. That led to meeting Chester Metcalf, a young stockbroker on the rise and a cousin to the man she was stalking, Philip.

Before that though, while still in Georgia, Angela soaked in every nuance of southern culture, and assumed a nickname, Dixie. Once writing as A. A. Audette, she penned a novel detailing her life as fiction. She called it *Sun and Sand*, both elements of warmth. Limited copies sold, but the romance allowed Dixie to pass a little money on to Irene for Georgiana's care.

She and Chester enjoyed a love match with no room for scandals, or children better left in the past. It would only confuse the child. It would only upset the delicate balancing act Dixie managed with Chester's family. In time, Dixie and Chester climbed the career ladder to social prominence as a team, an exclusive team.

In time, Georgiana was relegated to shadows.

Those shadows now lived in the sunlight of South Florida within the walls of Merry Acres, when, decades and decades later, Dixie Metcalf learned Georgiana's fate.

The detective employed initially needed more information. She could hardly call Irene with whom she hadn't spoken for ages. Dixie procured details another way, by ingratiating herself with Sharon, the Barrier Isles Golf and Country Club's social director. In the club office one day, Dixie learned the woman was leaving early for a doctor's appointment. Opportunity knocked. Dixie slipped into the club's business office and riffled membership application files. She ferreted out Georgiana's social security number.

From that, the investigator furnished a full report on her daughter's tragic life in foster care.

It was too late to make amends. Other relations in Chester's family would hardly welcome news of another rival for inheritance upon Dixie's death. They didn't know of her failing mental faculties and she wouldn't be the one to tell them, instead surrounding herself with allies.

Gloria came in. "Mrs. Jessell is here. Let me help you into that dress."

≡ ≡ ≡

Though weeks had passed, Karl's death hung over the next BILL meeting like the black netting of a widow's veil. Susie Esterhause wasn't there. She'd left for Miami after her son convinced her to promptly list the house for sale and head south.

Everyone in Merry Acres was shocked when the house sold so promptly.

Buzz was, the offer—"as is" at a fire-sale price, just like the Mendez house—resulted in the prompt transaction. In the current market, most agreed, better something now than more later, and having a property languish.

If Karl's demise wasn't downer enough, Dixie was keeping to herself. More depressing than that, Augusta, too, had stalled out in a public funk.

The combination put everyone on edge.

"What's wrong with you," I asked Augusta, "the Esterhause death?"

"No," she snapped. "Why?"

I shrugged. "You're so subdued. I mean, I know Karl's death hardly puts any of us in high spirits, but—"

"Yeah, I know." She glared. "Augusta is not her usual life-of-the-party self."

Augusta, tall as a lighthouse, cast a broad, bright light when the beam was on full strength. Conversely, she cast a long, dark shadow when it wasn't. "Exactly my thoughts."

"I'm a decade older than you, Georgie. My mortality calendar looms large of late. You've got lots more years padding yours than I, all things being equal. One never knows when the light bulb of life will darken with a big pop." She sighed. "Hell, even I'm tired of this black mood I'm in. Let's eat, drink, and be adventurous. How about we blow this joint for Punjab Palace?"

"Considering lunch will be served in about two minutes, how can we?"

"Easy, eat light."

Becca struggled through her hostess job and the BILL luncheon slogged along. Dixie half-heartedly brought up the subject of a fashion show. The idea was not met with enthusiasm.

Lourdes spoke up. "I volunteer to command the next meeting in two weeks." She looked around. "Plan on a surprise to liven things up."

This brought about poking and grinning. Even moody Augusta perked up. "You mean big, tall, strapping, male escorts will attend?"

Lourdes' eyes flashed at the droll remark. Anybody with eyes could see that whatever was off-kilter between those two remained so.

Lourdes said with studied patience, "Wait and see. News flash. For those who don't know, Carlos prevailed. We're moving to Miami within the month." Everybody groaned. "I know, more changes. Hey, Janet, why don't you keep the treasury duties? One less shake-up, okay?"

Janet looked around. "Don't everybody fight to take the duty from me."

Augusta said, "Let's give Janet a big round of applause." She stood and clapped, moving her hands in a circle as she did so.

After the clapping died down, Sharon strode in with two waitresses and served. "That ovation for us? Gee, thanks. Gazpacho and salad plates today, ladies. Must be getting close to bathing suit season."

Well-dressed women reflexively patted their pouch-like middles and shifted on their padded rears at her allusion.

Becca said, "No, Sharon, I'm the guilty party. Guess my husband's fetish for all things healthy finally converted me, or

I'm the victim of some seed pod from outer space."

Augusta leaned over to Georgiana. "We lucked out. The light meal works in our favor, which leaves tummy room for samosas."

"Stop it," I scolded through clenched teeth. "My mouth is already watering for a cool glass of *namkeen lassi*."

Augusta's smile wasn't as genuine as smiles past, but it was a smile. She'd worn nothing but a frown since crossing the threshold to today's meeting except for that brief clapping exhibition.

The group sped through the light lunch.

"That's it." Becca, visually thrilled, brought down the gavel she'd borrowed from the unresponsive Dixie.

"Meet you there," I practically sang to Augusta in the parking lot. I hopped into my white Toyota SUV and sped north.

As excited as a child on a field trip, I arrived first. Written up in several magazines, Punjab Palace had only recently opened for lunch. No one was seated. The hour was late, almost three, and the host who greeted me in Nehru jacket and turban looked pointedly at his watch. "We stop serving at three." His facial expression brightened when Augusta walked in.

"*Namaste*, lovely Augusta." He bent from the waist, his hands together, his head bowed.

"How's it going, Raj? I brought a friend so dazzle, dazzle." Augusta was suddenly her normal self.

"This way, most distinguished diner."

"Raj, you old devil. You've given us the best seat in the house."

"I could hardly do less." She smiled, and he smiled as insincerely, and replied, "Lest an unattractive word make its way into the local papers."

"Told you." Augusta jabbed me in the ribs. "Illusion is everything."

Seated against a backdrop of gathered material, shirred yards of saris sewn together in an exotic pallet of color and design, we ordered.

It wasn't long before I closed my eyes in ecstasy, and then sipped the cool, thick, mint-flavored yogurt drink. "Yum."

"You should see this place at night. With the light from all the hanging lanterns bathing the room, it looks like Scheherazade's tent, as radiant and as seductive as post-coitus afterglow."

"I'll bet." I wrapped a piece of spicy lamb in a slice of naan after offering a piece to Augusta.

Augusta refused the bread. "I'm happy with my whole wheat chapati, thanks just the same."

My mouth still full, I spooned tomato chutney on meat, layering that on another wedge of bread. Forcing myself to slow down despite the tantalizing taste sensations on my tongue crying for more, I made small talk. "Poor Daniel gets meatloaf tonight."

Augusta swallowed. "Ran into your dear hubby yesterday. Well, not actually, though it was a near miss. Your neighbor is a speed demon in his damned golf cart. Doesn't adhere to the cart paths, either. Anyway, after the screeching brakes died down, we all chatted a while. I understand dance lessons are on your horizon."

"Latin." Odd Daniel hadn't said anything about a near run in. "Speaking of dancing, what's up with Dixie? Has she seen a neurologist?"

Augusta sipped her chai. "Her mind's wandering appears to be a temporary blip. Eat up, you're not holding up your end and you can use the extra pounds more than I."

The curt answer meant Augusta could not be pressed on the matter. Maybe she didn't know and was covering up her ignorance. Maybe she was exhibiting loyalty to Dixie. I changed subjects even though curious about what cloud forced ever-sunny Dixie into shade today. I was more curious about why Daniel hadn't mentioned the minor traffic mishap. Probably didn't want to worry me. Our neighbor took on another personality whenever he climbed behind the wheel of his cart. Then, too, Augusta cosmically landed in spots enabling her to learn minutiae about anybody, anywhere.

"I've been exploring volunteer ideas—"

"Working at the library isn't enough?"

"Obviously not," I snipped. "I called up a community service program. All sorts of agencies referred me to at-risk programs. One of which was a shelter, HELP. That stands for—"

"Homes Enveloping Less fortunate People," Augusta finished.

I took a bite and chewed slowly before saying, "They allow abused women, and very rarely a man or two on the mend, to stay there a week or two, you know, until they can move on.

They desperately need money. With Becca's help, maybe the BILL could put together a cookbook and sell it, giving proceeds to HELP."

"My advice, dearie? Go by the place. I hate to sound uncharitable, but most people there are able bodied. They could wash windows, pull weeds, or do something for gainful employment. No, they'd rather make the rounds at flop house and these shelters. HELP isn't the only such shelter around. I investigated this, oh, maybe a year ago. You know, while I was on the prowl for my Pulitzer."

I stiffened. My aunt had mentioned more than once that my mother and I had "flopped" in such a place when I was a child, before I was handed off to said aunt. Before Mommy Dearest disappeared. "Hmmm." Dropping the food from my fingers, I wiped my hand on a napkin. "I just figured with so much time on my hands, I'd do something useful."

Augusta set down her cup. "Aw, I've hurt your feelings." She studied her short, clipped nails. "I hit close to home, huh?"

"All's well that ends well. Let's drop it."

Augusta held up her hands. "Fine with me."

Raj seated another customer, a man.

Ever alert, Augusta looked him over. "Well, if it isn't a member of Merry Acres' finest. What's up on Mendez?"

The man, around forty, hunched his shoulders. "Not much."

"Georgie, that's Detective Mike Morgan. You want to know somebody good at reading people, he's your man. Mikey is also the sort who'll take secrets to his grave. Ain't that so?"

The detective, by now far enough away to present only a vague physical impression, gave a half-hearted, four-finger wave before sitting down with his back to us.

"We can take a hint, Morgan." Augusta lifted her hand and signaled Raj. "Check, please."

"No, no, lovely Augusta. Punjab Palace could not take your money."

"Thanks, Raj. Look for a glowing word or two in my column soon." She looked at me and winked.

Outside, I tilted my head downward. "I sit in the presence of a master."

"Guru, I believe, is proper nomenclature in these parts."

We laughed.

"I'm off to hit the practice range, maybe work in a fast nine holes. My golf game suffers and my tennis game is going to heck, too, because of my column."

"All right, but let's get together soon. Mae Chens?"

"Alas, Georgie, this is our last lunchtime adventure for a while. I'm exploring health food, solo. I suppose Becca inadvertently planted the bug in my brain at today's BILL luncheon. I figure the subject might make a good column and I've got another tiring deadline two days hence. I have a sick relative I must visit after that. Maybe I'll come up with some health remedies to pad the piece. And, I better eat better. I'm older now, no kids, don't want to end up at the whim of some seven dollar an hour rent-an-aide. Be back in a few. Catch you later." She shook her hips. "Have fun cha cha cha-ing with Danny boy."

I watched the long strides of fast-departing Augusta and climbed into my car. The topic of my childhood settled heavily in my gut, causing indigestion.

Not a day passed I didn't rankle over my misfortune. Really, knowing who your parents were, was that such a stretch? A mother and a father? Even a ratty family unit was better than none.

Dredged up again that day were memories of when I'd searched inside a forbidden chest of drawers in Irene's room. I found my birth certificate, naming Olympia as my mother, not Irene's imaginary friend. My father's name was "unknown."

Being a bastard was bad enough, pawned off on a reluctant family member and then pawned off on child services was akin to abandonment. Abandoned. Unwanted. Unloved. Who could surmount that?

Aunt Irene, a woman with whom I hadn't communicated in ages. The woman, near eighty now, probably still clung to Greek customs like sweet syrup to baklava.

I'd bet Irene still worked in her yard, mowed grass with a push mower, and drove from Ft. Lauderdale to Tarpon Springs for the blessing of the shrimp boats every spring. Never mind there were plenty of Orthodox churches nearby with attendant rituals mere miles from her Broward address. She insisted on the annual drive to Tarpon Springs. She was tough, no-nonsense, and possessed the patience of a gnat.

In other words, a perfect maiden aunt but a ghastly mother substitute. The sort of woman who wanted a trophy child, a doll to dress up. Not a living, breathing, feeling, curious, mischief-making, human little girl.

And my father? Were there that many sexual dalliances on mother's part? Who knew? When I was little, I fantasized dad had been killed in a plane crash on a mission of medical goodwill with an organization along the lines of Doctors Without Borders. What else had I but whimsy?

And Mother? A blank I tried to flesh out but never could. "Mother" remained forever the image in the last family photo taken of Olympia at sixteen, a girl, pretty in a typically Greek American way.

Blood ties were severed permanently after I ran away from Irene for the third and final time, each time desperately trying to find Olympia in New York. The family took Irene's side, as usual, viewing my act as ungrateful treason. They didn't believe I was blood.

I never made it out of Florida, never mind all the way to New York.

Lucky for me, the case worker assigned by the State's child services program wasn't yet beaten down by a broken system.

She placed me with a wonderful family. Mr. Briggs was a teacher, his wife a former social worker, and their twin boys were cute, cuddly four-year-olds. They put a part of the state's monthly stipend into an account for me, my rainy day fund, as they called it. I blossomed under their care and my grades soared.

When I turned ten, the Briggs were attacked and killed during a home invasion. A misguided guardian angel had sent me bike riding a half hour before the attack occurred or else my own troubles would have ceased, too.

Much later, I found out a sour drug deal was the motive behind the killings. Proving, once again, nothing and no one could be trusted. Good old Mr. Briggs supplemented his meager teacher wages with foster care money and the odd drug deal. Something apparently went wrong and the four Briggses ended up dead, execution style.

More foster homes followed after that because I grew resentful and rebellious again until I gave up and went with the flow. Good grades were my only salvation. When I hit puberty, I buckled down and studied hard. Nor did I make further waves in any of the foster homes.

Happily, I was never abused mentally, physically, or sexually, allowing the street-savvy girls I shared space with—most families took in two or three children at a time—to display themselves for hungry-eyed husbands. While they reveled in revealing budding charms, I hid mine under baggy clothes and stayed out of sight, too, preferring kitchen or bath cleanup chores. The ploy worked. I never had troubles with the wives or much interest from the husbands.

Considering the extreme neglect and woeful financial mismanagement of state money allotted each child, no one was surprised that monetary abuse was virulent. I learned the value of money. It could buy freedom.

Attending night classes at a junior college, I gained experience from daytime administrative assignments booked through a temp agency during the week. I waited tables on the weekends. Tips were middling for a born introvert. I dated, usually older guys, always searching for that missing link in my life, a father. I broke things off when they wanted to get physical, but finally lost my virginity at twenty. Sexual exploits after that were few and selective.

Unwanted pregnancy was the last thing I wanted.

I gave up on ever finding Olympia. For all I knew, she was some bag lady or drug abuse statistic picked up on a New York street and either incarcerated or buried in potter's field.

Years later, the insurance company where I worked became my de facto family. Alas, the aging owners eventually put it up for sale and I didn't make the cut when employees were culled. I lived for a while on a severance package and modest 401(k) funds, minus the hefty early-withdrawal tax penalty.

My luck changed for the better when I answered an ad in the paper one fateful day and met Daniel during a second interview.

Daniel was gentle, attractive, and fatherly. He had a knockout sense of humor, too. He hired me after the interview. A small snag. Besides his sense of humor, Daniel also had a wife, but that didn't matter, at least not at the time.

Daniel was the closest thing to a knight in armor I'd ever known. Energized, I changed my hair, makeup, and clothes. I made sure he noticed me.

Later, when our relationship grew intimate, I allowed Daniel to think he had seduced me. More than once in my life

I'd witnessed the positive harvest guilt could extract and I mined it for all it was worth. Finally, Daniel set aside his family and married me.

Things between us were wonderful, at first. Ultimately, however, guilt worked against *me*. Ongoing alimony harangues chipped away at happiness. Dour visits with his children took a toll, too. They said cutting and cruel things to me, more hurtful for their validity.

Then, eighteen months ago, Daniel's second brush with middle-aged folly came along. Her name was Rhonda and she was a family friend.

CHAPTER SIX

A week later, I was running errands when the long line at the pharmacy counter of the local drug store sent me to the cosmetic area. There, I tested blushers, lipsticks, and foundations before choosing a new lip color and strode to the end of the aisle to check on progress over in pharmacy. The line was down to three with one leaving and two customers waiting. I walked over, wondering about the worthiness of my doctor's advice. She'd referred me to a therapist for depression. As if Daniel and I could afford weekly $150-per-hour therapy sessions on top of everything else.

I accepted the prescription for an antidepressant from the clerk, stunned silent when he announced the charges. I shoved my credit card at him. "Here."

"Hey, you look like I do when I get the bill. Sticker shock?"

Becca's husband smiled at me as I signed the credit card slip. "Oh hello, Ben. How's Merry Acres' resident author?" I hurriedly stuffed the Rx bag in my roomy purse. Had he perchance read the contents? I'd met Ben once or twice after BILL meetings when he chatted with us on his way to the fitness room. He played cards once in a while with Daniel's group.

He looked sheepish. "Promise not to tell?"

I played along and pinched my index finger and thumb together and then moved them across my lips.

"Ticker." He thumped his chest. "CHF—congestive heart

failure." He pointed to his swelling ankles.

"Oh dear."

"Yeah, great promo for my heart-smart book, right? Doc says it's genes. What can you do?"

It was then I noticed his pronounced shortness of breath. It must be symptomatic. "Hurry up and get published is my suggestion."

He laughed. "That's good advice. Now I gotta add potassium pills to all my other prescriptions."

"Daniel subscribes to lots of health newsletters that promote supplements for your illness. Want me to give them to Becca at the next BILL? You could discuss them with your cardiologist."

"I know about them. I better stay with what my doctor recommends, but thanks for the thought. Hey, I saw one of your BILL buddies in here. Guess she can't sleep because she was stocking up on sleep aids."

"Who was it?"

"Augusta St. James. She was rude to me when I approached her. Strange duck, that one."

"She can be abrupt, but she's up against deadlines so the Sandman probably gives her sleep habits a fit from time to time. Sleep deprivation makes you cranky."

"If you say so. Becca enjoys those BILL luncheons, by the way. Gives her time away from me and allows her to unload on you gals."

"Nah. She has only complimentary comments about you. She's lovely, Ben. You two are so lucky. You know Daniel and I are taking dancing lessons. Why don't you and Becca sign up and join us?"

Ben smiled. "This book is all I can handle now. That and walking."

"I understand."

"Take care and say hello to your husband. I don't know him well since I live on the jogging trails and he lives on the links. We'll have to change that one of these days. But, not dancing."

"Sorry to cut this short, but I have to stop at the grocery store. Hug Becca for me."

"Sure thing. See you."

As I exited the pharmacy area, I glimpsed Augusta studying greeting cards. I started over, but decided not to seek her out. She might be in a hurry, too, and I really needed to finish marketing at the grocery store if there was to be any dinner. On the way out, something made me look up at the large circular mirror mounted in a corner near the automatic exit doors. Augusta, now at the prescription pickup counter, was chatting with the clerk. Ben was nowhere in sight.

Had Augusta seen Ben and me at the pharmacy? If so, I prayed the clerk would use discretion if Augusta asked about my prescription. How self-absorbed was that? Augusta had mentioned a sick relative. Maybe she was saving the person a trip to the drugstore.

I mumbled as she left the store, "You're allowing anger at Daniel to make you unhappy and you're getting paranoid. Stop it."

While marketing, I picked up poultry and an impulse buy, a couple of herbal plants on display in the produce section. I stalled dinner to work outside for a bit, arranging a container garden for the herbs. I liked cooking with them since they added zing to recipes. Fresh ones cut from the garden would look nice on the kitchen counter and infuse the air with a pleasant, earthy scent, too.

Daniel came home. He bent down and pulled my soil-covered gloved fingers to his chin. "Great news! We won! My partner and I won the club tourney. Know what that means?"

"Not exactly, but I'm thrilled for you."

"It means a two hundred dollar prize and an award ceremony. Tonight."

The entry fee had been fifty bucks, so the return on investment was sizeable. The recognition was an ego boost for Daniel. Pumping him up further, I cried, "That's terrific." I rose and kissed his cheek and then offered him a seductive glance. "How about a preliminary prize?" I removed a glove and stroked his thigh.

Daniel jumped back as if bitten. "Thanks, but not now. I need to shower if we're to make the ceremony on time. You, too, earth mama."

Hurt, I gave him a long look. "Sure. First I'll finish repotting the parsley, sage, and rosemary." I put my glove back on. "Is dinner included with this shindig?"

"Sort of, heavy hors d'oeuvres. It starts at six, so we haven't much time."

I would have suggested showering together, but refrained

after his snub. "Go shower, then. I'll sponge off and slip into something."

≡ ≡ ≡

The Barrier Isles Golf and Country Club was awash in light when we arrived. Cars jammed the circular drive. Inside, Sharon the social director and her staff had worked miracles in little time.

The dining room was magical. Transparent ribbons were strewn like iridescent crepe paper. White cloths were overlaid with blue, square toppers on which floated stenciled golf balls.

Every table flaunted an attractive arrangement of mums, greenery, and miniature novelty items: plastic golf clubs, golf bags, etc.

A scoreboard was set up behind a dais for the award show later. Daniel and our neighbor's names were highlighted in gold as was their winning score, sixty-eight. Four under. Not bad for the geezer group.

There was an impressive ice sculpture in the shape of a two-foot tall golf ball, complete with realistic dimples, smack in the middle of a food spread any Pasha would envy. Crab cakes, shrimp, miniature hot dogs for the under ten set, all of about six children. A few teens, and a handful of the collegiate crowd were there thanks to Spring Break.

Catching sight of one of my personal faves—finger sandwiches including the much-coveted cucumber—I plucked five of those off the tray and set them onto my plate.

"Hello, there," Dixie drawled. Her eyes lacked sparkle, as if tired. "Pretty dress."

"Thank you. A catalog buy." My square-neck dress in daffodil yellow, on which romped white hibiscus petals with yellow stamens, had been a bargain. I had made do with last year's bone-colored wedge sandals, hoping hastily applied toe nail polish served as an instant pedicure.

"Congrats to Daniel. Gloria and I are homeward bound now that our bellies are full." Dixie covered her mouth and yawned. "Pardon me, darlin'. Trip here from Georgia gets longer each time."

"I'll relay your message."

Daniel flitted here and yon, no doubt bragging a little while reliving the entire eighteen holes that went into sudden death.

I saw him pocket greenbacks along the way and suspected he was collecting on private bets. He looked happier than I'd seen him in ages, tanned, sparkling, confident. The old Daniel.

Becca and Ben Bernstein were presently part of a group clustered around Daniel. Becca saw me first as I approached. "Hey, you." She hugged me. "Aren't these goodies divine?" She assumed a dreamy expression as she munched. "First calorie-laden food I've had since I snuck into a fast food place for a kid's meal during my granddaughter's recent sleep over." Becca snickered. "Poor darling, I practically ripped French fries out of her little hand."

We laughed over that and then Becca excused herself to speak to another lady, one who wasn't a member of the BILL.

Lourdes ambled by. She was lovely in a bodice hugging ruby-red tank top under a gauzy matching safari jacket and fitted white pants, even though Memorial Day was a week away. Aunt Irene always said a lady never wore white before Memorial Day or after Labor Day.

"Congratulations, mija. Little bird told me you and Daniel are taking dance lessons. They might come in handy."

"What?" I could only offer a blank stare.

Lourdes smiled. "Oops. This punch is spiked with something. I've said too much already. I'm off to give your hubby a congratulatory kiss. With your permission?"

"Of course, make his day. Where's Carlos?"

"Somewhere." Lourdes found Daniel in the throng and reached up to kiss his cheek. They turned back in my direction and waved. I waved back and blew my husband a kiss. He beamed.

The night wore on. I managed to make small talk and smile until I felt the muscles in my face ache. I felt the void of Augusta's absence and regretted not having seen her for a week, not counting that glimpse at the drugstore. Wherever a crowd gathered, gossip ruled and usually there was Augusta, but not tonight, perhaps visiting that sick relative.

Finally, the award ceremony took place. Daniel gave a rousing speech and magnanimously handed the single trophy to their neighbor, his partner. Daniel was a generous soul, a good soul, a kind soul. And sometimes, a duplicitous soul.

I counted my blessings, feeling a thaw in that glacier under my skin. Maybe Daniel and I would right the ship of our union after all. Merry Acres was good for us.

At home that night, Daniel had an amorous reversal from the afternoon. So what if it the adrenaline rush of winning a trophy, or the bets he'd won, or the scotch he'd drunk was the cause and not a rekindled love for me?

We made love for the first time in months like we both meant it. Afterwards, I lay in Daniel's arms and allowed the contentment of this moment to warm me.

≡ ≡ ≡

Later that week, while women throughout Merry Acres consulted wardrobes for what to wear that day for the BILL luncheon, Augusta St. James trotted along the main bike path circling the course, holding a lunchbox-sized cooler.

Ben Bernstein happened by on his daily run.

"Hey, Benny. How's it going?" Augusta fell into step with him.

"Okay." He was race walking today, not jogging.

Augusta noticed Ben's face was red and he was slightly winded.

"This is fortuitous. I've been stood up," Augusta said. "A buddy was supposed to meet me on the trail. Now I have an extra smoothie from that new health food store. Hear about it?"

"No."

"They make delicious drinks, healthy stuff. Guess I'll have to toss this, unless you could help me out by drinking it. You're probably stuffed from some gourmet goodie Becca crammed into you though, huh?" She extracted one of the plastic cups from the cooler. She sipped through a straw. "Yum."

Ben stopped and bounced in place. "She made my favorite breakfast, banana pancakes, but that was around seven this morning. I was going to breeze by the grill room and down some bottled water. Is that cold?"

Augusta made a show of wiping condensation across her forehead. "Yep. Really tasty, too. A great way to work in those four or five servings of fruits and veggies. Sure you don't want the other one?"

"Better not."

"Okay, I'll just throw it away at the next trash receptacle I find. A shame, but—"

"I could use a short break. I don't have much oomph to-day."

"I hear you. I hate to waste things, don't you?"

"Yes," he said hesitantly, as if debating. "That's probably got stuff in there I shouldn't have. And high calorie, too, I bet."

"Look at me, Ben. Do I look like I need a fat-laden drink?"

"Actually, you're pretty trim."

"Thank you. Because, usually, I watch what I eat. This is only smashed up fruit. If you don't want it, you don't want it. My loss. It's okay. Really."

"Give me the damned thing."

"Thanks, Ben." She put her empty cup in the cooler and took out the second one. She removed the lid and handed it to him. "Isn't that good?"

"Refreshing."

"Invigorating?"

"In a way, yes."

"Good, a second favor when you're through with that. I need competition to rev my jets. Race-walk me half a mile."

"If you don't do this regularly you could injure yourself."

"I'll take my chances. Come on. Scared I'll beat you?"

He laughed. "Wouldn't bother me if you did."

"That's where we differ. I'm competitive and registered in a charity run. It's a dash, not a marathon, thank God. I don't want to enter the thing if I can't win. Today, I need incentive to walk a half mile let alone get my rear in gear. You'd be helping me out big time."

"All right." He finished the drink.

"Give me that." She put it with the other stuff and zipped the cooler. "Ready?"

"Whenever you are."

"Let's go."

Several minutes later, both were puffing pretty good.

Augusta said, "Uncle. I've got to stop. Thanks, Ben. You go on. Maybe I'll see you later."

He smiled triumphantly before he continued his exercise routine.

Not much longer, Augusta came upon Ben sitting Indian-style on the grass. Ironically, he was fewer than ten yards from the soggy growth surrounding the pond where Karl Esterhause had drowned.

"What's wrong, you don't look so hot?"

"Tired."

"Uh-oh. By the way, I'm sorry I was rude to you the other day in the drugstore. Forgive me?"

"Sure."

"You didn't mention to Becca that I was stockpiling sleeping aids, did you?"

"No, I forgot all about it, actually. I did mention it in passing to someone else."

"Yeah?"

He nodded.

"Oh, you mean Georgiana Duncan. I saw her in the store that day. She's discreet. I don't have to worry about her. You really look done in, Ben. I'm going to jog up to the security gate and have one of the guys come back and check on you. They know emergency CPR."

"No. I'm fine. I have my cell. I'll call 9-1-1 if I feel worse. I just need a breather, that's all."

"Oh, yeah, you have your cell. Sure you don't want me to get someone? Only take a sec."

"Yes."

"All right, then. Hello to Becca. Thanks for the competitive push."

Ben coughed. He choked out, "Good luck in the race."

Augusta called back. "Good luck to you, too, Ben." She added hastily, "On your book."

She called Dixie from her car. "Sure you aren't up to entertaining the troops today? I've got you covered, if you don't. I want to stop by and change at your place, if that's okay. I just finished a jog and your house is practically on top of the clubhouse."

Not five minutes later, Gloria let Augusta in. "Dixie is resting. She told me to thank you for taking up the slack her not attending would leave. She owes you."

"Forget it. She'd do the same for me. Where can I change?"

Dixie's companion showed Augusta to a guest room with its own bath.

"Mind if I shower?"

"Of course not."

Augusta had long ago mastered the five-minute shower. She dressed in record time and, falling prey to natural inquisitiveness, opened a second door off the room. It led to a small office. She entered and looked around. She didn't have much time before she must dash to the BILL meeting.

A bright blue file folder on the desktop caught her eye. It was turned the opposite way from a few manila files over and under it. Another talent Augusta had learned in the newspaper biz was how to read upside down. Her curiosity popped when she made out the word G-E-O-R-G-I-A-N-A. She checked the hallway. Nobody nearby. She grabbed the file. To be on the safe side, she retreated to the guest room bath, shut the door, and restarted the shower while she stood outside, fully dressed, and scanned the contents.

Very interesting.

Gloria called from just inside the bedroom doorway. "Everything okay?"

"Yep, can't resist a long shower. Won't take a sec to dress. My mother always said I should have been a fireman."

Gloria laughed and shut the door behind her.

The only snag for Augusta was how to return the file because now someone was on the phone in the adjoining room used as the office.

As forgetful as Dixie was, would she notice it missing? Augusta had no choice but to take the risk and filch it anyway.

"Hey, Dixie, I see you're up and about," Augusta said a few moments later from a screen door leading to the massive covered porch overlooking one of the fairways. Dixie tottered around the brick-floored patio on heeled mules, fiddling with orchids.

"Hello, Augusta. Want some sweet tea?"

"I can't stay, dear."

"No? Where do you have to rush off to?"

Augusta glanced at Gloria who nodded sadly, indicating she, too, realized Dixie had already forgotten about today's event though they'd discussed it again after Augusta called from the bike path.

"I'll take a rain check on that tea, but if time permits, I'll stop by after the BILL meeting and tell you both all the exciting details of my dance debut." If she could just get out of there before the file worked its way out of the top of her panty hose. Here she'd thought the rutched band beneath her waist a design flaw that made her look like a pregnant flapper. Turns out, it worked in her favor.

Dixie's mind must have slid back into the present. "You better," she said. "By the way, Augusta, break a leg."

≡ ≡ ≡

After I'd finished dressing for the BILL meeting, Daniel came into the closet. "Nope, wear this."

"Oh, honey, I can't. I wore that at a club function. They'll remember it."

"Mark my words, you'll thank me."

"Do you know something I don't?"

"My lips are sealed." He leaned down and kissed me. "They're available for kissing, though."

I chuckled. "I'd oblige your fashion sense, but everybody in the BILL saw this sunshine-bright number at your awards dinner. How about this?" I lifted a hanger holding a cobalt blue sundress with spaghetti straps and a matching short sleeve jacket trimmed with a ribbon of white polka dots.

Daniel said, "Maybe. Put it on."

I modeled it for him.

He came over and tipped me in a dip.

"Ow. The straps cut my shoulders when you do that."

"Won't do. Wear the yellow."

I gave him a suspicious look. "Lourdes said something about dance lessons being handy. You aren't roping me into some dance exhibition, are you?"

"Time flies. I'm late for our golf pro's homily on accuracy in hitting the green. Lectures I don't need. The eyesight of the thirty-year-old lecturer is what I need."

"Be mysterious, why don't you? Very well, I'll wear that yellow frock and perish from curiosity in the meantime."

He pecked my forehead. "I love your practical nature, dear."

"Go, learn." I flicked a hand at him. "Listen well. Maybe you'll win another tourney and I can enjoy more cucumber sandwiches."

He snatched what looked like a suit from his side of the closet. "Anything for the dry cleaners? I'm making a run later."

"No, thanks."

"Wow, I'm late. Bye." He saluted me and turned on his heel military style.

I put on the yellow dress and added a jacket before making my way to the garage.

In that area of the clubhouse dining room where the BILL was meeting this time, sheer drapes were closed against the bright sun streaming through the tall glass windows. A screen was off to the side, which normally wasn't in use during their meetings.

Lourdes, presiding over today's affair, was aglow in a to-mato-red sheath and matching red leather stilettos. Attendees took their seats at tables decorated with white linen cloths, red carnations, and black napkins.

"Snazzy," Janet said.

"Sharon and I worked on the scheme," Lourdes said. "I can't use the gavel. Dixie still has it and her friend Gloria called to say Dixie couldn't come today. Which is really, really too bad."

Women, who had not yet settled down since lunch, were in high spirits. Everyone raved over the club's version of arroz con pollo. The Spanish chicken-and-rice dish had been Lourdes' nod to her own ethnic tastes. It was a welcome change, especially after the ultra-light meal Becca had ordered at the previous meeting.

Instead of a gavel, Lourdes snapped her long, red-tipped fingers, which sounded like admonishing castanets. It stilled the cackling hens at this session of the BILL.

"Okay," she began in her soft, barely noticeable accent. "No old business, but a surprise. We have a distinguished visitor today, ladies."

She clapped her hands twice. Victor Herbert's "Merry Widow Waltz" blared from behind the screen before someone adjusted the sound. Daniel appeared in a tuxedo and top hat and bowed.

I was struck dumb.

Everyone's eyes flew from him to me.

"My wife is speechless, a first," Daniel teased before he held out his hand.

Mortified, I shook my head. "Uh-uh. Not me." So, that was a tux he'd sneaked out of the closet today pretending it was going to the cleaners. He must have dressed in the men's locker room. Pretty clever. I crossed my arms.

"See how she treats me?" He looked my way. "I'm saving my second dance for you, darling." He grinned. "You're not leaving this room until you and I... tango." He then addressed

the members. "As my better half has"—he cleared his throat—
"turned me down." A showman, he let the crowd react. Sympathetic "Awws" followed before he then said, "May I present
my backup dance partner since Mrs. Metcalf isn't here today?"

Suspense built. Whispers about Dixie flew, but were cut off
when Daniel started speaking again.

"Known to us all in Merry Acres as the wicked-witted
woman with a golden pen, welcome please, Ms. Augusta St.
James."

Muted applause greeted Augusta's name. Again, eyes flew
to and fro from Daniel to me and I felt my face was redder
than Lourdes' dress. I grew more self-conscious when I
sensed their suspicions. Not even I quite knew if my heated
face was from shock or anger.

Waiting a theatrical beat or two, Augusta appeared in a
tea-length silk dress of silver lame, skimming along in medium
high, French-heeled shoes, no doubt chosen so she wouldn't
best Daniel's six feet as she very well might have if she'd worn
high heels.

Her hair was darker, too. No grays peeked out, meaning
she'd sprung for a color job for the occasion. She embodied
the look of a patrician woman straight out of the 1930s. Augusta brandished a long, black, cigarette holder with a thin,
unlit cigar in her gloved hand. She was art deco personified.

"Quick, someone call Hercule Poirot," Janet Jessell joked.
"No, wait. Who needs him? I'll bet the next thing we'll hear is
that Gussie has solved the Mendez murder."

Augusta returned a stare that could freeze molten steel.
"Not yet. And, it's Augusta, if you please." The latter words
mimicked the tone of her ultra cool look.

Janet uttered a huffy, "Well, excuse me."

I snickered, thinking of the many times I'd endured Augusta's "Georgie." Reminding myself this was part of the
show, I tried to be a good sport. Probably rehearsed, for all I
knew. Golf lecture, indeed. Why hadn't Augusta told me about
this? Or my husband? Post traumatic syndrome attacked and
Rhonda popped into my head. What else were Daniel and my
friend keeping from me?

On cue, Daniel and Augusta glided over the carpet as if
they were finalists performing on a popular television show.
Although very good, neither was a dancing star of that caliber.

I squirmed. If Dixie had been the intended partner, when

had Daniel practiced with Augusta, and where? Their moves were too practiced, too smooth, to have happened within the last few hours.

Well, hell. I remembered Augusta's brassy remarks concerning Daniel the first time they'd met and thought of Rhonda. Again. That got my blood pumping. Shy or not, showman or not, I would tango all right. The mood I was in, I'd give sex appeal new meaning once I turned my tango with Daniel into an Apache dance.

The waltz ended.

Everyone, regardless of their feelings for Augusta, stood and clapped. The dancers bowed. Augusta disappeared, but not before glancing my way with what looked to me like a cruel smile. The music changed to "Orchids in the Moonlight." Daniel held out his gloved hand for me.

I strode to him, seeing nothing but Daniel. Old wounds reopened. My pulse raced as I recalled his affair with Rhonda. I took my position in his arms and muttered, "So, how often were you...uh...*waltzing* with Augusta behind my back?"

He looked aghast, then quickly readjusted his expression for the onlookers with a fake smile. He said, "Exactly the mood for a tango."

"You think?"

"This wasn't exactly planned, Georgiana. Dixie couldn't come to half the practice sessions. I'm happy, however, despite your mood, if it goaded you into dancing in public."

Hyper-aware, I felt the beat of his heart as we performed what was essentially a rough sex act to music, in public. "You didn't answer me about how much time you spent with Augusta."

He twirled me out, then reeled me in. I sneered at him, digging my index fingernail along his cheek but not deep enough to draw blood. I heard every musical note over the voice in my head screaming, *bastard, bastard, bastard.*

He entreated, "Augusta was kind enough to fill in for Dixie Metcalf. It was the only way I knew to make you show these gals what you could do on the dance floor. We practiced waltz steps a couple of times. *Nothing else.*"

The music ended. "Liar." My eyes raked his face more sharply than my nail had.

His eyes pleaded, but I gave no mercy. The ovation brought me to the present. I tried to remove my hand en-

closed in Daniel's, but he would not relinquish it. Stuck together, we bowed as I bestowed upon the BILL members a
stare ten times colder than Augusta's had been.

Ripping my hand from Daniel's, I stalked to my chair,
grabbed my purse, and started to leave the room. I was too
hurt and angry to cry. Humiliated in public, again.

Alarmed at the turn of events, Lourdes looked over at
Janet and signed a slicing move against her neck. She
mouthed, "End it."

Janet dashed behind the screen and turned off the music.

I tracked toward the double-door entryway like a train, but
Lourdes ran after me. "Don't be angry. Please, Georgiana, lis-
ten. Dixie couldn't come today. There's nothing between
Daniel and Augusta." She blurted, "It's not like her and
Mendez." Lourdes' hands flew to her mouth. "God, forget I
said that."

I stopped and took a much-needed breath. "Interesting.
Homicide just crossed my own mind. Maybe Mrs. Mendez once
felt the same way."

Lourdes went pale.

Another BILL member meowed. "Watch out. Rumor has it
Augusta's affairs start in the men's card room then move to
the bedroom. Maybe this time, she stopped off on the dance
floor."

"Shut up," Lourdes snapped. "Drink your wine and keep
those comments to yourself. Besides, the men's card room is
off limits to women, just as ours is to men."

I searched Lourdes' face. "Yes, that's true, isn't it?" I
grabbed the lifeline of a shaky truth.

"Sure it is. Now, you go over there and make up with your
husband who only did us a favor."

Before I acted on Lourdes' suggestion, the social director
rushed in, practically knocking us aside. A uniformed police
officer followed.

Sharon scanned the room and zoomed toward Becca
Bernstein, indicating Mrs. Bernstein should follow her behind
the screen. Standing just outside the screen, the officer said
something.

Becca came out from the screened area, went white, and
swayed.

Daniel, the only other man present, rushed over in their
direction. "What's wrong?" He brought over a chair and the

officer helped Becca into it.

Sharon wrung her hands.

"No, you're wrong. It's a mistake." Becca wailed in decibels that would put a commercial airliner's jet engine to shame. "Benny would have called me if anything was wrong. He always carries his cell phone when he jogs. My Benny's not dead, I tell you. He can't be. Certainly not from any goddamned heart attack."

CHAPTER SEVEN

"That's it, gals." Janet took over for Lourdes who was still occupied with my temper fit.

Janet promptly dismissed the BILL members, no doubt ad-libbing when she said, "Details about the next meeting will follow by phone or e-mail."

Women gathered in clumps around hysterical Becca. Finally, after spending the last of her passion and the waterfall of tears slowed to trickles, Becca turned stoic. Lourdes left me for Becca, where she patted her shoulder. "I'll take you home. Come along, now. We'll all help you through this."

"How? You're leaving town," Becca said. "My children! I must call them."

"Of course," Lourdes soothed.

Daniel and the police officer, awkward guardians, stood by.

"Georgiana." Daniel signaled me over with his hand. "Why don't you take Mrs. Bernstein home in your car?"

I wanted to shout, "Why don't you, Casanova?" Yet, I answered the call for help. Having nothing against Becca, I obeyed. "I'm so sorry, Becca. You can call your children from home."

Becca looked at the officer. "Where was Ben when...? At home? Is his body there now?" She looked horrified at the thought.

The young officer looked at his feet. "Someone discovered

his body on one of the jogging trails and alerted the security guard who called 9-1-1. Your husband's body is at the County Morgue, Mrs. Bernstein," he said gently. "You'll need to iden-tify the body then contact a funeral home. They'll know how to proceed after the body is released following an autopsy."

"Autopsy?" Becca cried. Her bosom shook with another wave of grief. "Oh God. Don't tell me my Ben's on some cold slab. Sliced open and gutted like a fish? No, I won't give per-mission."

"It is customary under the circumstances. I'm sorry." The officer, quite uncomfortable, looked around one last time and strode out.

Becca could not be comforted.

Augusta, gone now, would be furious she hadn't been in the thick of things. At least the woman had enough decorum to make herself scarce after that waltz routine. I concentrated on a grieving Becca. "Wait until the medical examiner issues his cause of death. That will answer your questions."

Becca wiped away tears and sniffled. "That sounds rea-sonable." I walked her out. On the way to the door, Becca looked back at her BILL sisters. "Keep us in your thoughts and prayers." She started to sniffle again and I rubbed her back.

"Daniel will drive your car home." I looked at my husband who nodded stiffly in agreement. Becca fished in her purse then threw the keys on a chair.

At the outside entrance to the club, I said, "Wait here, Becca. I'll come around for you. I didn't use valet parking so I have to get my car. Meanwhile, lean on that cement column, dear, if you feel weak. "

Becca, compliant now, did so.

We drove to the Bernstein residence in strained silence.

"Don't come in, Georgiana. I have to, you know, let Ben's death sink in. For that, I want privacy. After, I'll call our kids and...our Rabbi." She looked into my eyes. "I'll be all right."

She worked to shift her stocky body from the SUV. With slumping shoulders, she moved in the direction of the front door. I heard a doleful sob before the door shut.

At least Ben's death had changed the wagging tongues of BILL members from peccadilloes to deaths. The last thing I wanted was to face Daniel so I drove to the mall. Listless, I walked around.

On a whim, I stopped in a store that specialized in electronics.

"May I help you?"

Taking a breath, I said, "Do you sell surveillance equipment? I have a pet sitter I'm not sure about. I guess I want a nanny cam."

The man assisting was probably the proprietor. About eighty, with kind eyes, he said, "A nanny cam, eh? For your...uh...pets?"

God help me, I blushed. "Yes. I'm not sure my little darlings are being treated as kindly as they deserve."

The man said, "Follow me."

He showed me some stuffed animals. "These are naturally more than they first appear. A small camera records visual activity via the toy's eyes. There isn't any audio, however. For that, you might try a small voice-activated recorder and place it in a remote spot. You might need more than one. They're not inexpensive. I have older, outdated models I could sell at a discount."

"How much for one voice-activated recorder?"

"Twenty-five dollars."

"I'll start there. Would it work under the driver's side of a car?"

He stopped boxing the recorder. "Odd place to monitor a pet sitter."

I looked down at my purse.

"I'm a retired therapist. May I make a suggestion? Forget this device. Go home, make your husband a nice dinner, put on some soft music, and get reacquainted."

"Thank you for your advice," I said tartly. "You didn't answer my question."

"Yes. There would be engine and road noise to consider. This isn't the top of the line equipment. See, allow me to show you how this works."

After he showed me once, I tried it myself. On the third try, I grew competent with its workings.

He boxed it. "Thank you for stopping in. Good luck with the...er...pet sitter."

I huffed out and drove to The Athenian Garden for Greek coffee.

Was that man right? Was I creating mountains from mole hills? Things picked at me. The time Augusta had dropped by with the candle and overtly complimented Daniel. The time

Augusta mentioned almost sideswiping Daniel and our neighbor in the golf cart and Daniel's never breathing a word about it.

Stop it. It was a near miss, and no one was hurt. My gut said something wasn't right. Maybe an affair with Augusta had yet to begin, but Daniel couldn't be trusted. Augusta either. She was an instigator, probably some borderline personality type who lived through the drama she caused in the lives of others, having little in her own life as far as I knew.

Since the restaurant lot was full, I parked at Barb's Book Nook. Waiting out the lunch crowd, I went into the bookstore. The effort was useless. I couldn't read titles for the tears prickling my eyes. What if Daniel was sleeping with Augusta? The same old thoughts looped over and over. We had no assets to split. Another thing, I'd taken something that wasn't mine years ago, and for that I had to pay. And pay. And pay.

Wanting to forget my guilt over breaking up Daniel's home, I sought warmth, familiarity and safety. Lost in my own thoughts, I told Barb, the bookstore owner, "I'll be back later." I started across the street. Still distracted, I walked behind a car pulling out of the lot and was nearly run over. The irate driver blasted me with the car's horn, forcing me to watch where I walked with greater care.

Somehow I found myself inside the café. Angry and frustrated, I dug my nails into my hands, staring into space.

Sensing distress, I guess, the owner came over. "Are you all right?"

Wonderful, make a spectacle of yourself. "Yes, thank you, Joe." He stood near the hostess stand and greeted another diner while I made an excuse for my weird behavior. I whispered to the woman at the cash register who was about my age, "Night sweats are keeping me awake."

The woman nodded. "Oh yes." She signaled to Joe. "Water."

I accepted the glass and drained it dry. "Thank you."

Joe exchanged a knowing glance with her before he sat me at a nearby table.

"Coffee and baklava are what I need."

He grinned. "A whole one this time, eh?"

I smiled. "Yes." As if I could eat.

Allowing the caffeine to boost my sagging spirits, I picked at the dessert.

"Guess I wasn't as hungry as I thought." I paid my tab. Not wanting to go home, I returned to the bookstore.

"Hello, again," Barb said. "What can I show you? Some romances?"

"No! I mean, I'm up to here with that genre"—I moved my index finger across my forehead—"How about"—I fought for something convincing—"a murder mystery?"

"Those are on the shelves over to your right. Shall I suggest something?"

"No, I'll just browse. Thanks."

Brass bells strung over the door clanged, announcing another customer. Barb left me and moved in the direction of the storefront. A minute later, after making a show as if I were really looking at the books, I said, "Sorry, nothing grabs my attention today."

The owner nodded, assisting a woman busily stacking several books on her arm.

On the drive home, I thought of Dixie. How soon before the Merry Acres version of Blanche DuBois would learn about today's fiasco and call me to "sympathize"? In a proactive mood, I swung by Dixie's golf villa and rang the bell to preempt such a call but there was no answer.

I stopped at Mojito Joes and ordered a mojito. But I wanted it my way, telling the bartender to make it with lime, seltzer, tequila mix, and vodka.

"That's not a mojito, ma'am."

"It is, in my opinion."

I paid the tab and sipped, allowing the liquor to act as a magic elixir to ease pain. After I'd reached the last drop, I quit feeling sorry for myself and planned to drop by the HELP shelter with a sack of paperbacks in the trunk.

After consulting directions I'd scribbled down weeks ago, I soon parked on the street in front of a modest house in a working class neighborhood. I navigated a chunk of broken sidewalk heaved up from the advancing roots of an ailing oak. Who'd planted that, way too far south for its own good? Someone had tried to jolly up the place with flowers. Scraggly Blue Daze and some yellow lantanas, a hardy bush that could take neglect, pushed against the front stucco wall. An untrimmed Areca palm, with yellow-tipped fronds begging for magnesium, shaded some of the porch.

I hoisted the bag onto a receptionist's counter. "I brought

some books."

The harried woman barely acknowledged me. "Just leave them."

My eyes pored over two poorly dressed children holding jelly sandwiches. They stared at the books and then me for a minute, before they went tooth-and-tong over a toy between bites of their snack. A woman no more than twenty handed the older one a wet cloth. "Wipe your face, Will. After him, you wipe yours, Ethan."

The children argued with her and she popped the eldest on the arm. They wiped their faces.

"Books, huh?" She pointed to the brown bag with a finger tipped by nails too long and too bright. Her clothes were clean but clingy. She wore flats with rundown heels. Flax-colored blonde strands extended several inches beyond three-inch dark roots.

"Yes."

"Thanks." Her tone implied little gratitude. "We don't have a lot of time to read around here."

I suspected a twenty dollar bill would be much more appreciated than used books.

The woman went back to the kids. "You know I have to leave for work in a few minutes and I don't want any arguments or fighting after I'm gone. You'll get us tossed out of here before our time's up."

I wondered what kind of employment awaited this woman. My upbringing hardly engendered maternal instinct, but that was a positive so far as already-a-daddy Daniel was concerned when our illicit romance began.

Acting on the spur of the moment, I walked back to the receptionist. "Do you accept donations?"

The word donation brought a smile to the mouth of an African American woman standing nearby. "Sure do."

"I wish I could give more." I wrote out a check for thirty dollars. "My address is on the check. Send a receipt, please, for tax purposes."

"Sure thing." Three lines rang at once. The receptionist answered with "H-E-L-P." She prompted callers to hold and then answered one of the lines. "Line one for you."

"Excuse me." The woman who'd taken the donation went into a room that apparently served as her office. The receptionist checked on waiting callers. "Amy here, How may I direct your call? Hold, please, she's on another line." Frankly, I was surprised she answered giving her own name and the shelter's name. That would hardly put off unwanted searches by abusive spouses and others. Deadbeat dads wouldn't care and maybe the name the receptionist gave wasn't her real name. Or she was an employee, not a resident as I'd first thought.

Compared to these women, my life was a bowl of peaches and cream. I'd see this place got some money if I had to go back to work. It occurred to me I didn't need a shrink, I needed gainful employment. Work was the only therapy I'd ever known. Paying off Daniel's gambling debts was more likely if I brought home a paycheck. Still, helping others in some way would get my mind off my own marital mess.

I drove around Merry Acres a while. Someone had said Merry was buried on the grounds. I wondered where, since I felt a kindred spirit with her. I drew the line at killing Daniel, but that didn't mean I didn't feel like it. I never found the grave.

It was after six o'clock. Ready or not, it was time to go home. I took the long way home, driving well under the speed limit all the way there.

≡ ≡ ≡

"Where've you been? I've been frantic." Daniel rushed out to the garage. "I called Mrs. Bernstein; she said you'd left hours ago."

"Out."

"We need to talk. You have the wrong impression about Augusta and me."

"Leopards change their spots, do they?"

He glared. "That's unfair."

"Unfair?"

He groaned. "Just when we were doing better."

"Just. I ate a substantial lunch at the BILL meeting and snacked at a restaurant later so I'm not hungry." I wanted to scream, *You take away my appetite.*

"I'm not hungry either. I'll make a sandwich."

"Whatever. I'm going to change clothes."

He opened a bottle of beer and then slumped in a dining room chair. "Welcome home," he said sarcastically.

"Home," I said in reply, "just another four-letter word."
Détente was over.

≡≡≡

Days later, I paid the handyman who, at long last, showed up and fixed the doorbell, as well as completed remaining repairs. Daniel was out on the course, probably making bets. I no longer cared as my volunteer work kept me busy. I spent four hours once a week at the HELP house, dropping the library from my volunteer roster. I forgot about mentoring, too. I wasn't in the mood to present some bright, happy face to a kid who would see through my ruse in five minutes.

Taking stock, I realized the BILL wasn't panning out either. Visits to HELP were therapeutic, but I remained bored. The therapist said boredom was another form of anger. I read snippets about the Mendez murder investigation, which was not progressing. Household and marketing chores left little time for snooping into the Mendez case, but I desperately needed another distraction, so I called a friend at Daniel's old insurance agency.

"Hey, Lilly, how are you?"

"Georgiana. Wow, it's been a while since we talked, huh? I got your earlier message, what, a few weeks ago? Sorry, first there's work and then the kids came down with colds. You know there's no rest for the wicked. How is Daniel?"

Sipping on a soda, I said, "Fine. I wanted to ask a favor of you."

"What's that?"

"Next time you call the state to check corporate officers for corporate umbrella and product liability policies, run a name by them. Manny Mendez, probably Manuel Mendez." I filled my former work buddy in on the auto dealership name and address details. "See if he happens to be listed as a corporate honcho for any other corporation. I'd like to know. No rush."

Lily said, "If and when I can. Might be a while. Again, I'm sorry."

"Whenever is fine, and thank you in advance."

Now to get ready for tonight.

We'd argued about it over breakfast, but agreed to make our last dance session since it was paid for. We could use time away from the house at night anyway. A bath soothed my nerves, but I hadn't a clue what to wear for the event.

"Anybody home?" Daniel called.

Through the vanity mirror I saw him enter the bedroom and heard him toss his money clip on the dresser and dig change and golf tees from his pockets. Breathless, he came into the bathroom.

When he looked my way, he averted his gaze and said, "I need to shower. I decided better here than in the men's locker room."

Not keen on displaying my nudity, I grabbed my robe from a nearby hook while Daniel stripped and entered the shower stall. At the vanity, I pulled my hair back into a severe chignon and hoped the pins wouldn't fly out of my fine, straight hair before the dance routine ended. After lining my eyes with a heavy hand, I used a lip plumper lipstick that made my lips tingle. Ready except for slipping into a dress, I lacked enthusiasm.

My final selection was a dress culled earlier from a cedar chest and discarded. It was a ruffled affair in red cotton eyelet I hadn't worn in years and was shocked it still fit, if too snugly. I decided to wear it.

Tonight, we would perform the *paso doble*, a fast-breaking Latin number that Daniel had taken to as easily as Fred Astaire to tap shoes. I, as usual, would stumble around as best I could.

Content with a pseudo-Spanish look, I might at least look the part while I lurched around. It didn't matter. Daniel was the type of dancer skilled enough to maneuver anyone so artfully others in the class wouldn't find my moves completely laughable. All I worried about was tripping. I didn't need a broken limb as well as a bruised heart.

Dance lessons, the reconciliation ploy, were to have brought Daniel and me together, off the dance floor as well as on. It had, briefly. So much for good intentions.

And so, Mr. and Mrs. Daniel Duncan arrived five minutes early for our final session. We entered the studio in a cautiously optimistic mood, having, on the way over, chitchatted more as roommates than a happily wedded couple.

Still, partly cloudy skies were better than thunderstorms.

The session ended. Daniel danced so well the studio owner asked him to work part-time. "No, thanks, but I'll keep the offer in mind."

"Yep, a real Valentino, that guy," said I to one of the spectators, not the least bit hurt when no such employment offer was extended my way.

Back at home, I spurned Daniel's overture for a nightcap and retired earlier than usual to read. I must have read nearly twenty books in a two week span. Reading the last line of the current novel on the bedside table, I yawned before adding this paperback to the hefty bag of used books I'd take to the shelter.

Lately, I'd learned to "suffer the little children" at the shelter. I even started a garden in the backyard flower bed beyond the sandbox. Some of the preschool children "helped" by watering the plants. If they continued with their enthusiastic and well-meaning "care," the plants might live a couple weeks, tops, before root rot set in. I'd visited a few consignment and thrift stores, talking them into donating unclaimed clothes to the shelter, which I worked into suitable work wardrobes for a couple of the women. I even helped one or two construct a résumé.

Daniel played golf and cards daily, foregoing tennis after he came home with a severe limp and an ACE bandage on his ankle. We passed on a club outing invite from the next door neighbors featuring a club dance. For the time being, our days of dancing together were done.

I hadn't seen or heard from Augusta. Or Dixie. The HELP shelter claimed more of my time. Good thing, too, since I'd actually started wondering whether Karl Esterhause's death was accidental.

Who would profit?

For something to do at home and to keep my mind off marital and financial problems, I discovered the name of the carrier underwriting the Esterhause policy. Turned out I knew someone who worked at the company's home office.

That source revealed that while the policy amount was sizeable, it wasn't out of the ordinary for people living the retired, resort-community lifestyle. The same went for the Bernsteins' policy issued by the same insurance company, written by the same agent, another Barrier Isles club member.

Closure came rapidly for the Bernstein family after the autopsy, which Becca's son, a prominent attorney in Miami, pressed buttons to rush through. Honoring Jewish traditions, Ben was buried within twenty-four hours after the body was released to the funeral home. Becca didn't turn a hand. Her son handled everything. At the service, Becca mentioned their personal physician had consulted with the county medical examiner with whom he played golf. Extensive drug tests were made but it would be weeks before a final formal report was issued. However, nothing odd popped up in the initial lab results.

As if there could be any suspicions about Ben or Becca.

Ben's cell phone wasn't with his body, Becca said. Police figured he dropped it when he fell and, later, a stranger picked it up. Possibly whoever called to report the body on the walking trail to security guards. Becca promptly cancelled the service, disappointed no one turned it in to the club's lost and found.

As for Dixie Metcalf, she was linked in my mind with Ben's death, but only because she happened to be absent from the BILL meeting that day and had not been seen since.

That mystery was solved when I ran into Janet Jessell at the Merry Mart. According to Janet, Dixie had returned to Georgia where she was undergoing treatment in an assisted care facility specializing in Alzheimer's patients. No shock there. Didn't matter. I never seriously considered Dixie a murder suspect What was her motive in any of the deaths?

Susie Esterhause was a different matter. She hadn't appeared especially close to her husband. She liked to shop and spend money. So what? If that was a valid motive, every woman in Merry Acres would be rounded up for processing at the local jail.

The life insurance payoff was within reason. Nor had Susie profited from the sale of her inherited Merry Acres property. According to that ever-dependable info source, Daniel's card buddies—the friend of a realtor that one of the card players knew—related that Susie, in fact, lost money when she accepted the first offer presented in this buyer's market.

These random thoughts were no more than mind play. Besides, no further mishaps overtook any of the remaining married men of Merry Acres.

≡ ≡ ≡

Daniel dropped a stunner at the dinner table one night not too long after Ben's burial. "Heard a rumor in the card room today. The Bernstein house sold. Same deal as Mendez and Esterhause. Off shore bidder, as-is, prompt sale. Even better, they all resold! Some lucky speculator with a Midas touch flipped three properties in a down market just like that." He snapped his fingers.

"Weird."

"Uh-huh." Daniel nodded, eating his pot roast and mashed potatoes. "Out of fifty-some-odd listings in this place, the Mendez, Esterhause, and Bernstein places all sold within weeks of the listing date. Of course, there were extenuating circumstances not attendant to other listings languishing on the market."

"True. Selling on the cheap to leave behind bad memories." *Been there, done that.* I sipped bottled water. "I have a request for you. It requires a dance instructor."

Daniel looked wary. "Sorry, I've hung up my dancing shoes."

"Come on. It's for a good cause."

"I'm not agreeing until you tell me what's involved."

How times had changed. Once, he would have agreed instantly so long as I asked and tripping the light fantastic was in the offing.

I cleared the table alone. Daniel no longer helped out. Instead, he plopped into his recliner post-dinner. "The kids at HELP are so-o-o-o bored. I can't dance, nor am I into kinder care. However, I thought you could teach them some dance steps."

He laughed derisively. "Sorry, I don't do the bunny hop or hip hop."

"Really, Daniel." I tried to tone down the whine in my voice before I continued. "They might take to it. What do you have to lose?"

"Precious hours of my aging life, for one thing. Who would be my partner? You?"

I didn't like his unflattering emphasis. Much as I didn't want to include Augusta, I'd rather not dance with Daniel myself. That would hardly inspire the kids anyway. "No, I thought I'd call Augusta, the drama queen, and mend fences, and possibly provide her with fodder for her column. You two could reenact your waltz routine."

Daniel shook his head. "No way."

"Look, Daniel, things could not get any worse between us

if you fucked her in the middle of the dance floor."

"Only way I'll get laid."

"True. Oh, and I would very much appreciate it if you would keep certain details of my childhood private, like the fact my mother and I once spent a *brief* period of time in a shelter when I was a toddler. That is not for public consumption. Augusta mentioned it at lunch one day. I wonder how she knew?" I lowered my head and put my index finger to my chin in a grossly theatric posture.

Daniel looked like he'd been shot in the gut.

So, he had gossiped about my past to the guys he played cards with, and Augusta. "All you"—I made angry, exaggerated quote marks with my fingers—"'guys' talk a lot over cards, huh?" I stormed back to the bedroom and slammed the door. Then opened it for only a second. "Feel free to sleep in the guest room." I slammed the door again.

Not so long ago, he would have followed after me to make amends.

No such conciliatory action was forthcoming on either side.

≡ ≡ ≡

The next morning, Daniel, bleary-eyed from having slept in the guest room with its eastern exposure and gauzy window covering that allowed the full force of the morning sun to blast him into the new day, extended an olive branch.

"Tell you what. I'm a sport. If you get Augusta to agree to your entertainment project for the HELP kids, I'll do it."

I gloated. "Deal." A two-for, no, a three-for: keeping hubby close and a possible enemy to our tattered marriage closer, as well as furthering a good cause. I'd watch them as they practiced together. So help me, if I caught Daniel and Augusta in a single compromising scene, I would divorce him.

Aware my husband hadn't slept well, I noisily unloaded the dishwasher.

He looked over-anxious, the way he did when hiding gambling debts. The kernel of angst in my stomach ballooned into a knotted fist punching at my insides. Anything affecting my security unnerved me. Especially now. I slammed the dishwasher door. "Everything all right?"

He bobbed his head a couple of times. "Just peachy." However, he took his coffee cup and went outside to read the paper there.

"I'll bet," I said under my breath and took my own coffee back to the bedroom.

That afternoon, after striking out on both Augusta's home phone and cell, I dialed the *Gazette*. "Augusta St. James, please."

"Hold, please."

An eternity later, Augusta inquired, "St. James, here. Whoever the heck you are, I'm behind schedule. So whatever it is you want better be easily answered."

"Hey, it's me, Georgiana."

"Well, as I live and breathe." Pause. "Excuse me, I'm puffing on a ciggie. Unfortunately for me, my little prop in that stupid waltz number for the BILL reactivated my tobacco desire receptors." She paused. The sound emitted was like smoke escaping her mouth. In a nasty tone, she asked, "How the hell are you, *Mrs.* Duncan? Still seeing 'other women' behind every bedpost?"

Gritting my teeth, I convinced myself this ploy would not only allow me to watch body language between Daniel and Augusta for clues about their loyalty, but give the women and kids at the shelter a night of fun.

Augusta's sarcasm wasn't an especially auspicious beginning, but the columnist hadn't hung up. I casually replied, "I'm well, thank you. And, if I recall, your prop was an unlit cigar, not a lighted cigarette, so don't blame the BILL." Smoking, eh? Maybe Augusta was worried about something other than her column. What could it be, a breakup with Daniel?

"Just so you know, Georgiana, I've frequented the men's card room where I played poker and gin rummy with Daniel and his buds. I get in 'cause I'm considered 'one of the boys.' I play cards for money. It's another source of income. You okay with that? Too bad, if not."

"No problem." I went one-on-one with the levity queen, adding a spunky, "so long as you let Daniel win once in a while. We need income, too, you know."

"What can I do for you? I'm on a really, really tight deadline, like five minutes ago. Fact of the matter is the copy editor is glaring over my shoulder as we speak." She adjusted her decibel level even higher. "Might say I have an on-the-job injury known as singed shoulder blade."

"I have an idea for your column." I couldn't help poking

fun at Augusta, so I decided to return the favor of using an unflattering nickname as she had with me. "That's why I called, Gussie."

"Gussie?"

"Turnaround is fair play. Nobody but you calls me 'Georgie.'"

"What idea?"

"Dancing at the HELP shelter. Wait, don't hang up. This idea is a gem. It involves charitable works, current trends, and you play a major part in the story."

Pause. "I'm listening. Wait a second, I simply must confer with this *vexing* copy editor."

A string of cuss words followed by lots of mumbling. The only clear thing I heard was Augusta saying, "One more minute." Then sounds like lots of pages turning. "Damn, you're right. Mine is the wrong usage." Keyboard clicking followed and more puffing sounds before Augusta said to someone, "I hate it when you're right." A brief silence was followed by smoker's cough. "Okay, Georgie, I'm back."

In the zone, I out-purred the late Eartha Kitt, "You and Daniel could recreate your waltzing wizards number for kids at HELP. That might encourage the kids to learn ballroom dancing. Their mothers watch that dance show on television so they might be encouraged to try dancing on their own. I might convince the dance studio to throw in some free lessons for good publicity."

Pause. Puff. Puff. Sigh. "I'll think about it. Bye." Augusta hung up.

Nonplussed, I stared at the receiver as if it could interpret Augusta's mindset on the idea.

I stalked to the laundry room, dried some towels, and was shuffling toward the linen closet in the master bath when the phone rang. "Yes! Augusta bit." I dashed for it. "Hey."

"Georgiana, it's Lilly. I've got some information for you, got a pencil?"

"Oh, hello. I'm sorry, I'm never prepared. Give me a minute." I scrambled over to my night table drawer and extracted a pen and pad. "Ready."

"That Mendez guy was registered agent and everything else, except treasurer, for a corporation on file with the Florida Secretary of State known as Sun And Sand, Inc., a realty company, in addition to the auto dealership you mentioned.

No tax returns for Sun and Sand, but the entity was only a few months old. If the treasurer filed for an extension, that's reasonable and perfectly legit."

"Who's listed as treasurer?"

"Hold a sec." Georgiana heard Lily shuffling things on her desk. "A. A. Audette."

"Drawing a blank. Thanks, anyway, Lilly. I'll buy you lunch next time I'm on the west coast."

"Deal. Regards to Daniel. Bye-bye."

I went back to restocking the bathroom linen closet, disappointed Lilly's return call hadn't yielded better results, like naming Augusta as treasurer.

Who the heck was A. A. Audette?

CHAPTER EIGHT

The next day, I was surprised when I opened the front door to Augusta.

"Hello, Georgie." Augusta held up a white paper sack. "I brought a smoothie. Did I mention I'm researching health food? Lucky you, this is a tasty treat unlike the herbal grass drink I tried last week. Ick."

I eyed Augusta. "A white bag, as in a white flag? I know, it's a peace offering for not telling me beforehand about plans for a waltz routine with my husband for the BILL. And you were rude when we talked on the phone yesterday."

"Sometimes a smoothie is just a smoothie." Augusta's lips slowly bloomed into a grin. "Mind if I come in and sit down at your kitchen table? You have such a cheery kitchen, so well ordered, so unlike mine."

We walked to the back of the house and sat down at the small drop-leaf table.

Augusta removed two tall take-out cups and handed me one along with a long straw. "Strawberry, banana, and yogurt blended with vitamin-laden protein powder." She sucked on her own straw. "Not bad, as far as this stuff goes. You ask me, some rum and a little umbrella would help."

"Freebies? Or did you purchase these at a discount?"

Augusta's look soured. "No, in fact I paid full price. Can you believe that? No respect for the power of the press. That's okay, though. Wait and see if the health food store gets mentioned by name in my article."

Augusta reached for the prescription bottle abutting the salt and pepper shakers. "What's this?"

I snatched the bottle. "Nothing." I jumped up and shoved the pills into a cabinet.

"Touchy. Where's Daniel?"

What, you don't know? "Golfing." I looked at my visitor. "Presumably."

"Drat, I wanted to tell you both at the same time. I've thought over your suggestion and I think, since it might make reasonably good copy for my column, I'll dance with Daniel. That is, if you and the HELP staff arrange it on a day that doesn't hinder my limited time for golf, card play, or writing the column."

"That certainly limits it." I was pleased Augusta wanted to address me *and* Daniel. "I'll set things up and let you know. If you can, you can. If not, I'll dream up something else."

"Aren't you going to at least taste it? Another reason I dropped by, I want to buy another candle like the one I gave you. The holder is unique. Trust me, I've looked. There's no more at the local store so I thought I'd search online for one. Would you mind if I looked at it? Maybe there's something etched on it to help narrow the search."

"Not at all. Actually, I prefer bringing it to you." I didn't want her to put one foot in my bedroom, innocently or not. "I haven't cleaned our bathroom today."

The phone rang. "I'll take this in our bedroom since it's on the way to the master bath. I'll be back in a second. Go on, enjoy the rest of your smoothie. I'll drink mine while I get the candle and talk on the phone."

A few minutes later, I returned with the candle.

Her usual tactful self, Augusta said, "You look horrible, somebody die?"

"I just heard from a ghost named Rhonda." I sucked down the rest of the smoothie and hurled the cup into the trash. "Don't ask," I said hoarsely.

Augusta busied herself with the candle and made notes on a small spiral-bound pad in her purse. "Look"—the foot of her crossed leg bounced and her voice was chock full of remorse, whether genuine or not, who knew—"I can see you've got things to do and thoughts to think. Relay my agreement to Daniel and call me." She slowly rose. "I'll see myself out."

I barely nodded in reply.

When I heard the front door shut, I laid my head on my folded arms and wept. Rhonda "just called to see how things were on the east coast." I suddenly felt very tired and closed my eyes.

Sometime later I woke up, outside the garage, on the hard cement of the driveway.

Daniel bellowed. "What the hell are you up to?"

Groggy, I replied, "What?"

"That was bright, Georgiana, really bright." He huffed, pulling me to my feet. "For heaven's sakes, shutting yourself up in my Corvette with the motor on and the garage door down. Come on, get up. Let's go inside before the neighbors see us."

He pulled me to our shower, started the water, and shoved me in. "Wake up. Wake up." He slapped my face for good measure.

"Hey."

"That's nothing. What I'd really like to do is wring your neck. What the hell were you trying to pull? We can forget therapy sessions. You're worse, not better. Damn it all."

Cold and wet, I shivered. "How did I get into your car?"

Daniel ran his hands through his gray hair. "Oh come on, Georgiana. It's too late to play innocent now. I caught you, and just in time, too. Otherwise, I'd be a novelty around here, a widower and not a widow. What brought this on?"

"Rhonda called, I remember that."

"For crying out loud, how long will I be on trial? They parole convicted armed robbers after serving half their sentences. I'm sorry about Rhonda. It's over. Done. History."

"She called today."

Daniel's puffy anger deflated instantly. "Oh my God."

I started shaking.

Daniel held me. "I have no idea how she knew our number, it's unlisted. Forget her. Let's get you in some dry clothes and into bed. I'll make you some hot milk."

He rustled around. Before too long, I was in silk pajamas I seldom wore and between crisp, fresh sheets I'd put on earlier. Sipping the hot beverage, I let the warmth soothe me. "I don't remember going out to the garage, or getting in your car, much less starting it."

Daniel grunted as if he found that hard to believe. When I

finished the drink, he took the empty mug. "Get some sleep. I'll make something for dinner."

"Feed yourself. I'm not hungry. Just shut the door on your way out."

"Okay. I'll check on you later."

"Oh, and Daniel, you can sleep in here tonight."

"Whatever. Though you do need a keeper, apparently."

When I heard the door shut to my dark cocoon of comfort, I slept.

The next morning, we both walked on eggshells.

In an overtly cheery voice, I started a conversation. "Augusta came by yesterday. She brought me a smoothie, as a peace offering, I suppose. She said to tell you she'll dance with you when I can arrange it with the HELP people."

Daniel looked up from the paper. "Are you sure you can handle my dancing with Augusta? Are you sure it won't trigger something like...yesterday's episode?"

How could I convince him I really didn't know what happened yesterday? The experience was too terrifying for my mind to get around. How could I have committed such an act without conscious thought? Rhonda's call had been upsetting, of course, but that much? "Yes, Daniel, I'm sure."

After dressing, I drove to the shelter where I spent a couple hours helping with office paper work. The staff was thrilled with my dance idea but couldn't promise cooperation from the kids. The women in residence, and the staff, would certainly enjoy the diversion though. They all put their heads together and decided the best day would be Tuesday next, around four in the afternoon.

I discussed the date and time with Daniel first, then called Augusta since it didn't conflict with any of Daniel's goings on.

"Works for me, too," Augusta said. Her tone implied she was in a rare down mood. "This health food thing is going nowhere copy-wise, and I've got to turn in something. Maybe I could get a photographer out to the shelter." I listened as she drummed her fingers on some hard surface. "This is a wild, out-there idea but maybe, just maybe, I could get a local television channel to cooperate. You know, community outreach, et cetera, et cetera. No promises."

"Oh, Augusta, that would be so cool."

"Easy for you to say. You're not the unphotogenic woman making an ass of herself posing as an aging, wannabe dancer.

Anyway, see you next Tuesday, with...uh...bells on."

"Wonderful! So you know how much I appreciate this, I won't feed my dear hubby garlic for lunch next Tuesday."

"You're too kind. Goodbye."

I jubilantly ran in place. "Think of the publicity," I said aloud. "Money might eke in to the shelter." It occurred to me Daniel was right, my mood swings were dangerously diverse. I put on jogging clothes and went for a long walk.

The warm weather had yet to reach hellish temperatures and the daily sticky monsoon rains that pummeled the area in the summer months. Black olives towered over the trail, providing some welcome shade in this little part of the subtropical South Florida world.

Merry Acres was a thousand acres sandwiched between State Road A1A on one side and a strip of very expensive sand, five miles in length, lined with condos on the other. That was separated by a fingernail-width stretch of water surrounding an even more exclusive stretch of sand—an island worlds away from the daily life of folks in Merry Acres and most anywhere else.

I came across a makeshift memorial against a frangipani tree. The small brass vase held a single, wilting, white rose. Wasn't this near the spot where someone had found Ben? Since Becca had moved out of the area, I wondered who had replenished the tribute flower.

Thoughts of mortality and my queer trip to the garage the other day sped me past the marker.

At home, I found Daniel's note. He'd stopped by after I'd left. Card pals had invited him south to Delray for card play. Consequently, I should count him out for lunch and possibly dinner, too.

Crumpling the paper, I prayed this engagement wasn't way south to some dog track in Broward or horse track in Dade County.

With fingers crossed, I called our bank's automatic teller number and entered the account number and PIN. I checked the balance with our check book. Daniel had withdrawn $1,000 earlier today. "Oh boy." I rubbed my forehead.

Were other women in Merry Acres so very merry? What marred the gloss of happily ever after in their marriages? Maybe some hurts could only be healed by drastic action, like drowning someone looking for golf balls, or doing something so that a man suffering from congestive heart failure would succumb to his genetic destiny.

"You are getting way too imaginative."

Heading for the sink, I drew water in a glass to brave another antidepressant. After what had happened days before, I hesitated, holding the pill in my palm. Weren't there a billion side effects printed on the warnings sheet I'd never read? Reports of suicidal thoughts for instance?

However, I needed some crutch to face Daniel when he came home either overjoyed from a win or despondent from a loss. So, I took the drug. I would see BILL members tomorrow and keep my eyes and ears open about remarks concerning the recent deaths. At least concentrating on the woes of others would keep my mind off my own with Daniel.

This angst-y mood lifted a half hour later when the pill took effect. That was good because a visibly shaken Daniel returned shortly before the dinner hour.

"You're back early. Have a nice time, dear?" I inquired with feigned merriment, mixing meatballs for our spaghetti dinner, knowing he hated pasta.

"Capital. Where's the television remote?"

I pointed to the side pouch on his recliner.

"Thanks." He retreated to his safe place without another word. Silence from Daniel was anything but golden.

We could kiss goodbye the $1,000 he'd withdrawn today, I thought as I busied myself with cooking. Aunt Irene once counseled, in one of her few philosophical moments, that adulterers were bad, drunks worse, but a gambler was the worst sort a woman could tie herself to. Daniel fit two out of three.

Who cared? I floated along, happy my antidepressants were keeping my emotional boat on an even keel.

≡ ≡ ≡

Augusta, in rare form, begged a moment from the BILL hostess and hogged the lectern. "Guess what, ladies? I'm going to be on the little silver screen. Catch me on Channel Two next Tuesday at four. Yes, I know, it interferes with Oprah, but you won't be disappointed. Some do-gooder put me up to this." She looked my way. "It's for a good cause, my column."

Chuckles followed.

One lady asked, "Details?"

"Uh-uh-uh. Tune in and see. Okay, back to today's pro-gramming." She bowed and left to take her seat where she shuffled cards and gabbed with her table mates.

After the luncheon, many promised to watch. Augusta gave me a wry look as if to say, "We'll see."

≡ ≡ ≡

Tuesday came. Around three that afternoon, Daniel and I drove in jittery silence to the HELP shelter. Daniel wore his tuxedo. I wore a cobalt-dress and black pumps. Nervous, I toyed with the gold-tone chain handle of my black purse which was fabricated from woven leather straps.

My hair had rebelled and I had done what I could with it, pulling half of it back and securing that with a band. The rest fell to my chin ending in a natural, sixties-look flip.

Few pieces of good jewelry remained in my jewel box— Daniel's debts had made sure of that—discounting the en-gagement ring I never wore for practical reasons. It caught on things and I was afraid of losing the stone. Earlier, I'd peeked in the box, hoping memories would lift my spirits. My heart sunk. The box that held my engagement ring was empty. I'd meant to put it in a safety deposit box in my name but never got around to it. Well, there were the simple, gold-hoop ear-rings in my ears and a snakelike chain, also gold, grazing my neckline. These were my own purchases. He at least hadn't stooped so low as to pawn those.

Daniel looked haggard, understandable since he hadn't slept well since returning from his card junket further south. He didn't volunteer details and I didn't pry.

My new motto, don't ask, don't tell, worked for me. If an entity as monumental as the military utilized it, so could I. The pills helped, too, and I'd popped another before we left the house. At least Daniel lost his place in a card game this after-noon due to the event.

I erased an image of the county sheriff knocking on our door with an eviction notice after Daniel lost our house in a card game.

"Ha, ha, ha."

"What's so funny?" Daniel asked.

"Nothing." *Great job, pills.*

Augusta, already on site when we walked in, was attired in

the same dress she'd worn at the BILL luncheon and dashing around as if a silver comet. She gabbed easily with the television crew. They, she, and some of the heftier women at the shelter pushed the few raggedy pieces of furniture against the wall. If she was nervous, no one would guess. She gave her dance partner a nod. Daniel reciprocated. Augusta smirked at me before taking out a pad, busily jotting down the names and notes she needed from the HELP staff.

Television people were setting up equipment, stringing cables, and adjusting their portable lights.

At five minutes to four, my erstwhile friend was still wearing her reporter's cap. Anyone not knowing Augusta's true feelings would never guess the contempt in which she held the women she interviewed.

The cameraman bellowed, "Showtime."

The dance went off without a hitch even though "Fred" and "Ginger" hadn't practiced a single step, at least not that I knew of.

The television crew left.

Daniel graciously danced with one or two of the shelter women bold enough to ask. Augusta made a swift exit, citing her all purpose, get-out-of-anything excuse, "Deadline."

The kids meanwhile romped with Daniel, who seemed genuinely pleased for the interaction.

"That's right. Slow, slow, quick, quick. By jingo, you've got it. You're a natural, young man. You too, missy."

I wondered if he wasn't reliving happier times with his own children for a moment or two.

His charm paid off. One young boy took his instruction seriously. By the time they left, around six o'clock, that boy and a little girl were chanting, "One, two, three," and duplicating a pretty good box step.

Daniel asked. "Mind if I borrow a bathroom to change?"

"If you can find one that's unoccupied." Mama Smith giggled. She showed the way for Daniel. Later, he came out in a spiffy sports coat and dark pants, wearing a peachy pink polo I'd given him for his birthday last year.

The best news was that as we walked out the door, the phone was ringing. According to the grinning receptionist, pledges of coming donations were promised.

If checks didn't follow, I figured no one in this place would give broken promises a second thought. Sadly, I'd learned to substantially discount promises, too. Oh, Daniel and I had tried. *Look forward, not back.* That platitude from marriage counselors rankled. How well did *they* handle infidelity?

Honesty could be brutal, discretion, worse, and deception, worse still. Then there was that good old "give and take" recommendation. Over the years, we'd both given it our all and taken about all we could stand. A happy coincidence that night was I hadn't observed overt hanky-panky between Daniel and Augusta. That didn't mean they weren't sleeping with each other, but somehow, discreet slipping around didn't mesh with Augusta's in-your-face personality.

On the drive home, after turning in his rental tux, Daniel said, "How about dinner at the club?" Either the dance routine or the kids had put him in a relaxed mood.

Ten minutes later, we drove under the Barrier Isles club-house porte cochere.

"Good. José is our valet. He's great, always treats my golf bag—and car—with care. Some of these guys." Daniel shook his head. "Pftt."

"True, but I usually park myself and make the long walk *past* the valet parking area up to the clubhouse. It's good exercise and inexpensive." A two dollar tip here, a two dollar tip or more there, added up, after all.

The maître d' greeted us. "Mr. and Mrs. Duncan. So nice to have you."

"Hello, Gerald," I returned. "This was a spur-of-the-moment decision so we don't have a reservation. Can you seat us?"

"This time of year there is no problem, especially on a Tuesday evening. Right this way. In fact, I have a window seat available."

The wintergreen-print drapery fabric blended well with the burgundy-print commercial carpet and traditional furnishings. The décor was upscale men's club. The drapes framed the window where we sat. The sheers were opened, allowing diners to view the setting sun and the eighteenth tee.

In the distance, on another fairway, a lone golfer slung his bag over his shoulder and walked into the dying embers of the orange blaze horizon as if he was calling it a day. Club rules spoke against "renegade" walkers. It meant the club received no rental cart fees for one thing. Some thought it diminished their club's perceived tony atmosphere.

When peak season waned, however, course rangers, the law men of the links, took a more relaxed interpretation of the rules unless a special club tournament was in progress.

Elizabeth, our favorite server, appeared with menus. A minute later, she reappeared with Daniel's single malt scotch and unsweetened ice tea for me, since more often than not I drank a half glass of wine with dinner. The rest, I gave to Daniel.

Elizabeth set the drinks down and recited the specials.

A no-brainer for me. I said, "I'll have the lamb, and cabernet. No appetizer or salad tonight. I'll be satisfied with the grilled vegetable that accompanies the meat."

Daniel smiled at the friendly, plump, gray-haired woman. "I'll have the same, thank you, Elizabeth."

Daniel sucked down a long drink from his glass and then looked at me. "I have some unsettling news."

I braced.

"I sold your diamond engagement ring."

I hunched my shoulders reflexively as if the matter were of little import. "Big surprise." I looked out at the dusky shadows, remembering the joy the ring had brought me when he'd proposed. I seldom wore the two carat marquise-cut diamond cradled in gold. My working hands were happy wearing only the matching gold wedding band. Or had been.

"No interrogation, no berating comments?"

I sipped my tea. "Nope."

Daniel slumped. He looked old and tired.

"I'll *really* worry when you sell your Corvette."

My half-jest elicited no flippancy from Daniel. "So, we're that far gone?"

I scratched the nape of my neck, and then crossed my arms before fashioning my mouth into what I hoped was a bemused smile. "I'm afraid so. We came close to reigniting the flame recently, but the pilot light went out. Any spark to re-light it—"

"Is gone."

We ate the meal in silence, declined dessert, and Daniel signaled for the chit.

"Leave a generous tip for Elizabeth." Thinking, *there but for the grace of God go I.*

Daniel tipped José handsomely, as well, when he brought the car. We slid into the SUV. Our valet shut my door with a jaunty smile and sent us on our way with, "Good night, Mr. and Mrs. Duncan."

Daniel brought up the weather and the stock market on the short drive home. I bemoaned interest rates versus the plunging dollar, and looming raging inflation ignored by the Federal Reserve Board.

At home, we readied for bed. Though we were sharing a queen-sized mattress, I knew there was a wide gap between us. As I hugged the edge of my side, Daniel did the same on his.

Something troubled the edge of my fitful sleep and half dreams. I kept seeing that golfer in the setting sun and the sand trap. Something about the combination teased and taunted until I awoke fully at two.

Daniel was gone.

Once I would have risen to find him and encouraged his prompt return. That was then. This was now. Our relationship in flux, reformed, morphing into... whatever. Let Daniel sleep where he would, as would I.

Yes, widowhood prevailed in Merry Acres, both the factual kind and the theoretical. I was living proof of the latter.

CHAPTER NINE

I woke at nine to the scent of coffee.

Daniel had left the house, but a fresh pot waited for me. Perhaps our marriage could survive on the currency of small kindnesses.

Paying monthly bills that included remittance for my final trip to the therapist, I knew Daniel was right on that score. We couldn't afford sessions that were expensive and, so far, unrewarding. Thankfully, the couple of times I'd taken the medication since that dragged-from-the-garage episode, my anxiety calmed without further mishap. Still, I was playing with fire. I needed a prescription-free coping method, so I changed into swimming attire.

My hourglass figure grew more pear-shaped with each year, but I couldn't complain compared to others my age. I added a thigh skimming knit dress and slipped into backless Keds. Today, I'd walk to the clubhouse and spend time at the pool for amusement.

Once there, I stretched my legs, tired after their unaccustomed trek. Removing my cover up, I reapplied sunscreen, and languished on a chaise, cheered by a sky as clear and blue as the pool water.

I was the lone singleton. A few couples lounged on chaises lined with fluffy white towels provided by the club. Scattered as they were around the Spray-Crete deck, they reminded me of clouds. I heard the couples murmuring now and then and watched as they massaged each other with lotion-coated hands, wondering what message their fingertips imparted to each other.

Sad again, I focused on a paperback, a boring tale of angst about a group of women my age adjusting to their current stage in life and love. Putting the book down, I sipped cranberry-flavored iced tea I'd ordered from a roaming attendant and scanned the poolside again.

Odd, not seeing Karl preening like a peacock and sunning like a contented crocodile before slicing into the water for a few more laps.

Susie hadn't called, nor had her name surfaced during the BILL luncheons, at least not to me. Susie was gone, like her husband.

What had happened to the Mendez case? It, too, had disappeared from the subject of conversations and the local news. Mrs. Mendez had sent a thank you for the finger sandwiches and promised to drop in at one of the BILL luncheons, but she never did. If Lourdes knew where she was living, she didn't say.

Lourdes, too, would be gone before the next BILL session, the only woman my age within the BILL group, and only married woman other than me, for that matter. Not that we clicked. Lourdes was Latina. Lourdes had children. Lourdes had a life. Was her marriage a happy one? She hadn't sounded enthused about Carlos' decision to move south.

I let the sun warm my skin.

After an hour, I started home, showered, dressed, and drove to the shelter. Utilizing my organizational skills, I whipped haphazard filing into shape. I took over the phones, too, while the volunteer receptionist ate a late lunch off premises.

I surprised the kids when I helped one little boy with homework. Time flew, and my four hours were up. I dreaded going, feeling more at home here, among battered women and their children, than with Daniel in our Merry Acres home.

Stalling that final turn into our driveway, I drove a block or two then circled the golf course. Carts rolled along cart paths in the distance. Shouts of joy and despair rang out depending on the course taken by the little white ball. Daniel was out there somewhere. Gambling?

Jealousy of Lady Luck was a culprit in my fractured marriage. I hadn't known of his predilection until after the wedding. Guilt had spurred him on the self-destructive path when he'd left his wife for me. Sure, we'd talked about it over the years. He tried to stop, but the lure pulled him back time and again. He'd enjoyed a successful career on the back of risk-taking. Alas for him, his personal life didn't mirror the success of his professional gambles.

A few days later, dressed in slacks and a sweater set in colors to brighten my weary hazel eyes, I drove to the clubhouse for the next scheduled BILL meeting.

I sat next to Janet, and we speculated about Mrs. Mendez and expressed dismay Mr. Mendez's killer was still at large. Time neared for the meeting to start.

"Where is Augusta?"

"I wondered the same thing," I said. "Nobody works a room as well as she does, mining for gold for that column."

"Incidentally, I caught her dance number with Daniel on the telly. Better watch out, Georgiana, there definitely seems to be chemistry between them... at least on the tube."

"Really?" I wondered if Janet had mailed in a contribution or was merely enjoying an excuse to drop a concerned warning into my lap. "If Augusta doesn't show up, I'll call later and find out the reason she abandoned us. Could be she's ill. She's not the type to skip a venue to strut her stuff, and she knows most of you watched her and Daniel on television."

Janet fiddled with her wine glass.

"Do you know Missy Youngblood?" I asked, filling an uncomfortable silence. "She's the hostess today."

"Nope, don't know her. I do know she's new to Merry Acres. And married."

"Hooray for that."

Janet said, "I know her address and phone number since she mailed me a check to cover her dues. I've sort of taken on treasurer duties permanently. We should raise dues next season. That would give us a reserve. Maybe we could go on some shopping trip out of the area. You know, hire a sightseeing bus for the venture."

"Great idea." The thought of escaping Merry Acres for a half-day fun trip sounded divinely inspired. "Why don't you bring it up today?"

"Oh no. Treasury detail is the limit of my largesse for this thing. As founder, you should broach increased dues."

I gave Janet a sour look. "Thanks."

A petite redhead, presumably Missy Youngblood, moved to the fore and faced the seated BILL members.

"Hello, everyone," she began. "I'm happy so many of you came. Looks like almost everybody on our roster, for this time of year, that is. You all have made me feel so welcome in such a short time, I couldn't wait to get up here and tell you."

Missy had the presence and flair of a natural born speaker. After a few warm-up jokes, she recommended a pool party in the coming months since the weather was warming, which she would happily chair.

This was met with sparse enthusiasm. Few members were Missy's age or had her figure. Still, after some comments for and against, especially since Missy would do all the work, a half-hearted okay gave the go ahead.

I leaned over to Janet and whispered, "We have a winner." I raised my hand. "Hello, Missy. We haven't met. I'm Georgiana Duncan."

Missy smiled warmly. "Oh yes, the originator of the BILL. Nice to meet you, Georgiana. Do you have something to say?"

"I was wondering how we felt about taking our show on the road, so to speak. I'm referring to a bus ride to Palm Gardens Regional Mall, perhaps, for lunch and shopping. Or further south. I laud the pool party you've suggested, by the way, and wonder if a raise in dues might be in order."

Missy clicked her teeth as if debating how to respond. "Oh, my." She looked around the room. "A show of hands. Who would prefer to leave things as they are, with no dues increase?" Missy smiled. "I know nobody wants to be a public party pooper. Let's have a secret ballot. We'll vote yes or no on blank cards at our next meeting to provide anonymity."

Good luck with that, honey. I said pleasantly, "A diplomat. We should make you Madame President and permanent leader of the pack."

Missy gave a modest "aw shucks" smile. "Actually, I love leading things. Often wrong, but seldom in doubt, as my Jack says."

Everyone giggled.

Personally, I rejoiced—another married member presented a golden opportunity to make Missy the permanent chairwoman. Let them stew over the dues increase. Besides, not everyone on the summer roster had yet taken a turn as hostess. I glanced about. Actually, the only one left untested was Augusta, who should have manned today's luncheon.

After Augusta's turn, I'd officially put forth the idea of making Missy the official head of the BILL. I knew one thing. Missy would joyfully accept the position.

Missy's luncheon menu was interesting: cold melon soup, poached chicken in a creamy wine sauce, and bread pudding for dessert.

As the ladies chatted and ate, Sharon, the social director, came into the room.

Immediately, a hush descended. Sharon had the unfortunate reputation of being the angel of death, having brought news first of Mendez, and then Ben Bernstein.

My heart raced when Sharon marched straight for me and Janet. Unmarried Janet took my hand, offering comfort, and said, "It's okay, whatever it is. There's no cop with her."

"Mrs. Duncan, a word please."

Janet dropped my hand, allowing me complete freedom of movement, but I was fixed stone still. My clenched hand felt like lead in my lap and my voice came out high and tinny. "Yes?"

"Mr. Duncan's at Merry Acres Memorial. He's banged up, the victim of a hit and run, but able to ask for you."

I fled from the room, blaming myself for dark thoughts that had brought bad luck to Daniel.

≡ ≡ ≡

Pulling our SUV into the parking lot, I straddled two spaces when I finally stopped the car, jumped out and then half-jogged to the emergency room and inquired about Daniel.

Inside, an aide led me to an examining area.

"Daniel, what happened?"

Daniel had a cast on his left leg. "I'd like to say, you should see the other guy, but I can't. I never saw him, or her, as the case may be. What really hurts is my new golf cart is wrecked."

"New cart?"

"I won it fair and square on an eight-foot putt, downhill lie, mind you. I digress. See, I was test driving it on the way home. A shame, too." He frowned. "It was red and white, a beauty."

"Daniel, what happened?"

"You know how people in Merry Acres fuss if you ride carts on the bike paths? Well, I stayed on the road, as we're supposed to. I came upon a malfunctioning fire hydrant spewing water into the street and I moved over to avoid it." He looked at me. "My mouth is dry, hand me that plastic water cup."

I snatched up a turquoise cup filled with water and a straw already inserted, and handed it to him. He sipped and handed it back for me to replace on the ledge of a rolling cart loaded for bear with bandages, boxes of gloves, and other medical paraphernalia.

"Next thing I knew there was a flash of white. It looked like a panel truck, or van, but I couldn't swear to either. Whatever it was swerved my way. Naturally, I jerked the cart's wheel in the opposite direction. The cart took the brunt of the hit, or I'd be at the morgue. I was not unscathed. In addition to my black eye, I have a cracked collarbone, too, and the bum leg. Some bruises, too. They're starting to hurt big time now that the adrenaline's worked out of my system. They gave me a prescription for mild pain killers."

"When can I take you home?"

"I've been patched up and discharged." He smiled. "Just awaiting the discharge nurse. I suspect our HMO doesn't want me in here an hour more than absolutely necessary. No dancing dates for a while, I'm afraid. Just when I was warming to those kids at the HELP shelter, too. Well, I'm sure they'll get a kick out of signing my cast."

I flagged down a nurse who eventually brought the discharge nurse who went over medications and doctor's orders, then made Daniel sign a release form before she summoned an orderly to transport him to the ER exit. Twenty minutes later, he wheeled Daniel to the glass doors, but beyond that, we were on our own.

After pulling up to the emergency driveway, I helped Daniel into the SUV. "Good thing I wasn't driving the Vette today."

"I'd nod in agreement, but I've been told to keep my head immobile."

"I'll take you home and then take that prescription to the drug store."

Later on, Daniel was still resting in his recliner I'd lined with pillows to brace his neck and leg when I administered the first dose. Normally stoic about pain, he eschewed aspirin. He took this pill without protest. "I hopped around and took some vitamin C while you were out. Ol' Ben Bernstein swore vitamin C was so potent it could cure cancer."

"Didn't do much for his heart, did it? Tomorrow, we'll investigate crutches for you."

"I've already called that doc-in-a-box place. It's a walk-in clinic, but I made an appointment for ten so we won't sit in the waiting room for hours. This isn't rocket science, after all. They can furnish crutches or lead us to a medical supply store that can."

"Did anyone call the police to report your accident?"

"I called 9-1-1 from my cell. A patrolman came and wrote up a report. We chatted, and the Mendez case came up. Actually, I brought it up. No leads, not that he'd tell me, of course. Anyway, my supplemental insurance will cover anything Medicare doesn't, thank God."

I had mixed feelings about the change in circumstances. Daniel wouldn't be playing golf anytime soon, but cards were another matter. He could still gamble. "Do you need me to call anyone on your behalf?"

"Are you kidding? Word is already out. I've heard from a couple of guys." He held up his cell phone. "I'm out of the game until I get proficient enough with this monstrosity on my leg to drive to the club."

"No way."

"It's my left leg. I should be able to drive the SUV in a few days. It's an automatic."

"Your pals are welcome to play to cards here."

He gave me a broad grin. "We'll provide real *Odd Couple* charm. I appreciate your sacrifice, however."

"Want a sandwich?"

"Yes, thanks."

"I'll get out of these clothes and make you something. Meanwhile, are you all right? Do you want anything before I leave the room?"

"No, I'm good. The pain pill is helping. I may nap a while."

"Wait, if you can, until after you've eaten."

He gave me a cautionary yawn. "Hurry."

After quickly changing into shorts, I returned to the kitchen and rummaged through the refrigerator for Daniel's favorite lunch meat, hoping we weren't out. After what he'd been through, he deserved a treat.

In luck, I made him a roast beef on rye with a smidge of horseradish sauce mixed in the sandwich spread. I put the sandwich, a pickle, and a few chips on a plate I placed on tray with a bright, cheery yellow napkin. A man, he wouldn't notice, but I did.

After debating the wisdom of it, I poured some beer into the tiniest glass available, a wine glass one size up from a cordial glass. "You probably shouldn't drink alcohol with the prescription, but..."

"Beer in a wine glass. How novel. I don't think six ounces of beer will kill me. Hmmm. On second thought"—he looked both ways—"I better not say that too loudly in Merry Acres."

"Very funny." I gave him a quelling glance. "I've got some calls to make. Holler if you need anything."

Augusta answered her cell phone, "Hey, Georgie."

Caller ID had spoiled my surprise attack. "Hear about Daniel's bust up?"

"Yeah. Sheesh."

"How'd you know?"

"Happened to be in the hospital visiting somebody when they brought him in. He didn't see me and I figured they didn't need me hovering around him in the ER."

Convenient. "I see. We missed you, today."

"Gosh, you know what? I forgot all about the BILL what with the excitement over my plum assignment. I covered the opening of that new store in Merry Acres Mall, the one that caters to the spoiled canine set, Pampered Poochies."

"Sounds thrilling."

"You know it. Tell Danny Boy I'll be by soon to pay a convalescent call. I'll let him win at cards if we're allowed to play."

Miffed at what sounded like a proprietary tone toward Daniel, I said curtly, "I'll tell him. Bye."

I walked back to the den and removed the tray to the coffee table, grabbing more stray toss pillows for Daniel's comfort. "Lean forward a tad. Let's even out your neck." I lowered his head onto the pillows. "So, tell me, dear, do you and your friends ever discuss recent deaths around Merry Acres when you play cards? I mean more than a casual, 'oh, too bad' the day it happens?"

"Kind of. You know their hackneyed theories as well as I. Jealous husband, spurned woman. What's to speculate about

Esterhause or Bernstein? Natural causes, the first by drowning and the latter from heart attack. Why?"

I took the tray to the kitchen. "Nothing. Augusta says she'll come by to play cards when her schedule permits. She'll allow you to win out of sympathy for your condition."

"I'll take her up on the offer. She's good."

No doubt, and I wasn't talking about cards. A sudden malicious thought cropped up like a weed in my imagination. How well had dear old Augusta known either Karl or Ben? Well, not Ben. He and Becca were—had been—too close.

I considered saying something to Daniel about my suspicions, but the combination of pain pill and beer sent him to dreamland. I snatched a throw off the sofa and covered him before going about routine household chores.

An hour later, when Daniel's attention was enmeshed in yet another movie involving a serial killer, I tried to sit through it with him but gave up. "The weather is grand. I'm going outside to read until time to start dinner." I'd rummaged through a closet and extracted a big brass bell, a holdover from some Christmas pageant or other when Daniel was roped into filling in for one of the handbell ringers. "Ring if you need me."

He laughed "A dinner bell? How posh."

Outside, distracted by my thoughts, I couldn't get interested in the book even though it was one of my favorite authors.

I reviewed what I knew about Mendez. Mendez had apparently engaged in a little fling with half the members of the Barrier Isles club and a third of the women residing in Merry Acres. Some, like Augusta, opined that whoever killed Mendez had performed a community service, at least so far as a whole bunch of scorned women were concerned, or cuckolded husbands.

Mendez died by blunt trauma. A tire iron, wasn't it? Would officials divulge such telling details as the murder weapon, or allow media to report it? Where had Dixie heard about it? Leaks were possible. Police couldn't control them. Augusta must have heard it and passed it on to Dixie, but I couldn't be sure, and Dixie knew scores of women. She could have heard that tidbit from any one of them.

Theoretically, a woman's ability to overpower Mendez wasn't realistic, but what if the woman was tall and strong? Like Augusta.

Lourdes had let knowledge of an affair between Mendez and Augusta out of the bag, and she would know since she was tight with Mrs. Mendez. Maybe Augusta gave Mendez an ultimatum, marry me or else. That didn't wash. Augusta never made sounds like she wanted marriage.

Esterhause? Hard to picture Susie with a chunky, middle-aged man like Mendez. As for Karl and jealousy, hard to imagine Karl falling for anybody but Karl so he wouldn't care.

Word was Karl had tangled up on snaky reeds and discarded junk, like old appliances dumped into the ponds long ago. His half-filled tank hadn't been sufficient to allow him time to disengage and resurface. Why would Susie kill Karl?

She liked to shop, everybody knew that. Even though their life insurance policy wasn't overly grand, it meant she could spend it any way she wanted. She was an experienced diver. She might have known when Karl left the house how much air was in his tank, and possibly which pond he'd targeted to dunk for balls. Her alibi was her scrapbook group. Augusta had been taking photos, but perhaps that photo session had been much earlier. And were there really other women over there?

But that pond. Yuck.

Still, if Susie wore a wet suit covering every inch of her, maybe she'd brave it. The thought gave me the creeps and I shuddered. Alligators, snakes? No woman would go to that length to kill her husband.

Then there was Ben. Nothing suspicious there, just tragic.

Daniel's hit-and-run. Augusta hadn't been at the BILL luncheon, but she had a perfect alibi, an assignment for the *Gazette*. Some kid probably hit Daniel then panicked and drove away. Wait. How many kids of driving age lived in Merry Acres? Then again, these were the fading weeks of spring break for some schools.

Facing facts, I was injecting Augusta into fanciful murder scenarios because I was hurt and jealous. And embarrassed. Former pal Augusta had learned about my foster care background and probably Rhonda, too. And where had she unearthed this? Directly from Daniel, while playing cards.

I forced myself to concentrate on the boring book.

CHAPTER TEN

Except for essential errands, today was the first time in a couple of weeks I'd been out of the house. Pleased with myself, I had so far endured, with aplomb, four card games in our house. Fortunately, there were no smokers in the bunch. That could change, but so far, so good.

In the mood for something Greek, I dressed for lunch. The Athenian Garden reminded me of the food Aunt Irene had taught me how to cook during the time I lived with her. The brief time our lives had intersected pleasantly.

"I'm eating Greek for lunch, want to come?"

Daniel, who was strictly a steak-on-a-plate kind of guy, frowned. "Pass."

"I'm also going to work a few hours at the HELP shelter afterwards. Will you be all right?"

"Fine."

Daniel had grown proficient on his crutches.

"If your card buddies show up, forage for yourselves. There's cheese and cold cuts in the fridge and fresh bread on the counter. Don't forget to seal it back up, if any is left."

I wanted to caution him against reckless betting, but saved my breath.

At a stoplight, a white van pulled alongside me in the left turn lane. I noticed *Merry Acres Gazette* emblazoned on its side. On impulse, I followed it, greatly irritating the cars behind me when I changed lanes at the last minute. Though the left turn lane was clear when I zoomed over, I barely made the caution light.

When the van stopped at a convenience store, I followed the driver inside. I didn't want to bring attention to myself so I purchased a bag of chips, watched him fill racks in the store, and then followed him outside.

"Excuse me," I interrupted while he stocked a coin-operated newspaper stand. "Have you got a second?"

"I guess." He was around thirty, beer-gutted, ruddy-skinned and sandy-haired. Nice brown eyes, though. "How can I help you?"

"How many vans are owned by the paper?"

"Gee, lady, I don't know, two, three? Why?"

"I don't want to upset you, but my husband's..." *Should I substitute the word car for golf cart to avoid any possible working-class prejudices?* "...vehicle was struck by a white van. I guess every time I see one now, my mind questions whether it's the one. I'm not suggesting you hit him, but maybe someone else who worked at the paper might have. Do employees often use the vans?"

"Hey, I don't want to go there. Talk to a lawyer or something."

"Please."

"Don't mention me."

"I don't know your name, and won't ask."

"Okay then. Vans are used for deliveries. Sometimes employees run errands for the paper. Rarely, a reporter uses one if his company car's in the shop or something."

"Does anyone at the *Gazette* keep a log of who drives one at any given time?"

"Matter of fact, yeah. Look, I gotta go. You want info, talk to the manager of the transportation department. Nobody's told me any rumors about one of our vans being involved in a hit-and-run though. That kind of news travels. See, no damage on my van."

I'd already looked. "That's all right. Like I said, it's only because of this freak accident I even noticed your van. Have a good day."

He nodded, climbed in the truck, and drove away.

At The Athenian Garden, I ordered a house specialty, the Athenian-style Greek salad with potato salad in the middle, married beautifully with lettuce, tomato wedges, rings of green bell pepper, boiled egg, and, of course, olives and feta cheese. It came with pita bread.

My mouth watered reading the menu. When it came, I dug in. Stuffed, my stomach acknowledged today's repast was wonderful. I contemplated ordering coffee and a baklava when a man walked in. The restaurant was packed with lingering diners and he sat in the only available space, a booth across from me.

I recognized him as that unmarried detective Augusta had introduced in the Indian restaurant. That settled the matter. I called the waiter over and ordered coffee and the sweet. Maybe I could work up enough nerve to approach the detective about my theory about the *Gazette* hit-and-run. And the Merry Acres deaths.

When he ordered the salad, I looked in his direction. I glanced his way now and then, but my feet refused to move. Instead, I accidentally emptied an envelope of sugar into the coffee and stirred and stirred. When I put the spoon down, I took a breath and walked the couple of feet to his booth.

He looked up. "Yes?" His salutation was brief and impatient.

"Hello. I was wondering if I could talk to you a minute about some odd goings-on in Merry Acres."

"I suppose so." His dark eyes appeared glazed. He blew his red, bulbous nose.

I stood well back. "Cold?"

"Allergies."

"Melaleuca blossoms?"

He nodded.

"A South Florida curse. For some."

"Sure are."

"You don't remember me, but I was in Punjab Palace a while ago. I was having lunch that day with Augusta St. James of the—"

"I know who she is." The waiter appeared and held a salad in the air as if uncertain what to do. "Your coffee is getting colder by the minute, and I'm hungry." He looked at the waiter. "Why don't you serve me and bring the lady's coffee and dessert over here. Frees up a table for you, too."

"Thanks." I slid into the booth across from him and watched the waiter comply with the man's directives.

I looked down, averting my gaze when he stabbed a

forkful of salad, so as to not watch him eat. "I'm sorry to invade your privacy."

He hitched his shoulders. "How can I help you?"

I felt my neck and face light up in a raging blush that extended to my hairline.

"Relax, the only thing I'm biting today is this salad. The baklava here is good. Eat yours."

His comment made me a little less nervous, so I cut the tip from the diamond-shaped sweet and forked a tiny bite, savoring the nuts and flaky phyllo dough. I wiped my mouth with the new napkin the waiter had provided. "How much is left on my face?"

"It's all gone. You're safe, at least until the next bite." He winked.

That put me more at ease. "I live in Merry Acres. You know about Mr. Mendez, of course. That business with the tire iron. Well, I was wondering about—"

I stopped talking because the man's expression had changed. He wasn't kidding around or winking now, that was certain.

"About what?"

"You'll think I'm crazy, but I was wondering if maybe the recent deaths that looked like accidents, and were ruled that way, really were...accidents, or natural causes."

"I have no idea which deaths you mean, but nothing on my desk—and I work homicides—pertains to that planned community, except Mendez."

"I'll just go." I felt foolish. "Sorry to have bothered you."

"Wait a minute. Finish your coffee and dessert."

Since it was more a command than request, I took another tiny bite. I'd ruined the coffee by adding too much sugar.

"I have a question for you in return. I'm not sure Ms. St. James introduced us. If so, I'm sorry, I've forgotten your name."

"Mrs. Daniel Duncan. Georgiana." I actually gulped. This was ridiculous. I was almost a decade older than this guy, but he made me feel as if I were six years old. "What's your question, officer?"

"You've forgotten my name, too. It's *Detective* Morgan. Mike Morgan. And, for the record, I hate the name 'Mikey.' Where'd you hear about a tire iron?" He continued eating.

I stammered. "I-I read it in the papers, didn't I?"

He put his fork down. He looked hard at me. "No, you didn't."

"Oh, right." I fiddled with my hair. "I remember. I belong to a sort of lunch-bunch group for women in Merry Acres. Well, actually, we're all members of the Barrier Isles Golf and Country Club."

"Stay on topic. The tire iron."

I felt as if some hidden video was recording this conversation. What had I said to provoke the change in his attitude? Was he going to arrest me? Did Daniel know any lawyers? With his leg still in a cast, how could Daniel safely drive to the police station to bail me out? Was there enough money in the account to make my bail? "A woman in my group mentioned it during a telephone call."

"Who?" He took out a worn leather notebook.

He wrote down the name *Mendez,* then *Duncan*, then *Daniel*, then *Georgiana*. He scribbled *Merry Acres* and the country club's name after that and then the words *tire iron*. He also jotted down the date and the restaurant's name. Why would he make sure I saw what he wrote? He went back to eating his salad. "I'm waiting."

"Dixie told me during a phone call." I swallowed hard. "Gosh, I'm so nervous, I can't remember her last name, but she doesn't live here anymore. Oh yes, Dixie Metcalf. She's in Georgia now. She—I don't know if she'd want me to say more."

He sipped something that looked like iced tea. "I strongly suggest you do. That is, unless you want me charging you with withholding information germane to a murder investigation. Gotta tell you that further intrusion on my lunch hour, if I must invite you to my office, et cetera, et cetera, will not put me in a pleasant mood for questioning."

I drank the disgustingly sweet syrup from the demitasse to lube my dry mouth. "Dixie's suffering from the early stages of a mental disability and is residing in an assisted living facility. In Georgia."

"So you said." He scribbled that down. "Let me get this straight. A lady named Dixie Metcalf, who is a member, same as you, of some social group at the Barrier Isles Country Club told you, during a telephone call, about a tire iron being the murder weapon in the Mendez case."

I nodded.

"What's your address and phone number?"

I told him while my stomach knotted. Why had I talked to this man? I squeaked, "Are you going to arrest me?"

He smiled. "No, but don't leave town without checking with me." He handed me a card. "How do you know Augusta St. James?"

"We met at the same social organization."

"Which is?"

"The BILL. That stands for the Barrier Isles Ladies of Leisure."

He chuckled. "Who dreamed that up?"

"Me."

"It's clever. Really. Sure you don't want the rest of that baklava?"

"Positive."

He reached over and forked it into his mouth. "Now, tell me about the other...uh...deaths that may or may not be accidental. Or natural causes."

Happy to get his mind off pinning the Mendez murder on me, I turned his attention to Karl. Speaking my thoughts aloud to this man, I grew chagrined at how ridiculous I sounded and must appear.

He scratched his head. "Frankly"—he leaned toward me—"that's conjecture. However, would you be kind enough to drop off a membership roster for that BILL thing? Any time, no rush. Just mark it to my attention, Detective Mike Morgan, and drop it off at the station. Leave it with the Desk Sergeant."

"Sure." I blushed again. "One more thing." I was knee-deep in trouble, why not go all the way to my neck?

"Can't wait."

"My husband was the victim of a hit-and-run. Ended up in the hospital with a broken leg."

"Yeah?"

"Police came to the scene and filed a report." Detective Morgan didn't respond. "Daniel didn't really see what happened because it all happened so fast." I tugged on an earring, my brain warning me to censor the part where my husband ventured into the *other* traffic lane to avoid water from a wacko hydrant spraying his precious new golf cart. "But he thinks he saw a white car, panel truck, or van prior to the collision with his golf cart. I've learned the *Merry Acres Ga-zette* owns white vans. Augusta St. James works there, as we know."

He looked blank. "Is there some connection?"

"I don't know."

He leaned an elbow on the table and bracketed his face between his index finger and thumb. He stared past me and blinked once or twice. "Nope, I don't see a connection." He was slightly playful again. "Excellent creative thinking though."

Of course he saw no connection. Not being a married woman with someone like Augusta circling like a predatory bird eyeing a husband, what could he know? Maybe Daniel had spurned her, too, and she'd reacted by running him down. To shun Morgan's stare, playful or not, I lifted my shoulders, communicating that I understood how he could pooh-pooh a link.

"Thanks for the baklava."

"Don't mention it." I remembered Dixie's remark about Augusta buttering up the Merry Acres police with pastries. Maybe Augusta was this guy's buddy. *Not good.* If so, I prayed Morgan would keep this discussion private. "May I go?"

"Why not?" Still resting his head on his hand, looking like a man with a migraine, he flicked out his other hand, inviting my departure.

Wonderful, I'd probably just spilled my guts to Augusta's chief contact on the police force. I snatched my tab, gathered my purse, and raced to the cashier before fleeing outside to my car.

CHAPTER ELEVEN

Tapping my nails on the steering wheel at each traffic light, I pushed down hard on the gas pedal. What would Detective Morgan tell Augusta? Wait. He hadn't seemed overtly thrilled at seeing the columnist at the Indian restaurant. Maybe he could be an ally. That was only if I ever ginned up enough courage to face him again.

Meanwhile, what would Daniel say when I told him what had just occurred?

If I told him.

I came home to find food left out on the counter, soiled dishes here and there, and a despondent Daniel twiddling his thumbs in the recliner. The television set wasn't on. No book lay open in his lap either.

Now was not the optimal time to delve into my quasi-psychotic conversation with a cop. "Bored?

He nodded.

Apparently, his card-playing buds had moved on without him. At least for today. "I'll change clothes and play a board game with you."

"I love the play on words, b-o-a-r-d, or b-o-r-e-d."

"Let's go international with Chinese checkers. Or we could play cards. I excel at Go Fish."

He rolled his eyes. "Chinese checkers."

"Good choice." I returned in a few minutes barefooted and wearing a terrycloth romper. After rummaging around in one of the built-in bookcases, I withdrew a board game. Moving a lightweight, cane-seated bentwood chair from the kitchen closer to his recliner, I set up the game board on the tray used to serve his meals.

"What color do you want?"

"Black. Fits my mood."

Aha. The guy was really down. "Okay, I'll take red."

We placed the colored balls into the slots and I told Daniel to make the first move. He did. I followed.

"Men find Augusta appealing. Why is that?"

Daniel groaned. "Is that a loaded question?"

"Just curious, dear. Think of me as one of your pals for a moment. How do you all discuss her in the card room? When she's not present, of course. Pretend I'm just a fly on the wall."

Daniel scowled. "I don't think so."

"She's no spring chicken. She's not fat or frumpy, but she's not the least bit pretty."

He moved again. I did, too.

"I'd like a man's perspective."

He jumped three of my marbles and made it to the corner of my territory. "She has a kind of been-around-the-block sexuality. She's comfortable as an old shoe. You know, no demands, no scenes. Great wit. Damn good card player. To sum it up, a tomboy with, shall we say, experience." He looked at me. "Not that I ever considered anything but card playing with her, or dancing, and that was a fluke."

I swallowed my doubts.

Daniel beat me two out of three sets. I repackaged and put away the game box while he left his chair and hobbled over to the sink to take one of his pain killers.

"Is that necessary? Are you in pain?" Daniel, who never took an aspirin unless in excruciating pain, worried me. He was growing ever-more dependent on the things.

He ignored me and plopped back in the recliner. He used his hands to lift the cast onto the ottoman and hit a remote control button, bringing the plasma television to noisy life.

Okay. I busied myself in the kitchen, glancing his way from time to time. His head nodded.

I adjusted the special neck pillow we'd purchased for him when we bought the crutches and left him in his drowsy state. I then went outside to prepare the grill. Red meat might perk him up. I could use some, too. Steak and potato might lift his spirits. Maybe I could get some broccoli down him. And a piece of fresh fruit for dessert. Maybe.

No, I'd use up the failing fruit on hand. I'd throw a bruised banana in the blender with some fruit juice and the sad strawberries on their last legs, add a glop of yogurt, and whip up a smoothie.

The blender whipped my concoction into a creamy froth, which I adjusted for taste, adding a teaspoon of honey. For the proper texture, I added a drop or two of milk and tasted the final result. Voilà, a smoothie, as good as the one Augusta had brought.

Random pieces floating aimlessly in my mind abruptly coalesced. Ben's comment at the drug store about the sleep aids Augusta had purchased. Augusta's surprise visit presenting me with a smoothie. Rhonda's calling on that very day, at that very hour, seemed too convenient for coincidence. Perhaps someone, alerted by Augusta's signal seconds before she knocked on our front door, had pretended to be Rhonda.

I relived that afternoon.

The phone had rung on my way to the master bathroom. Augusta would know a call from Rhonda, or a poser, would divert me. Augusta could have then sneaked something, like a handful of over-the-counter sleeping tablets, into my smoothie while I took the call.

Augusta hadn't left at all.

The sly minx had opened and shut the front door, then waited until her potion took effect. Then she hauled me out to the car. Moving dead weight wasn't easy, but given our size differences, it was possible for Augusta.

Face it, after the words, "Hi, it's Rhonda," I had gone blank-o. What had jolted me most, the voice or the mere word "Rhonda"?

Forget that. I *knew* Rhonda's voice. As if I could ever forget it or any other minute detail about the woman. For instance, her preference for Castleberry knits, cloying perfume, red shoes, and red lipstick and nail color. It had been Rhonda on the phone. This acknowledgment hurled the Lady X accomplice into oblivion, which, in turn, detonated my theory about Augusta's drug and drag act.

I woke Daniel when supper was ready. "Go clean up,

change clothes, and come to the table. No trays tonight." I must get the formerly independent Daniel moving again.

He grumbled.

"Let's act civilized. No changee, no eatee."

"You're taking your penchant for Chinese checkers to the extreme."

"Go on."

When he balked again, I told him the menu.

His eyes twinkled. "Steak!" He reappeared in new clothes with a clean-shaven face. With minor difficulty he plopped down into the chair.

I grilled the steaks. Afterward, we ate and shared a glass of red wine. I had made it a point lately to leave the liquor cabinet bare.

Daniel skipped the broccoli and buried his potato in butter and sour cream.

He was gaining weight, but I bit my tongue.

Two heads were better than one. I didn't know what, if anything, was up, but I wanted to be prepared if another bizarre occurrence like naps in closed garages or traffic accidents befell us in the future.

I couldn't very well mention possible attempted murder to Morgan. He already thought me some bored country club kook with too much time on her hands. What witnesses were there? None. Augusta could say she'd visited but left after I received an upsetting phone call. Which was true. Thereby setting me on the path to suicide.

When I gave Daniel his smoothie, I reacted testily to his expression. "Just try it."

Reluctantly, he sipped. "Hey, this is pretty tasty."

"Thanks." I cleared away the dishes and loaded the dishwasher, watching him now and then until he downed the drink. Yay, he'd consumed fiber. "I want to discuss something with you. This is going to sound irrational, but hear me out."

First, I told him about my conversation with Morgan.

He stared at me and then looked questioningly at the remains in his glass. "What was in this?"

"Fruit and milk."

"No LSD? What you just told me is plain squirrelly."

"Think that's wacky? Try this." I told him about my thoughts on possible attempted murder, finishing with, "I think Augusta drove a *Gazette* van into your cart."

"Why, Sherlock? Answer me that, would you?"

"That, I can't say."

"You need to go back to work, fast."

"You first. Clean the kitchen."

He grumbled, "I'm injured."

"Hop to it, pardon the pun."

"Talk about kicking a guy when he's down."

"That's the point, Daniel. You need to get back your pep. Get going. I'm going to play with the computer."

"Great world. I've lost my pep and you've lost your mind."

I booted up the PC in the spare bedroom and Googled the name Augusta St. James. Only her info as columnist came up. For the heck of it, I Googled Sun And Sand Realty, Inc. A notation cited a website but it had been removed. The only reference now was "this page cannot be displayed."

Marching in to the master bedroom, I retrieved the note-pad where I'd scribbled the information Lilly had imparted and entered A. A. Audette, expecting a third strike.

Five matches came up: one, an entrepreneur selling herbal products out of California. Daniel might find that fascinating, but it did nothing for me. Next, a group spear-headed by an A. A. Audette sought missing persons for their ten-year high school reunion in June of this year. Hadn't he heard of Facebook? Regardless, that put them well out of the age group I was researching.

Another Audette was a cat breeder.

One was a man marketing his own country and western songs.

The final was a fiction writer.

"That's promising." I followed that link, which led to an online bookseller's search engine. The only thing that came up was some tome, *Sun and Sand*, listing a publisher I had never heard of. Judging from the copyright date, the book was long out of print. I Googled the publisher. Defunct. "That figures." For fun, I checked out Amazon's used book listing. Nada for A. A. Audette or a book titled, *Sun and Sand*.

Dead end.

There was no connection between Mendez's company, a book that some romance writer's publisher marketed dec-ades and decades before, and Augusta St. James.

Augusta was the sort who, if ever published, would inform the entire world. Certainly, everyone in Merry Acres
would know about it, or at the very least every member of
the BILL would have heard of her past literary success.

I blew out one big breath, turned off the computer, and
went out to help my husband finish his cleaning chores.

That Sunday, while Daniel watched a golf tournament, I
sat with him, reading a paperback during commercials. With
only a stroke separating the golfers, the leader choked. A tie.
Play went into overtime. Now, it grew interesting. I watched
the players call the coin toss. One called heads and won the
toss. He elected to have his opponent go first. A first, or so
the network commentators said.

"That was dumb."

Daniel counseled, "Not necessarily. A tough hole, lots of
water."

The first man to play addressed the ball, swung, and hit
his ball smack into a sand trap. Play continued. The other
player won.

"Good thing, otherwise they would have had to stay over
and finish tomorrow," Daniel said.

I wasn't listening. *Sun and Sand*. That was what had net-
tled me that night we returned from the dance program at
the HELP shelter and dined at the club. Looking out the window, watching the golfer hit out of a sand trap as the sun
set, triggered a memory. I couldn't pull it from the depths of
my subconscious that night, but it flashed into conscious
thought now.

The hourglass-and-sun logo on that deck of cards Augusta had talked Daniel into giving her didn't mean time in
the sun as Daniel had suggested. The logo referred to Sun
and Sand Realty, Inc.

Had Augusta realized that then? Did it threaten her
somehow?

"Daniel?"

"Hmm?"

"Who left that unusual card deck in the men's card room?
The one you gave to Augusta? The one with the sun and
hourglass on the back."

"Told you before, I don't know. Could you make me some
popcorn?"

"Sure thing."

"Can I have a bottle of beer?"

"I'll split one with you."

He grunted, expressing displeasure.

"Better half than none at all."

I prepared the popcorn. While it popped, it occurred to me that half of something might be worth killing somebody for. What if someone were trying to cut out another party altogether? The offended person might kill and take half, speculating that was a wiser policy than taking it all. Cleaning out the pot, after all, would point a neon finger at the taker. Maybe Mendez reneged on some deal. Audette, whoever that was, didn't like it. Or vice versa, and Mendez found out, confronted Audette, and soon after looked a tire iron in the eye because of it.

I handed Daniel the bowl of popcorn, along with the salt shaker.

"I'm going to give myself a facial."

"What, you aren't up to more board games?"

Ignoring his snide tone, I said, "Watch the tube. I'll check on you later."

Perhaps Augusta was working the connection to Sun and Sand Realty, Inc. and discovered the identity of A. A. Audette. So what? Would she kill over a story? A beefy byline couldn't mean that much to her. She was no humanitarian, but the risk-reward was not there.

As I smoothed citrus-scented rubbery goo on my face, I looked at the bedside clock. My mask would harden in a minute or two. Detective Morgan's brown eyes invaded my mental space. Abrupt, acerbic, allergy-ridden, he was hardly Hollywood handsome and he'd scared the daylights out of me, too.

What a guy.

Something zinged my blood stream. Something dangerous. Something risky. Something new. A younger man. Hey, cougars were the rage, right? Not that he was *that* young.

Perhaps I'd mention my hypothesis to Detective Morgan when I dropped off the BILL directory.

Maybe not.

I refused to believe Augusta had tried to kill me or Daniel because of some story. But I knew one thing, I hadn't attempted suicide. And somebody had tried to hit Daniel's golf cart. Why should Augusta want to harm Daniel or me? Unless she had killed Mendez? And Daniel and I had accidentally stumbled on some clue linking her thereto. God knew what it was. Was there something about that deck of cards that threatened Augusta? More likely, I was going nuts as Daniel had said.

He had a point. First the paranoia and now these wild presumptions. I'd had a half-glass of wine and half a beer. No wonder these ideas were zipping across the synapses of my brain.

The only thing ambitious Augusta coveted more than a story to make her editors take notice was... money. Neither Daniel nor I had any money or any connection to Mendez other than happenstance, but only if that card deck pointed to Sun And Sand Realty, Inc. and Augusta St. James had some connection.

But what?

Slow down. I looked at my face frozen in green goo. *You're working Augusta into something unsavory in order to punish her. You don't know for sure she and Daniel are, or were ever, involved romantically.*

A smile broke up the dried, crusty facial mask. Wouldn't it be grand if I, little "Georgie," bested witty Augusta?

Wouldn't it be grander still if I bested Augusta while giving much-needed attention to a group of youngsters with very little in their sad lives?

Like the HELP kids.

Rinsing away the residue, I dried my face and applied a toner geared for women of a certain age. I didn't look too bad for a post-menopausal female. My olive skin stood up to Florida sun pretty well. Decent bone structure. My schnoz was a bit prominent, but not too much so. My eyes sparkled. My skin glowed. So what if a twenty-dollar-a-jar facial formula was responsible.

Tomorrow, I'd call the *Merry Acres Gazette* to investigate tours open to the public. HELP shelter children would love to get out of that place. They might even enjoy watching the workings of a newspaper, even if it wasn't some big city daily.

While the kids watched the drama of daily news unfold at the *Gazette*, I would arrange to "bump" into whoever kept the company auto logs. A trip to the newspaper's parking lot might provide a bonanza, a white van with some dents, even a few scratches, *and* red paint that might match Daniel's destroyed golf cart. I'd saved a sample after paying the service to remove the cart from Merry Acres grounds in case he ever wanted to match the color for another, cheaper cart. What if it did match?

Wouldn't that impress Detective Morgan?

CHAPTER TWELVE

The woman in the publicity department at the newspaper was positively gleeful. "We would love to oblige your request, Mrs. Duncan. Of course, we must have a signed permission slip from each child's parent. There are lots of moving parts in the print room. Little hands could possibly get hurt.

I couldn't help smiling. As rambunctious as shelter kids were, "hurt" wouldn't cover it. Mangled might. "I appreciate your concern and promise to provide any type of release form you require, signed by each child's mother." I hoped. "So, tours are given on Wednesdays, between three and four?"

"That's right. Thank you for thinking of your hometown paper, Mrs. Duncan. Bye, now."

"Goodbye."

The next stop on my get-Augusta agenda was the HELP shelter. I would first talk to the woman who ran the place. Mama Smith, naturally, had been thrilled at the money brought in by my dance idea, meager though it was.

Mama Smith and I discussed the field trip. She promised to talk to current boarders, and also asked for my help the day of the trip. Getting a group of young children appropriately dressed and transported to the *Gazette* required team-work.

"Transport might be tricky," I said, since Daniel was still out of commission. "If only we had a van." Brainstorming, we came upon an idea that killed two birds with one shot. If we could snag an additional *Gazette* vehicle, I might possibly garner info about the *Gazette* van involved in Daniel's accident. That is, if my theory proved valid. I called the woman in the publicity department at the *Gazette* and explained the problem. "Could we borrow a van? I'd drive it. I'd be happy to arrange matters with the transportation manager."

"I don't know about that, Mrs. Duncan. There are liability issues to consider. Even if you have a perfect driving record, you don't have a commercial driver's license. Let me see if I can help you some other way. It is for a good cause, after all. I'll get back to you."

Having worked in the insurance industry for years, I knew this, but hoped somehow the newspaper would make an exception. "Thanks. In the meantime, I'll try to work out alternate arrangements." Like what?

I called BILL members whom I knew golfed, exercised, played tennis, or shopped when they weren't at the spa. Surely one of them would rearrange her schedule for one day to help out. Augusta would find out, but she already knew of my affiliation with the shelter. A field trip shouldn't sound any alarms.

Even so, there was safety in numbers. I would be with a group when seeking clues tying Augusta to Daniel's accident. I would still keep one eye on the kids and another on the columnist. If she was working at the paper the day of the tour, a heavy drum of ink might "accidentally" fall from the ceiling on a direct path toward my head.

BILL members scotched my efforts when they offered a hundred lame excuses as to why they couldn't help. Later that day, when the newspaper e-mailed the necessary release form, a closing sentence indicated the *Gazette* could spare one van, with driver, for the trip. It could accommodate seven children. More than that must find an alternate mode of transportation.

I called the shelter, advising I'd drop off copies of the release form. At the same time, I asked Mama Smith to take time from her impossible schedule to call the lady at the *Gazette* in order to respond to questions raised by the publicity department about the shelter kids.

When I walked into the shelter a little after four that afternoon, kids of every age, race, and creed surrounded me.

They hollered questions. "Are we going on a trip?" "To the newspaper?" "Can I go?"

And those were only the questions I could decipher from the cacophony.

Mama Smith came out at the clamor and told the kids to go in the backyard and play for a while. They did. When Mama Smith talked, everybody listened and obeyed.

Turned out, fourteen children were going. Mama Smith refused to grant older students permission to skip school even one day for a field trip.

I addressed the group of disappointed tweens and two teenagers. "We'll do something you'd like to do in the near future." What that would be, I had no idea. "If you have suggestions," I encouraged, "talk it over with Mama Smith. Between all of us, we'll plan something fun and age-appropriate."

They gave me wary looks.

My heart broke because I knew they didn't believe me.

After they left the room, I explained to Mama and her staff that the *Merry Acres Gazette* van would pick up seven children. I would drive the others in our SUV, all of us packed inside like sardines. I even gave an oath promising to arrive early and assist with the kids.

The day came and, discounting the battle to bathe, groom, and dress fourteen over-excited children, there was little fussing, fighting, or name calling on the way to the *Gazette*. A miracle.

At the *Gazette*, I helped seven passengers from the SUV. They were happy to stretch their legs and the "bigger" children were ecstatic to get the "shrimps" off their laps. Thank heavens no police cars were patrolling the back roads I took or I would definitely have a citation to show for my reckless solution to limited seating.

In the lot, SUV kids collided with kids brought by van, and all romped in excited play.

"Children." I clapped my hands. The youngsters ignored me and wildly jumped around.

The van driver grinned. "I got this." He pulled a whistle from his pocket. "Coach little league." When they settled down, he signaled for me to proceed.

"Remember, Mama Smith is depending on us to be ladies and gentlemen."

"What's that mean?" one little boy asked.

I smirked, figuring he was playing me. "That means be-have as if your mother is right beside you." I fixed them with a stare. "Better yet, pretend Mama Smith is looking over your shoulder."

A curly-haired blonde girl pleaded, "Okay. Okay. Let's go inside, pleeeeaaaase."

"Single file, march." I stood shocked into silence when they fell in line. I sang out one parting threat. "If *one* of you acts up, they will send us all home immediately. Remember, people are working. We must be quiet and respectful."

Antsy, the kids replied with impatient looks.

Inside, a volunteer guide greeted us. The tour proceeded apace. No on-site injuries occurred and the kids had a ball. Reporters and editors took a shine to them as well. The pub-licity department gave them official-looking press badges and baseball caps with *I Read it in the Gazette* embroidered on the front.

My planned jaunt to look over the van fleet proved fruit-less. Except for the van that brought the kids, no others were parked in the lot. I casually asked where the transportation department was located. Told that wasn't part of the tour, I later snuck away to find it, but when I did, a nameplate indi-cating *Transportation Manager* sat on a vacant desk, thus providing a golden opportunity to peruse the logs, if I could find them.

As luck would have it, I did, and flipped hurriedly through a few that revealed nothing of importance to me. Then, a man passing by saw me.

"This room isn't part of the tour."

"Sorry. I got lost. Are you the transportation manager?" I should have shut the door.

His expression told me he'd caught me in a lie. "No, but I'll show you the way back."

With the tour over and hopes of viewing all the car logs dashed, I joined the kids scampering around outside.

To be fair, I insisted the children rotate so the seven who had driven with me would go back to the shelter in the *Ga-zette* van. There was minor scuffling at this suggestion. A sports writer noticed and solved the problem. Raiding the break room for straws, he cut each one in half and instructed each child to hold out his or her hand.

His natural affection for kids led him to make a game of it. "Hope there's a straw for me or I'll have to stay here and work." Of course, there wasn't one. "You are all so lucky. I wouldn't care what kind of transport took me away." Consequently, when short straws were drawn, allowing a lucky two to take round-trip rides in the van, no riot ensued.

I thanked him, and we drove away.

The kids in my car chattered about the tour, and many spouted aspirations to one day work at a newspaper. Too bad there wouldn't be any newspapers left by the time they'd graduate college, the way the Internet was growing.

They were still buzzing about the day when I pulled onto the street in front of the shelter. The kids who originally rode with the *Gazette* driver sang praises of his jests and jokes. These stopped only when I parked and stood out of the way as they leaped out of the SUV.

I offered the van driver a ten dollar tip, which he refused, asking me to donate it to the shelter. I thanked him as tears stung my eyes and his, too.

Not a wasted day, but not as productive as I'd planned. At least Augusta hadn't been at the paper. Nor were hospital visits involved. Then, an incredible coincidence presented itself. The very van chosen to drive the children back to the shelter exhibited a few scratches and slight damage on its right front bumper.

I liked the driver. I hated doing it, but while he was diverted by horseplay with the kids, I took out a fingernail file and scraped off paint from the dented area, putting the tiny chips on a sponge inside my compact. I casually mentioned the ding to him after he stopped playing with the children, but he vowed he hadn't noticed it before.

"Neither here nor there," I said.

I watched his reaction carefully when I told him about Daniel's accident. The driver looked nervous, but that didn't mean he had been driving this van.

"Don't worry," I assured him, "you won't get in trouble." *Unless you were driving the day my husband was hit. Or know who did.*

"You should talk to my boss."

"Good idea. What's his name?" I wrote it down on a notepad and stuffed it back in my pocketbook. In any case, our insurance carrier would be interested if that paint chip matched the golf cart manufacturer's list. Even with Florida no-fault insurance laws, the carrier might use the information to negotiate a settlement if the *Gazette* van was involved.

More than that, I felt proud of the accomplishment. And I now had a valid reason to call on Detective Mike Morgan other than delivering the BILL club directory.

≡ ≡ ≡

Tired but jubilant, I waltzed into The Duncan villa on Carnoustie Way.

Daniel, standing in the kitchen, greeted me. "You look positively radiant. I take it all went well."

"Swimmingly."

My glow dimmed considerably when I smelled cigar smoke.

He caught me sniffing the air. "Some people stopped by. So many that we're playing cards in the dining room. We have any more Swiss cheese?"

I put on a good wife's demeanor. The kitchen looked all right, although damage control might be required later in the dining room, which I had yet to observe.

"I'll look. I know it's hard for you to bend down too far." As I had during Daniel's entire convalescence, I pretended this was another normal, post-accident day in our life. "Yep, only two slices, however. I'll put it on my grocery list."

"Could you please cut it up and maybe put it on some crackers? We ran out of sandwiches and popcorn."

"Of course." *Mighty Maid at your service.* "Go back to the game. I'll fix snacks and bring them in."

"Many thanks."

After dividing the cheese to make cracker sandwiches, I dressed up the remaining crackers with deviled ham spread stolen from our storm supplies, rationalizing this was an emergency of a sort. I dotted each with an olive slice and placed everything on a lettuce-lined platter.

Eat your heart out, Martha Stewart.

This time, I took it into the dining room.

"Hi, Georgiana," the group chorused.

"Hello." Two guys I'd seen before, two I didn't recognize—Daniel introduced them as guys from Broward County—and a shocker, Augusta reigned at the other end of the table, studying her hand.

She glanced up. "Hey, Georgie." She looked back at her cards.

"Hi." I shoved the tray at Daniel.

"Thanks, honey."

It was then I recalled that BILL wag's crack about Augusta's affairs starting in the card room then moving to the bedroom. Our bedroom was too close to the dining room for my comfort.

I put on my very best June Cleaver smile and chirped, "My pleasure, dear. Well, I have errands to run. Back later." Now was the perfect time to visit the Merry Acres police station and drop off the BILL directory and the paint chip for Mike Morgan.

Outside in the driveway, I mumbled, "Silly ol' me." I started the car engine. "Looking for women behind every bedpost," I growled. But upon further thought, I grinned. Daniel's leg cast would hamper seduction scenarios.

As for *moi*, with luck, I would meet with Detective Mike Morgan. Checking my appearance in the visor mirror, I reapplied lipstick and recklessly unbuttoned the first button of my blouse. Then, the second one.

≡ ≡ ≡

"Ah, Mrs. Duncan," Detective Morgan said. "Nice to see you again." He drummed thick, tanned fingers on a document. "Sit. Please."

Disappointed, I resented his cursory salutation, delivered with as little patience as if he were standing behind a shopper with twenty items in the express line at the local grocery. "No thanks. I'm only staying a minute."

His office, a windowless closet, was no doubt a contributing factor for his impudent manner. Hammering progressed in the background as the civic center underwent a major remodeling. The noise would hardly help an already surly disposition, but God help me, even with a runny nose, the man... intrigued me.

Morgan's big brown eyes, more glazed than the half-eaten donut on his crowded desk, held my gaze before he snatched a handkerchief from his pocket and blew his red nose. "Sorry."

"Melaleuca blossoms still?"

He nodded.

"Like I said before, they're a curse. You know, like accidents while dunking for golf balls."

"Mrs. Duncan, don't start, okay. Karl Esterhause drowned. Accidental. ME said so."

"A man who nearly made the Olympic swim team?"

"Forty years ago."

"A man who swam laps daily."

"Ever heard of cramps? It happens."

"Things," I shouted over the grating sound of a saw, "aren't what they seem in Merry Acres, Detective."

He yawned, covering his mouth. "Sorry, a recent schedule change and prescription allergy meds are affecting my sleep." He looked through the directory. "Thanks for bringing this by." His eyes did grant me an admiring once-over.

This I soaked up like a desert flower accepting rain and returned one of my own before pressing on. "What about Ben Bernstein's heart attack? The man toiled daily on a book detailing his journey from triple bypass patient to prime specimen. Becca was incorporating heart-smart recipes into the manuscript. Heart attacks can be induced, you know." Now wasn't the time to mention Ben's congestive heart failure.

"Natural causes," he sing-songed. He sniffed and refolded his handkerchief for another pass. "What's the motivation to add one particle of credibility to your suspicions? You want to play 'what if,' then ponder this—familiarity breeds contempt, right? Husband underfoot gets old, for better, for worse, and for lunch, too. Who's to say a wife won't go nuts and off hubby herself?"

Blood drained from my head as I pretended no affront had hit home. "That's ridiculous."

"Maybe," he said.

His expression unsettled me. Had he looked into my heart?

He continued, "Life insurance money is a powerful incentive."

There was nothing factual there. "You're not implying—"

"Just speculating, same as you. Look." He pointed to several file folders stacked on his desktop—open cases. "See these jackets? Real murders. If you come up with something concrete, call me. Otherwise, enjoy that group of yours.

What is it, the Ladies of Leisure?"

Okay, enough was enough. I arched my brow. "Really."

"Haven't been to the Greek place this week. You?"

I shook my head and, despite his brush off, wanted to say something to prolong my stay, but nothing came to mind.

He shrugged and, with an apologetic gesture, tapped his watch, indicating he had to get back to work.

"I'm surprised you can hear anything," I said over more construction noise, and pushed away from the edge of an ancient green-metal desk. His jaw worked, but he said nothing before turning to his computer screen.

All business now, he swiveled back around in his squeaky chair and faced me. "Something else?"

The paint chip! How could I forget that? "Yes, there is. Here's a paint chip taken from a *Merry Acres Gazette* van." I produced the compact, extracted the sponge with the paint chip on it and set it on a file folder on his desk, a "jacket," as he'd called it. "Wouldn't surprise me if it matches the junked golf cart my husband was driving the day he was blindsided."

Now, his brow rose. "Doubt the sample is large enough, but, to humor a junior detective, I'll give it to the lab." He blew his nose again before gesturing toward the door with a soggy cloth. "Goodbye, Georgiana."

He'd called me by my given name. That was a plus. Maybe. How could I get him to notice me? Really notice me? Momentarily conflicted, I started to leave and then remembered Augusta sitting there at my dining room table looking smug. I remembered Rhonda, too. "Maybe I'll see you at The Athenian Garden."

His smile warmed dark spaces in my heart. "I eat lunch there on Thursdays, around one. In the meantime, be good and let us do our job, okay? By the way, nice blouse. Very nice."

I practically skipped out of the building and floated over to the car.

CHAPTER THIRTEEN

Augusta was cool when we met by chance at the Merry Mart a few days later. "You missed the BILL luncheon yesterday. I was host."

"Sorry. My hands are full with Daniel, presently."

"Uh-huh," Augusta said. "You know, with the recent deaths and such, I figured we could use some cheer around Merry Acres. I, therefore, put forth the idea of a costume ball."

"Oh." I hated affairs where adults, dressed in costume, looked and usually acted ridiculous. Allowing one's "inner child" to run amok in middle age was, to me, unseemly. Not that the way I had allowed that detective to play with my mind wasn't a prime example of unseemly in my own life.

Augusta crowed, "I convinced Missy she should take it on." She chortled. "She practically had an orgasm on the spot. She's all for it."

"Hmm."

"I also suggested hired escorts since there will be dancing, naturally." She gave me a slow smile. "You know, the theme might be Merry Acres Widows Waltz. Catchy, eh? Anyway, escorts are necessary to attend the Barrier Isles Ladies of Leisure's subgroup."

I tried with little success to ignore Augusta's searing reference to her waltzing exhibitions with Daniel. "What subgroup is that?"

"Oh right, you're married, aren't you? I nearly forgot," Augusta said. "I'm referring to the WDDs, widows without dates."

Disgusted with Augusta's chronic glibness, I retaliated, "What about Janet Jessell, the divorced member or"—I hesitated for emphasis—"our one single member? That would be you."

"Works for us, too. I think of everyone."

"Right." I rolled my eyes. "It would be rather difficult for Daniel to dance with his leg cast. He'd feel left out, so I can't attend."

"Don't be asinine, Georgie. You started the BILL. You have to be there whether Danny Boy comes or not. Appearances, you know?"

She had a point. "We'll see. I suppose someone will keep us informed?"

Augusta said, strolling away with a cart, "That's up to Missy. Unless you want to take on the task."

Not on your life. "No. Missy would handle that sort of thing far better than I."

I grabbed a wire basket and selected the few things needed to tide us over before a major marketing trip later in the week. Augusta approached the checkout counter at the same time as I.

She rushed her buggy in front of mine and put her items on the counter first. "Understand you and the HELP kiddies paid a call at the *Gazette*."

Aha. So that was the cause of the cold shoulder act. "Yes. They're still talking about it. Actually, one or two expressed a desire to become reporters one day. We're encouraging them, emphasizing how important reading and writing skills would be."

"Reporters?" She jeered. "They'd be used to substandard living wages at any rate." She reached in her purse for a debit card. "There's a rumor going round." She put her hand on her hip in a swift movement. "Who knows how these things get started, but I heard you accused the *Gazette* driver—who so very charitably drove those kids over to the paper—of a hit-and-run against Daniel."

My arm muscle quivered from holding the green basket filled with items like a quart of milk, a six pack of soda, cheese, and a loaf of bread. I adjusted the basket. "What if I did? That doesn't concern you." Channeling Aunt Irene, I worked up a dandy accusatory stare. "Does it?"

Augusta smiled slyly. "Furthermore, sources say you and Detective Morgan are getting... thick. Should Daniel be worried?"

"I don't know, Augusta. Ask him next time you play cards at our house."

The clerk asked Augusta to speed things along.

"Oh, sorry." Augusta paid and left.

The hairs on the back of my neck hadn't yet settled down. Morgan appeared to be a man who held his cards close to his vest. I paid for the groceries, mentally allowing that, although Augusta might not currently be the best of pals, she could be the very best of enemies.

Back at home, I put away the food.

Daniel came into the kitchen. "No beer?"

"Not until marketing day."

"That's days away. The only thing to drink in the pantry was a wine cooler."

"That's right." I whipped up tuna salad and made two sandwiches. "I saw Augusta at the Merry Mart. The BILL will be putting on a costume ball."

"We aren't going, are we? I hate those things."

"Me too, but as founder, I have to attend. You don't."

"Well, hobbling around on crutches at a social affair is pretty ridiculous, don't you think?"

"I'm not sure when it takes place. You may or may not be fully ambulatory. Liquor will be served, however."

"That's incentive." Daniel maneuvered his crutches toward the den, plopped in the recliner, and started playing with the remote.

I nearly insisted he eat at the table with me, but it wasn't worth another dispute. I slapped his hastily made sandwich onto a plate and set it on a tray before I tore off a paper towel and shoved it under the plate's rim. This, I ferried over to him with a glass of milk.

"Milk? Gee, thanks."

"You're welcome." I stalked back to the table, again wondering what the heck had happened to happily ever after.

Oh yeah, first Rhonda, then Lady Luck, and then Augusta.

≡ ≡ ≡

Dixie Metcalf felt grand. Why not? She was in Georgia among familiar faces and surroundings. She loved Georgia. If not for Georgiana, she'd never return to Merry Acres.

She adjusted her bifocals and studied a random Island Dreams Airlines passenger list while the seated board members of the Metcalf Foundation waited. IDA was a corporation she'd convinced Chester to buy for fun and profit. While outside the Foundation's duties, she consulted with its attorney from time to time on the airline and other matters. Her fingers hurt today and she massaged them, admiring Chester's diamond ring as she did so. She missed him so. Especially when she looked at the suits lining the table in a conference room deep within her exclusive assisted living facility in a small Georgia town "beneath the gnat line" as the smart set in Atlanta would say. It was so kind of them to travel out of their way for these meetings so that she could conduct them on her home turf, so to speak. Not much outside the facility seemed all that familiar any more.

At least today her brain was functioning normally, or nearly so, thanks to a heavier dose of her prescription and therapy—in the form of a specially-created computer game—and endless word puzzles. She glanced around at the throng of trusted friends, smiled, took up the IDA passenger list and frowned. "There's no extra seat on the IDA commuter jet." She chuckled. "I have no plans of using it. However, Chester's agreement, when he bought the airline, was one empty seat on every flight in case he or I ever wanted to jaunt to the islands. I've caught them twice before. In perpetuity means forever."

She looked at a balding man sitting two chairs down on her right. "Isn't that so, Charles? Time without end, infinity, eternity."

He nodded.

"Carlotta, send IDA an e-mail." Dixie's voice exhibited irritability. "If they don't want a lawsuit over breach of contract, they'll open up a seat. I want a new passenger list faxed to me tomorrow before five o'clock. Tell them we're sending someone to check. They don't have to know we're bluffin'. If they have to bump some poor soul, I'm sorry."

"Yes, Mrs. Metcalf," Carlotta, her able assistant, said.

Dixie then noticed a name there that worried her. Why would *she* decide to fly to Alandira Island? Dixie's radar was on full alert. Trouble lay dead ahead.

"Charles, seems I'm pickin' on you today. I don't mean to, but have you completed the codicil to my will?"

The lawyer, one of the six seated directors of the Metcalf Foundation, again nodded in the affirmative. "It's in front of you."

"Good ol' Charles." Dixie chuckled. "Thinks I'm crazy," she confided aloud. "But won't say so. Publicly, anyway. We all know my mind is fast fluttering away, but I'm right as rain today."

Carlotta piped up. "Amen."

"Hush, girl. Now, y'all can all attest that today I am in my sound mind. Consequently, watch me sign this document." She lifted the codicil and shook it. "You all will witness it, and Carlotta will notarize it."

The process took a couple of minutes because of arthritis in Dixie's right hand. "Lord, my signature resembles the scrawl of a third grader learning penmanship. If my mind doesn't worry me, my arthritis does. Somebody get me an aspirin."

Carlotta jumped up and made a call on an intercom.

A nurse rushed in with a glass of water and a pill.

"Thank you, dear, I don't need the water. I have sweet tea." She took the pill and waited for the nurse to leave. "Anybody else have business to bring before the board? Good. I'm tired. Carlotta, you stay. The rest of you chickens fly the coop. Go on. No. Wait, one more thing. I reckon this is our last meeting."

She looked at them. "Uh-uh-uh. No long faces, no drippy eyes. Best gift you can give me is a bright smile. That's the best medicine this side of heaven."

They looked at her and then down at their pads, or hands, or anywhere else but her face.

"Shoo." She waved her hands as if sending a gaggle of geese to flight. "Go on, now. Shoo."

When Carlotta shut the door behind them, she trotted back to sit beside Dixie, her note pad and pen ready.

"Everything ready for the annual powwow at Widow's Retreat?"

"Yes, ma'am. Invitations were sent; all but one RSVP'd they'd attend."

"Who didn't?"

"Susie Esterhause."

"Wonder why. Follow up. Perhaps she didn't receive the invitation. The others are coming?"

"Everyone." Carlotta made notations on a pad.

"Wonderful." Dixie sipped iced tea. "I'll go to my suite then for a nap. Tell the kitchen I'm hankerin' for low-country food and coconut cake. No, make that pecan pie. Well, what's the difference? I'll take a slice of each and a Coca-Cola to wash it down. My mind is a mite wobbly, but my appetite's robust." She chuckled. "Maybe I'll pass in a diabetic coma."

"Please, Mrs. Metcalf, don't say such things, even in jest. Also, I'm sorry to report, I've misplaced a file folder, the one you insisted on taking with you to Merry Acres. The blue one given to you by the private investigator."

Dixie appreciated Carlotta's diplomacy. Her assistant had really asked, "What did you do with that file once I gave it to you?" Trouble was, Dixie couldn't remember. "Maybe Gloria remembers."

"I'll ask her. Don't worry, it'll turn up."

"I'm sure it will." Dixie worried it would, but in the hands of someone who shouldn't have it. Her thoughts grew hazy again. She looked out a window where a male cardinal preened on the branch of an anise hedge. Oh no. She must keep it together. She must. "What were we speaking about?"

"Nothing important, a blue file folder that's been temporarily misfiled."

That triggered Dixie's thoughts about that unexpected name on the passenger list. "Before I head to my quarters for a lie down, bring that IDA passenger list to me. Then call Janet Jessell for me."

Within minutes, Carlotta came to the doorway. "Mrs. Jessell is on the line." She handed some papers to Dixie.

Dixie picked up the receiver. "Hey, Janet. It's Dixie. Pardon? Who was that woman who called with the Caribbean accent? Why, that's Carlotta." Dixie grinned at her assistant. "Darlin', you know I can't remember phone numbers real well anymore. She helps me."

Carlotta smiled before she left and closed the door behind her.

"I know about speed dialing, Janet. Problem with that is names float in and out of my mind." She looked at the papers, wondering why she'd asked for them. "Some days, arthritis makes punching even single digits difficult. Enough about my aches and pains."

Dixie scanned the list and saw the name she'd underlined.

Oh yes. Her. She leaned forward and rubbed her back, which was suddenly as knotted up as her neck. She clicked her pen open and shut, open and shut. "Tell me, darlin', what's new in Merry Acres?"

≡ ≡ ≡

On Thursday, I met Detective Morgan for lunch. He ordered a sampler platter of Greek food. I selected a small Greek salad and drank Greek coffee.

"Good news, bad news," he said.

"Good first."

"Paint matches. We got a copy of the transportation log and it says Augusta had the van around that date."

I brightened and then sobered. "Bad?"

Mike said, "Unfortunately, 'around that time' doesn't prove anything. Augusta could say she drove the van, returned it in perfect condition, and the logs were incorrectly maintained. Lots of holes. But, I am starting to think you might be on to something. So, watch your back, Mrs. Duncan."

"Correction—Georgiana." I'd also ordered a baklava and ate half the sweet, pushing the other half toward Mike. His hint of confidence meant a lot. "Don't worry. I don't intend to get within fifty feet of Augusta any time soon for many reasons. Hopefully, Daniel will avoid her, too." I shrugged. "But he's a big boy."

Morgan smiled as if he understood my meaning and sympathized.

"I've got to get home. Hope I see you again. Soon."

As I prepared to leave, he held up a broad palm, halting me. "You know, Georgiana, witnesses at one of those BILL things stated you openly declared you wouldn't mind killing your husband."

"Is Augusta the witness?"

"Can't say."

Hurt, I worried if his interest was strictly from an investigator's standpoint.

"Detective Morgan, if you arrested every wife who said that, you'd be far busier than you are now." I reached over and crammed baklava into my mouth, gobbling the remaining bit of my dessert before squaring my shoulders.

"Wait." He took my wrist. "I had a reason for asking that."

He released my arm, allowing me freedom to walk.

By the time I reached his side of the table to depart, he'd turned in his chair so his body was open to me. His eyes darkened. His expression pleaded, as if asking something...understanding?

Pulse racing, I went out on an emotional limb. "As a civilian?"

"Something like that." He rose, gently removed phyllo dough from my cheek with two fingers, and put them into his mouth.

My head cautioned he was using me. My heart didn't care.

≡ ≡ ≡

The next day at home, after I drove Daniel to the clubhouse card room, the phone rang.

"Hello."

"Hey, Georgiana."

My mind spun in circles. Mike's voice caught and held me like a lover's arms. "Hello." Unsure how to respond, I borrowed Augusta's snappy approach. "Checking up to see if Daniel's still breathing? Can't help you, he's not here. He's playing cards elsewhere." Speaking of breathing, I wasn't doing so well. My hands shook, too. How silly. How thrilling.

He snorted. "It's, um, a social call. That means I'm violating my code of ethics big time. You okay with that?"

"I'm breaking several moral codes myself, but, yes, I'm fine with that."

"It's my day off. Want to go for a drive?"

"Love to."

"Wear pants and long sleeves."

"It's warm."

"You'll understand."

We arranged to meet at a park where I transferred to his car, a spiffy new model Honda.

Disregarding his wardrobe suggestion, I'd slipped into a girlish, pink short-sleeved twin set and a flowery trumpet skirt. The weather hinted at the coming endless summer and I felt younger than my fifty years. Foolish, perhaps, but delighted all the same, especially when Mike's eyes approved when his words didn't.

"Ever hear about Meredith Montgomery?"

"You mean the myth?"

"Myth? What myth? I'm talking about her grave site."

More excited, I said, "You know where she's buried?"

"I think so."

"Think? She once owned the land on which Merry Acres sits."

"So, what's the myth?"

"Reportedly, she was an unhappy wife who attracts others like her to the place. Like me." I couldn't bring myself to tell him the part wherein Merry uses her influence from beyond the grave to create widows.

"Are you unhappy?"

I snorted. "Would I be sitting here otherwise?"

He looked at his feet. "No, I suppose not. I have nothing to offer you. I'm a divorced cop who is not looking to remarry."

Sugar coat things, why don't you? "Yes, well, I'm an older woman seeking revenge against an unfaithful husband. Call it serendipity."

"We'll see. Today, I'll show you Merry's grave, if I can still find it. I assume it's hers anyway."

"Unique first date."

He laughed. "What, you thought I'd whisk you to some motel right away?"

Wrapping my arms about me, I replied, "Not at all. I hoped you were sensitive enough to know that wouldn't work. Not with me. Not...now."

"You're in luck. The result of a recent sensitivity training seminar."

I laughed at that.

We drove back through the gated entry into Merry Acres and eventually veered onto a service road. Mike parked and opened my door. I smiled. It always started chivalrously with a man opening a woman's door.

He took a golf club from the bag in his trunk and handed me a blanket. "That's a pretty outfit you're wearing, and nice black leather ballerina jobs. Yes, in answer to your amused expression, I keep up with women's shoe fashions. Somewhat. Too bad they and your outfit will be destroyed. It's wild where we're going. Wrap this around your shoulders to protect your arms, or put on the sweater. Expect snags if you do. Or wrap it around your waist to protect that skirt and some of your legs. Good luck with the shoes."

We walked through a stand of pines, thousands of needles carpeting the way. A tangle of brush lay ahead. Our shoulders touched and our hands brushed each other as we worked our way in.

Mike led the way and used the club to hack through overgrowth and hold back branches and brush so I could follow.

A short time later, we came upon a small, semi-cleared area and a granite stone the size of a large index card. *MM* was carved into it.

Instinctively, I knelt down and cleared the stone of pine needles and dead leaves. "How sad, no one tends her grave."

"Maybe that's how she wanted it."

A soft breeze filtered through the pine boughs like a whisper. For an instant, I thought I heard it call my name, but that was fantasy from the influence of too much rumor. I rose, and with the blanket still wrapped around me, allowed him to take me back to the clearing.

There, I spread the blanket. "So, Mike, tell me about yourself."

He bit his lip. "Yeah. Don't you just hate first dates?" He smiled. "You could say Clint Eastwood was a good or bad influence, depending on your point of view. I went to a Florida university, received a degree in criminology, then police academy, graduated, was a traffic cop, beat cop, and moved up, finally, to detective. Over the years, made it to grade three. Married, no kids. Divorced due to long hours, worry, and neglect taking its toll."

"That's it?"

"Minor revision. I should insert someplace I spent as much time in the bar where my buds hung out as I did at home. We grew apart." He shrugged. "She found someone to hold her hand when I wasn't around. We parted company. Reasonably amicably. Okay, I socked her guy once. Hey, I came home. He was at my kitchen table. In briefs. She was wearing only a towel. A man's castle, you know?"

"I understand. Believe me."

"Hell, he was lucky I didn't shoot him. Her, too. Upshot? They'd planned it. If I didn't make waves in divorce court, he wouldn't press charges. A sham, you bet, but IA investigations are frowned upon and there would be one. She got the house, the contents, half the bank account and the car. I got what was left."

"You sound...bitter."

"A little, but who can I blame except the guy in the mirror? My profession isn't a good fit for marriage. You see too much human nature. Trust? Forget that. Okay, Georgiana, I showed you mine, show me yours." He twirled his palm, ending with an open hand.

I took it and traced his life line with a fingertip. The line was long and deep. His hand was warm. I touched his wrist and felt his racing pulse and then gave him an overview from Aunt Irene to Rhonda, leaving out—for the present—details about Augusta. I let go of his arm and we sat silently.

He rose, extended his hand and helped me up, but not before I snatched the blanket and neatly folded it, hoping I had left my scent on it.

"That's enough history for one day. Hungry?"

I smiled. "Starving."

"Good, I know this ethnic place you might like. They serve great Greek food."

We drove back to the park where I got in the SUV and followed him to The Athenian Garden café.

We went in separately, acting surprised to see each other.

Nikko brought our salads, baklava, and Greek coffees.

When we left, Mike steered me around the side of the building and kissed me.

I melted into him, smelling aftershave and musk. I tasted testosterone and that coppery tang of want. His hot breath set me on fire and I kissed him back, tonguing him.

He caressed my breast, but I moved his hand.

"Let's permit anticipation to build for a while."

He groaned. With short breaths between words, he said, "Your wish is my command."

"Thank you."

"Soon?"

I responded with the same short, primitive speech. "Soon." When I slid into my SUV, I allowed the heat of our brief embrace to slowly dissipate, and watched him drive away.

It wasn't young love; it wasn't pure love. But I'd learned long ago to settle.

When I picked up my dear hubby, I hummed all the way home.

At our fresh-start house on Carnoustie, I convinced Daniel

he needed a backrub, and then a hand job to placate his neglected prostate gland while I placated my guilt. The bed was crowded, for as my hand circled Daniel's dick, sliding up and down rhythmically, I was mentally hand-jiving Michael's member, and God knew who was playing around in my husband's head. Rhonda? Augusta?

Afterward, I prepared steak for dinner and endured another serial killer movie, from start to finish, which consumed almost two hours, including those intervals where Daniel flipped to other channels during commercial breaks before flipping back.

Nothing like a little guilt to rev up the kindness engine.

That night before bed, I showered. A long, languid, hot shower wherein I soaped up and rinsed off and lathered again, stroking my face, neck, arms, breasts, and my thighs, pretending my hand was the one I'd held that afternoon. I might not be happy in the purest sense, but by the end of that shower, I was sexually gratified.

≡ ≡ ≡

The night of the costume ball arrived.

Wondering if Daniel appreciated irony, I rented him a Don Juan costume and selected martyred Marie Antoinette for my getup.

The hardest part was hiding the device I'd bought at the electronics store and never used. I couldn't very well ask Daniel to help. Poor man had never fully recovered from my earlier suggestion that Augusta tried to kill him in his golf cart and me with a drugged smoothie.

My mind left Daniel and joyously settled on Mike until Daniel's grunts in the other room drew my attention. He, too, struggled with his costume, not easy with a cast to overcome. At least the cast would come off next week. I left my dressing area and trudged over. "Need help?"

"Not yet."

Back in the bathroom, I studied the contraption in my hand. It might be state of the art, but hardly matched devices I'd seen in films. Why hadn't I lucked into some situation like those I'd seen in movies, wherein beefy lawmen in a strategically placed van would wait for my SOS? I fussed and fumed over the microcassette, finally securing the voice-activated recorder under the powdered wig. Praying I'd installed the battery properly and the thing would work when needed, I poked the wiry microphone through the wig's fabric and wound it over one ear. I covered it with strands of my hair that I'd heavily dusted with baby powder to match the wig. This caused a coughing spree. Under my breath, I grumbled, "Maybe it'll pass as a hearing aid."

"What'd you say?"

"Nothing." The gown's neckline plunged into a tantalizing V. The intention was to have everyone stare at the top halves of my breasts. One guest in particular. Mike. Checking myself out in the bathroom mirror, I noted my skin hadn't yet turned to turkey wattle. Another plus, I didn't freckle as some lighter-skinned women did. No, mine wasn't the chest of a babe like Susie Esterhause, but not too, too bad.

With effort, I secured the clasp of a gaudy rhinestone necklace purchased at a thrift shop, hoping it, too, would take attention away from my ears, which I left bare for the evening. My thoughts wandered back a few days to a long lunch with Mike earlier in the week.

He'd selected an outside eatery in another county allowing the guilty pleasure of holding hands.

"You know you're driving me crazy. I think of you all the time." He looked at me with piercing eyes. "I want you to be sure about this. You strike me as someone who could suffer—"

"A broken heart?" I laughed bitterly. "Don't worry. Been there, done that."

"I don't think you're over Daniel. Not really."

"You could be right in a sense, but it's only from habit, and fear. I'm fifty. Daniel's older. He's at the juncture where there's less future and more past. I don't have much to gain by staying, but the devil you know is often better than the one you don't."

He looked away.

"I didn't mean you were a devil."

"I can be."

"Who can't? Know what I'm really thinking right now? I'm thinking how I'd love to be with you on clean, crisp sheets feeling you inside me. Oh my. Look. You're blushing."

"Don't tease, Georgiana."

"I'm not."

"Who's blushing now?"

I took a sip of ice water. "That's age-related, dear. It's called a hot flash."

"I don't buy that." His fingers danced along my wrist, brushing the skin ever so slightly.

What woman wouldn't enjoy the delectable torture? I inflicted my own by slipping off a shoe and rubbing my foot up and down his leg.

We whispered secrets, we teased, and we taunted, allowing sexual desire to build but remain, as yet, unsatisfied.

"There's a costume party I must attend for the BILL. We're hiring escorts for the unmarried and unattached among us. They'll be dressed as superheroes. No one would know who you were or why you were there, were you so disposed, and so dressed. We could dance and slip away to the terrace and neck."

"How you talk. Me in a costume? I don't think so."

"Aw, come on."

We'd parted without his commitment to attend, and his disdain of costumes unchanged.

Though later, in my bathroom, I could still hear his laughter ringing in my ears.

Racy Regency romances I'd read over the years often featured sizzling love scenes at costume balls. Maybe such a scene was in my future. Would Mike come to the party? He must. I liked that we had extended the time before engaging in sex, but a twinge of doubt attacked now and again as to why he hadn't pushed it. Was he involved with another woman while seeing me? He didn't seem the duplicitous type, but neither had Daniel.

That same day, before I was barely out of my meet-Mike-for-lunch clothes, Janet Jessell had called, complaining vociferously about being roped into helping Missy.

I held the phone away from my ear a moment until Janet's rant ran its course.

Janet also wanted to confirm that Daniel and I would attend, which I validated. Next, Janet reported the escorts had been instructed to pick up costumes at the same shop.

How many costume shops were there in this small community?

They were all to dress as superheroes for the occasion, Janet said.

That, I'd already heard from Missy. Clever Missy

Youngblood had a sense of humor, too. I giggled. Mike was my own personal superhero, regardless of his attire.

Janet went on that afternoon about BILL funds.

While I clucked in sympathy, I no longer cared. The club was a bust. I hadn't bonded with the Merry Acres women. The story of my life.

I'd stopped going to the therapist. Fantasies about Detective Morgan worked just as well. No, they worked better. My taking a job had also been discussed. It would cut time with Mike, but I knew the affair, once consummated, wouldn't last long. Mike was the sort who enjoyed the hunt.

I rejoined battle with the costume's head piece.

Daniel called out, "Hey, can you help me? I can't go half naked to this thing and I can't find the pants."

Taking a pair of pants from a hanger in the closet, I joined him. "There aren't any." I tossed the pants on the bed. "I told the costume shop to keep the fancy pants. I purchased a pair of trousers at a thrift store. I'm going to cut off one pants leg at the thigh to ease your cast through. Let's see where the cast starts." I'd glued on some decorative stitching similar to that on the jacket.

I marked the cut line with a pin and went to my night table for the scissors kept there.

"Be careful with those, would you?"

"Your manhood is safe but I am not hemming pants tonight. I meant to take care of this task earlier, but I forgot."

"I'm forgotten a lot, lately."

I cut the cloth. "Poor baby." I shoved the pants at him. "Okay, moment of truth. Slip them on."

He hobbled over to the bed and put on the first leg, the full-length one, and then the half-length. He used his hands to push off from the bed and hopped the few feet to the dresser where he'd rested his crutches.

"What do you think? Not perfect, but a passable match to the rest of the costume, if I say so myself."

I said crisply, "I don't do perfect matches."

He replied, "Me, either. You see, darling wife, we do have something in common."

"You look fine, Don Juan. I'll meet you at the door out to the garage. We have fifteen minutes to spare."

He brought his hands to his chest and said, with a flourish, "I count the minutes."

"Look on the bright side, Daniel. There's an open bar."

"That's why I'm going." He smiled. "I'll wait for you in the car. Don't tarry."

"Watch the step down into the garage. And be careful getting into the passenger's side. I'll be there in a minute, as soon as I figure out how to pee while wearing a hoop skirt rivaling a hot air balloon."

Daniel's crutches thumped away. He stopped suddenly. "Let's stay home."

Should I recommend he stay home? That would suit my purposes just fine, but I'd let him decide. "Really, Daniel, what's so difficult? We stand around an hour or so with masks on our faces, drinks in our hands, and say some vainglorious words. Then, we come home. What could be simpler than that? It's my swan song for the BILL."

"Well, there's that." Daniel lamented loudly, as he thumped away, "Stupid, silly, boring night ahead."

Thinking of Mike Morgan, I said under my breath, "Boring for some, but not all."

Shifting this way and that, I finally took care of personal business in the bathroom and washed my hands. I was acutely aware of the recorder grazing my scalp, my head already uncomfortably hot from the wig. A sure fire recipe for a major headache.

As to the goal to trap Augusta, thereby solving the Mendez murder and pumping up my ego—not to mention winning major points with Mike—my plan consisted of plying Augusta with drink and then asking her leading questions in a very public place.

I adjusted the wig for the tenth time. It stubbornly listed despite efforts to align it properly. This proved futile due to an attached crown of gold-colored tin, reminding me that Marie Antoinette had lost her head. Could I keep mine during a faceoff with Augusta?

And what about Mike? When Mike Morgan showed up and danced with me—and he would—could I keep my heart in check?

Between angst over besting physically powerful Augusta, and growing affection for a man who might not return it in full measure, I wondered how I could possibly keep my cool tonight.

CHAPTER FOURTEEN

At the clubhouse, cardboard screens painted in harlequin designs dotted the room. There must have been twenty at least. Tiny white lights, artfully suspended from the ceiling, were strung across the area. A jungle of potted plants, also dressed in the tiny lights, filtered air in the densely populated room. Every BILL member, their guests, and then some apparently, had come.

A red-haired Aphrodite and her abbreviated-toga-clad mate approached Daniel and me.

Missy Youngblood said, "Hello, Georgiana, or should I say Your Majesty? You're safe tonight, Marie, no guillotines were ordered for this affair. This is my husband, Jack Youngblood."

"Greetings." The man beside her bowed his leaf-wreathed head. "I'm Mercury, in case you missed the golden wings on my freezing feet." He lifted his leg to show off leather straps cutting into his flesh and leather sandals adorned with flimsy, gold-foiled wings. "Right now, I'm ready to 'fly' all right." He held up his old-fashioned glass. "Straight to the bar for a top-off."

Daniel laughed. "At least you have two legs to carry you there. Save room for me, will you, Merc?"

"Will do." Jack asked, "Ladies? Drinks?"

"None for me," Missy said.

"Nor I, thanks," I said.

He saluted us before taking his leave.

"Daniel, may I present one of, if not the most able, of our BILL ladies? Missy arranged tonight's party on our group's behalf."

He looked at Missy. "Charmed, Aphrodite. Everything is tops. I'm Don Juan, if you haven't guessed." He rolled his eyes. "Georgiana's little joke. It's hard to stay in character though. Chasing the ladies with only one leg and the other hampered by these abominable crutches is tough." He stood still and shoved out his cast a few inches for emphasis.

"Good luck then." She winked. "I'll see you two." Aphrodite left us to greet new arrivals.

"Don't worry about me, Daniel. See you at the bar, later."

He bowed his head slightly and then hobbled toward the area where many of the costumed men had converged.

I looked for Mike, but all the superheroes were on the arms of other ladies. Eventually, I found a lonely palm tree wanting company.

On the way to my target, I passed the dance floor where couples enjoyed music provided by a talented quartet seated behind them in near shadow. A plump Guinevere was on the arm of a portly Lancelot, or was it Arthur? I guessed he must be the latter since he wore a crown.

Another fleshy couple, bravely underdressed as Caesar and Cleopatra, tripped the light fantastic. Janet Jessell, Annie Oakley tonight, spun to and fro on the arm of a superhero escort.

One of the waiters, carrying a tray of drinks, whisked by, but not before I lifted a fluted glass. Sparkling cider? The open bar charges must have put a dent in the champagne budget. On the other side of the room, another woman served bottles of sparkling water. I would grab one of those next.

The hour proposed was deliberate. Well after the normal dinner hour, it was presumed revelers would have eaten. Judging from the hearty giggles and guffaws, guests were certainly enjoying the open bar. Perhaps food would have been the better option with a cash bar, but who was I to second guess Missy?

The music changed to a tango. A stalwart escort in a courageous hero's attire, and tall enough for NBA material, danced with an almost equally tall, and quite fit, Mae West, wearing a long, form-fitting black skirt, tight black turtleneck, extreme pumps, and a blonde wig sprouting feathers. She'd painted her lips red, and her eyes sported fake, inch-long lashes.

The pair was enthralling several onlookers, including me. Could it be? Yes, Mae West was Augusta. I lifted my glass when Mae looked my way. Mae didn't acknowledge me, either because of the tight posture demanded by the dance, or because she didn't deign to.

"The cut direct, eh?" I mumbled, and moved one of the familiar faux-bamboo folding chairs beside my palm tree sentry and took a load off.

After the last sip, I moved along to say hello to each of the women there. One woman I could never quite catch up to was dressed as the most realistic angel I'd ever seen.

In a little while, if my plan to catch Augusta unaware failed, I'd head to the bar, grab my husband, and go.

I chatted with Janet, who positively glowed after her dance. The man of steel-type with whom she'd danced now waltzed with Queen Victoria. Janet and I made small talk before I moved on to the next woman, and the next. How many members were there now? Susie, Becca and Lourdes were gone. Who were all these people?

Someone tapped my shoulder. "Dance?"

I knew that voice. My heart hammered when I turned to face a caped man with dark mask and pointed ears.

"Detective Morgan, I presume. Tell me, is that merely a costume?"

He laughed. "In fact, no. To prove it, my super copmobile is parked out back. I'll show it to you later, if you like."

"Oh, I'd like that very much."

"Where are my manners?" He feigned regret and made an exaggerated bow. "Forgive me, Your Majesty, where is hapless Louie?"

"Louie couldn't come. Don Juan brought me. Donny's presently at the bar."

Morgan glanced that way. "Ah, yes. The crutches are a dead giveaway. Care to dance?"

"Alas, I don't. Baptist background," I lied.

"That's not what I heard."

"Oh? Naughty detective, whatever gave you such an impression?"

"Doesn't matter. You're dancing with me. Now."

"Your allergies are better."

"New prescription."

I allowed him to whisk me onto the dance floor. As luck would have it, a tango began.

He pressed me to him and I pressed my face against his. "I'm not just idling about, you know. I'm working tonight," I said.

"Hmm. I didn't think royalty ever worked. You mean some new Ladies of Leisure project?"

"No. I'm going to force Augusta into a spectacular confession—"

"Confession?"

I gave him a theatrical frown. "Should I tell you? I think not. In any case, prospects at the moment look dim. She hasn't left the dance floor. As for you, the WDDs are waiting."

"Georgiana!" He pulled me off to the side. "Don't do anything stupid. I mean it. If you're on one of your junior detective jaunts, stop it."

Missy came by. "Excuse me, I see a lonely flapper at twelve o'clock. Go dance with her."

"Actually, I'm not one of your escorts, but a party crasher."

"Really?"

"Nevertheless, far be it for me to leave a damsel in distress."

"Thank you," Missy said. "I'll find out who you are yet. Oh dear, Jack is still camped out at the bar. Excuse me."

"Of course." Before Mike walked away, he gave me a tight smile. "Remember my advice. I don't want to rescue you, too."

"I'm holding you to that invitation to view your unique...automobile."

Before he could admonish me again, Daniel thumped over.

My superhero nodded curtly and stalked over to the flapper.

"Who was he?" Daniel handed me a Coke with a lemon wedge.

I smiled at the offering and its sacrifice. Bringing me a drink meant he couldn't manage one for himself, too, with his crutches, so he was going dry for the moment. "One of the paid escorts." I sipped the soda. "Thought I was one of the widows without a date."

"Can't blame him, what with your hiding behind a potted

palm most of the night. Shall we go out on the terrace and bay at the moon?"

"Why not?"

"Not so fast." Mae West bore down on us. "I want a dance with Don Juan."

He chuckled. "Sorry, Mae. I'm out of commission."

"Come on, Daniel, a minuet. All you have to do is stand there. I'll circle around you like the spokes of a wheel."

He hunched his shoulders. "I'm damned near drunk enough I don't mind if I do." He then looked my way. "Yes, no?"

"Be my guest." A temporary stab of guilt hit me. When had I stopped caring a fig about what my husband did? In fact, when had I started thinking not only if I'd connect with Mike, but when and where? Oh yes, that day I found Augusta in my dining room. The day I unbuttoned my blouse, inviting more than a glimpse of flesh.

In a short while, half the room surrounded the dance floor. Many held their sides, regaled in laughter. The improvisational skit Don and Mae were putting on was a hit. To the strains of some long ago court dance, Daniel's Don Juan stood at attention while Augusta as Mae circled him with gyrating hips.

Everybody clapped. Daniel lifted his crutch in response and Mae strutted, rolled her eyes, and in a sexy contralto, said, "You ain't seen nothin' yet."

Augusta then escorted Daniel to the bar where many of the guys, including Mercury, still hung out.

Minutes later, after a bottle of sparking water, and the soda, I had little choice but to head to the ladies' room.

Urinating at home had been hard. Maneuvering around this bathroom stall in a hoop skirt was as difficult as climbing Mt. Everest with only fingertips for gear.

When I emerged, Mae West lay in wait. "Why don't we go out on the terrace and talk?"

"Weren't you just at the bar? Did you fly in here?" On a broomstick?

"You know I move fast. Let's talk."

"Fine with me. Talk."

"I want privacy."

I made a show of looking in each of the empty stalls. "Perfectly private."

"Someone could come in at any minute. I want to talk to

you about disturbing comments I've heard from pals at the police department." She poked a sharp nail into my bare chest. "From you, concerning me."

Who was her contact? Mike? "Ask away." I jutted the ear with the wire toward Augusta, hoping the woman's natural earsplitting tone would activate the device. I heard a whirring sound, but that could be the reverberation of blood rushing in my ears.

"Outside."

"No."

"Yes."

I gave an offensive sound to show my irritation. "I said, no." I turned for the door. Augusta moved to block it.

"What? Am I your prisoner?"

Augusta pulled a small derringer from her sleeve. "How'd you guess?"

I felt weak. "What is that, part of your costume? Well, if it is, I'm not happy to see you, to misquote the real Mae West, and I'd like you to go and take your toy gun with you."

"Care to bet your life it's a toy?" Still aiming the gun at my heart, Augusta turned on all the faucets full blast. "I made sure nobody saw me slink in here." She held the gun level and started flushing the toilets. "No one will hear a bullet from this pop gun over all that."

I stood my ground. "I'm not leaving. Do what you will." I crossed my arms. "Let's start with Mendez. You're certainly strong enough to kill somebody with a tire iron, especially if you caught him off guard."

"Go fish."

"Go fish. Did you hold Esterhause under the water? You mentioned scuba diving lessons as an assignment for the paper."

"Imaginative, but no."

"Sun and Sand, does that ring a bell? You were treasurer, weren't you?"

Augusta glared. "That's why we're here, Georgie. A contact in the Secretary of State's office told me somebody checked on S&S. That didn't really bother me. The cops checked too. Nothing links me to Sun and Sand. Except a deck of cards I'd misplaced that showed up at chez Duncan."

"IRS auditors might be after you since no return has been filed."

"The corporation's accountant asked for an extension. Government bureaucrats won't squawk for months, if not years. The rest of the money will have been transferred into my account far, far away by then."

"Switzerland?"

Augusta grinned. "I'll never tell."

I felt perspiration dribbling down my neck. Would sweat eradicate any recorded words? "Who is Audette?"

"That would be me, or rather, my alias."

"You killed Mendez, why?"

"What makes you think I killed him?"

"Follow the money."

"You kiddin' me? Half the women in Merry Acres wanted his hide." Augusta shook her head. "What a laugh. No wonder Morgan ain't lifted a finger against me. As for Karl, he had an ego the size of several combined continents. According to Susie's waspish lips, Karl liked 'em young. When I say young, I mean jail bait. So as to not soil his nest like Manny Mendez, he hunted far afield. In retaliation, Susie started an affair with Mendez. He dumped her. Didn't sit well, especially when he threatened to circulate rumors of Karl's interest in young hotties if she ever made trouble for him with his missus."

"What about the tire iron?"

"I overheard interested parties discussing tire irons and blackmailed them."

"I don't get it."

Augusta smiled. "Doesn't matter, dearie. How did you find out about the tire iron?"

"A little bird told me."

"Dixie?"

"I don't remember."

"Yes, it was Dixie. My bad. I blurted out that salient fact once while she and I discussed the Mendez case shortly after the first BILL meeting. Wouldn't you know it? That was the one thing her ditzy brain held on to." She grabbed my arm. "Let's move outside in case Daniel wises up you're in trouble. He might inform a certain cop moonlighting as an escort. Morgan's here, isn't he? I've tried to snag a dance with that guy you tangoed with, but he's played a little too coy."

I could use a caped crusader about now.

"Come along, Georgie. I'll make my escape and leave you in the parking lot."

"Dead."

"Not necessarily. You could get lucky along the way."

I prayed Mike was paying attention to my whereabouts.

As if privy to my thoughts, Augusta said, "Mikey is watching Mae West, but he's been duped. He's stalking a decoy. Too bad."

About that time, my knees buckled. Please let Morgan's superhero car be gassed up and ready to race. "Let's roll," I said loudly.

"Relax, kiddo, with the water going in here, the music blaring out there, and joy juice flowing down everybody's tonsils, our BILL gals and their guys can't hear a thing."

"Where to?" I screamed, "The parking lot?" Please let someone be near the door.

Augusta snapped, "Stop it, will you? I waited until the evening wore on for our little chat. That way, party goers would be liquored up and harder of hearing than usual. Get goin'. Soon, I'll be in a tropical paradise. I earned it, believe me. Mendez was no pleasure. Yes, we had a little thing, but he got sore when he found out I'd tampered with S&S money. Imagine. That insurance money widows paid to keep my mouth shut about indiscretions helped grow my retirement nest egg. I convinced them to sell me their homes at fire sale prices, which I flipped for a song. Why should I care if they gave them away? It was gravy for me, regardless. For the first time in my life, I'm solvent and then some."

"You killed Ben Bernstein, too?"

"Now, that was hard. I liked him, and Becca. Ben was in the wrong place at the wrong time."

"The drugstore?"

Someone knocked on the door.

"It's a man. A woman would have walked right in. Get rid of him or I'll shoot you where you stand, and him too."

"Georgiana, are you in there?" came Daniel's slurred words. "I want to go home."

What could he do if I told him of my present danger? A one-legged man, lit up on liquor, and a wimpy woman were no match for Augusta with a gun.

"I told you, it's hard to pee in this dress. Run along to the bar. I want a...Bloody Mary. He knew I never drank liquor. That might sound an alarm, if he was sober enough to make the connection. Where was Mike?

In an instant, I took a risk, yanking open the door before Augusta could react, hoping to scream, but Mike was nowhere around and Daniel had already moved away. Augusta poked the gun in my ribs. "Don't make a sound. Move slowly. Don't look left or right. Back terrace. Go."

"So, you did kill Ben?"

"Shut up and walk. Wait." Augusta locked on to my arm and pulled me back inside the ladies' room.

"Ouch." My arm, practically ripped from the socket, throbbed.

A tipsy Queen Victoria opened the door. Augusta yelled at her, "Use the women's locker room, for God's sakes. We're having a private discussion in here."

"Well!" The woman in fifty yards of black silk turned her black veiled head in the opposite direction and rustled away.

"Georgie?" Now holding the gun at my head, Augusta scanned my costume's translucent sleeves and tugged on the bodice. "Are you wearing a wire?" She ripped the bodice. "Where the hell is it?"

"See, nothing up my sleeve." I held up the torn fabric to cover my breasts. "Where are you going?"

"Hell, most likely. Someday. It's not like I didn't try. I mean, I did like you. I staged a phony affair thinking you'd run off as you did after your marriage went south on the west coast. Nope, you two stuck it out. Then I tried to warn off Daniel by sideswiping his spiffy little cart. Well, maybe I did try to kill him, but there were no hard feelings. What happens? He survives with barely a scratch. There is one other thing you should know. Danny got in over his head with gambling debt. Not a first, right?" She sneered. "I suggested an easy way out. You."

"Me?"

"I wheedled Rhonda's name from him and discovered her phone number. Later, I manipulated her into calling you by first calling her from Daniel's cell phone and leaving a re-quested call back time and your home number as the call back location. Just prior to my doping you with sleep aids in the smoothie." She clucked. "Perfect set up. Suicidal thoughts are a side effect of your antidepressant, as you know. Your little fit after I danced with Daniel at the BILL luncheon fit my scheme perfectly. To all appearances, you were so enraged and de-pressed, you decided to end it all."

"Daniel saved my life."

Augusta smiled cruelly. "He did, indeed, after he'd agreed to my plan in a weak moment. Why not? Things were not well between you, his gambling debts were rising by hundreds each day, and there was my...uh...oh-so-soft sympathetic shoulder. After your funeral, we'd split your life insurance pay-off." She ripped off her skirt and blouse to reveal a black, mid-calf cat suit beneath.

"You're lying."

Augusta kicked the clothes under the ladies' room sink station. "He couldn't go through with it and pulled you out at the last minute. His loss. He's an accessory to attempted murder, if I'm ever caught." She ripped off her hairpiece and tossed it in the trash receptacle.

"I don't believe you."

"Why didn't you just leave town? I couldn't take the chance you'd figure out the link between me and S&S from that damned deck of cards. When my source in Tallahassee snitched, I didn't fret until I learned how close you and Morgan were becoming. I feared you'd blab your suppositions if you had any. No matter. By dawn there will be a new mystery in Merry Acres. Rather than the humdrum dead husband, there will be a murder-suicide. Depressed wife kills husband, then self in jealous rage. After my dance with Daniel tonight, it's a natural. Front-page crime copy and I won't be around to write it." She raised the gun. "End of story. Outside."

Still clutching my bodice, I lied. "I've told Morgan I suspected you drugged me and tried to kill me."

"So? Open the door, and remember, I have a gun and will use it. I'm fast and while everyone's twittering over you, I'll escape."

Resigned, I opened the door. Once outside, I'd somehow signal Mike or try a run for it along the way.

When the door swung open, an angel appeared.

"Change in plans." Augusta took aim.

Modesty be damned. I raised my arms in a defensive posture. "Help!"

Augusta screamed at the woman standing in the threshold. "Take your harp and find another cloud or you'll join the heavenly host for real."

Instead of fleeing, the startled onlooker hesitated long enough to read the dire circumstances. She pushed me hard left the moment the gun fired. Augusta knocked the woman to the floor. My stunned attention moved to my bleeding shoulder. Lightheaded, I staggered, but didn't fall. Augusta lunged like a panther, hitting me full force on the head with the gun.

Seconds later, I thought I heard a voice say, "That towel behind your head will help a little. Let's fix your dress, darlin'. Don't worry, baby, Mama's got you now."

There were sounds of scuffling feet.

"Let's go now," a woman said.

"No, not yet."

I tried to open my eyes. They refused to cooperate. God, my head hurt.

A voice said, "Repeat these words, IDA airlines. Island Dream Airlines. IDA."

"Huh?" My mind swam in semidarkness.

"I-D-A."

"You don't want to get mixed up in this. Hurry, others are coming. She'll be all right. Come along. That's right. Follow me." I thought I heard voices, but the sounds turned into a disjointed flow of noise.

With my mind floating, I repeated that one glorious word clinging to my tattered memory, "Mama?"

CHAPTER FIFTEEN

Mike Morgan knelt beside Georgiana. He called for help on his cell and propped open the door with a decorative trash bin. Despite grave misgivings, he wanted to gently kiss her forehead. Others crowding in solved the dilemma.

"Stay with me, Mrs. Duncan," he said with professional detachment. "Somebody get her husband in here. What happened? Where is Augusta?"

"Air."

"You need air. Why? Can't you breathe?"

"DIA. Air."

"What?"

"Mama came back for me at last. She couldn't before because she's an angel."

Morgan hollered, "Isn't that freakin' ambulance here yet?"

Missy Youngblood stood closest and cried. "The whole night is ruined."

Morgan swore. He finally staunched the remaining trickle of blood oozing down the left side Georgiana's head and worked on the arm wound. "Give me some paper towels, would you?" Waiting for Mrs. Youngblood to act, he ripped off Georgiana's wig. A small recorder was cracked in half and fell on the floor where it broke into even more pieces.

Again, he was tempted to say, "Nice try, Georgiana." All he could do was maintain appearances and wipe away the blood. Hoping she could hear him, and recognize his voice, he said, "Good news, bad news, Mrs. Duncan." He wondered who had put the towel under her head. Somebody had seen what happened, but who? "Can you hear me?"

Georgiana opened her eyes.

"How many fingers?" He held up one.

"Two?"

"Great, double vision. It's going to be okay. Stay awake." He molded his hand around her chin and forced her head side to side. "Listen, that wig and the recorder saved your life. However"—he paused—"doing so destroyed the evidence."

Daniel thumped in with a Bloody Mary in his hand. "What in the hell is going on? What, sir, are you doing to my wife?"

"Feel free to drop down and hold her bleeding head anytime you like. She has a concussion at best, a fractured skull at worst. She needs medical attention."

Daniel gasped and then snarled, "You know I can't get down there."

"Then shut up." Mike looked at Missy Youngblood. "Hey, Red. Quit groaning about your party and make yourself useful. Hold Mrs. Duncan's head. Talk to her, keep her awake. I'm a police detective. I need to go after the suspect. I can't do both."

"But my costume."

Morgan glared. "How does a charge of reckless endangerment sound to you?"

Missy leaped down and took Georgiana's groggy head.

"Duncan, give me that Bloody Mary in your hand. Mrs. Duncan can't drink it now."

"Aren't you on duty?"

"Nope. Cheers." He drank down the glass. "Ah, it's the best thing that's happened to me all night. My aching feet. You Ladies of Leisure might try dance lessons for your next project. " He looked at a shell-shocked Daniel. "I'll get backup."

Minutes later, a policeman and the paramedics showed up. The cop said, "Morgan?"

"One crack about my getup and I'll bust you. Follow me."

They ran outside to the parking lot. "Anybody see Mae West leave?"

Suddenly, two women dressed as Mae West appeared.

Morgan swore again. Under his breath, he said, "Way to go, Augusta." He knew then he'd been had.

Georgiana's plan had netted her a big bump on the head,

a bullet-grazed shoulder, a useless tape, inadmissible anyway, and no corroborating witnesses. Meanwhile, his career could be jeopardized by a married woman with whom he was personally involved, who might have learned something about the Mendez murder, but was fading in and out of consciousness. Who knew what she'd say and to whom.

He looked at his fellow law enforcement officer. "Unfortunately, the suspect got a full half-hour head start." Putting on his full professional mien, he said, "That injured woman moaned something like DIA Air. Does that mean anything to you?"

"No. Wait. Isn't there an island hopper out of Lauderdale? Island Dream Airlines?"

"That's gotta be it. Call them. Stop any plane going out tonight. If a passenger named Augusta St. James checks in, hold her and call local police. Put out an APB. Tall, Caucasian woman, salt-and-pepper hair, strong features, brown eyes, I think. Strong, possibly armed, and definitely dangerous."

Something was worrying Morgan. Why would Augusta have said anything about the airline she wanted to use for her escape? Something didn't fit.

He grabbed his cell and called the station, barking out orders. Ten minutes later, he scribbled down six private fields within driving distance, including those in Martin County, Palm Beach, and Lauderdale.

He exchanged looks with the other cop.

"It's a crap shoot."

Morgan said, "Yeah, and I'm not feeling lucky." He watched the EMS guys load Georgiana onto a stretcher. Her legs were showing since that oversized lampshade she wore stuck up three feet. He threw his cape over her dress.

They wheeled her out.

Mike wished he could accompany her, but it was just as well Daniel Duncan was furiously thumping along after her. Rumors would fly if he insisted on riding along. As it was, a certain person would not be pleased when she heard about this.

His cell rang. "Yeah, Morgan here." He nodded impatiently. "Uh-huh." He sighed. "Got it. Thanks." He looked at the other officer. "We're dead."

"What's up?"

"St. James was booked on an IDA flight for tonight. Some

scheduling problem the last few days resulted in her getting bumped from this flight. Whoever she's flying with, it's not IDA."

The other officer said, "We've got spotters at the airports in three counties."

Morgan bit his nail. "Call me crazy, I'm thinking private jets. We gotta check out Martin County, Palm Beach, and Lauderdale. Maybe Miami. It's going to be a long night."

≡ ≡ ≡

The Haitian pulled his ambulance up to the private Palm Beach clinic's rear loading area. He'd been paid handsomely in advance for this task.

A gurney was rolled out. On it laid a person wrapped in bandages from head to foot who looked to him like a fair replica of a mummy.

"Crowder Airfield in Miami." The man releasing the gurney handed the driver a duffel bag and got in alongside the patient. "It's a celebrity. Nasty burns, eighty percent of the body. We're going to a private clinic somewhere in the islands. That's all you need to know. A private jet is waiting. You know where Crowder field is?"

"Yes. You've called me before."

"Get going. There's another hundred fifty for you if we get off without any problems. Understand? No problems."

"You think I'm looking for problems?"

"Put it this way. Make sure problems don't find us."

A second orderly left them and moved back inside the building. The driver watched him disappear to the swishing sound of closing automatic doors.

He thought he heard a woman's groan. The driver looked over his shoulder and addressed his cargo. "Wish I be goin' to de islands, too, but not in your condition."

The two-and-a-half hour drive went smoothly.

Only one plane was parked at the airfield. Two people approached his ambulance, a man and a woman.

They talked to the man who'd accompanied the burn victim. He heard the tall, white guy introduce himself as the pilot while mentioning the woman with him was his sister and co-pilot.

The Haitian opened the rear door of his vehicle and assisted the orderly with the unloading task. The patient groaned loudly when he and the medical attendant, whom he assumed would fly with the burn victim, rolled the gurney toward the plane.

"Wait. Don't you need be signin' some paper?"

The medical attendant looked at the pilot, who in turn, looked at the co-pilot, before saying, "A release, huh?"

"Yeah."

The crew grinned at each other as the cabbie returned with a clipboard. Handwritten on a piece of paper was the word *Release.* Underneath was scribbled, *Received patient at 2330 hours* and the date. The pilot signed his name, John Jay Johnson, and printed it beneath.

The Haitian had a cell phone hidden in his fleshy palm, camera function on, record feature activated. "Okay, Mr. Johnson. You accept the patient from the Beverly Clinic in Palm Beach County, yes?"

"Not exactly, buddy. I accepted the passenger from Able Ambulance Service."

"Ta-ta." The Haitian figured he better shut up and drove away. As he reentered the north bound section of the Homestead extension, he checked a plastic coin holder for quarters. He'd need plenty for the return tolls. It was then he saw a police car exit the highway, lights flashing. It took the road to Crowder Field. He gunned the gas and sped away in the opposite direction.

≡ ≡ ≡

Just as Officer Washington leaped from his squad car and hit the tarmac running, the jet's stairway began to disappear. He raced up to the jet. "Stop. Dade County Police."

The jet made no progress, but its engines remained engaged.

Washington quickly climbed aboard. "I'm looking for a tall, white female. Name of Augusta St. James."

The pilot left the cockpit. "I'm the pilot sir, hired by a private individual who wishes to remain anonymous." He lowered his head and whispered, "A celebrity, according to the orderly with her when they arrived by private ambulance. A burn victim en route to a private clinic on Alandira. Or so he said."

"Mind if I look?"

The female copilot joined her brother, and they stood on either side of the aisle. The pilot signaled by hand for the policeman to proceed.

"As you see, officer, one passenger, bandaged."

"Man or woman?"

"I don't know. Feel free to ask the passenger."

The officer halted when the passenger groaned. The voice could be male or female. The bandaging was such that identity of sex was not possible.

He looked at the man dressed in white seated beside the gurney. "Who are you?"

"Lance Davis, Medical attendant from Beverly Clinic in Palm Beach."

"Who is the patient?"

"Beats me. Burn victim is all I know."

"May we proceed?" the pilot asked. "We have a timetable and we're in a crunch. This is a time-share jet rented by several people and two corporations. I'm on a quick turnaround. Gotta be in Miami to pick up another party in a few hours. I'd like to squeeze in a nap beforehand."

The officer paused. He was torn. It seemed a tad coincidental to him, but he didn't want to face some police insensitivity interview. Or be responsible for some lawsuit for disturbing a patient. He debated.

The pilot again said, "Sir?"

"Give me the passenger list."

The pilot complied.

"A. A. Audette." How the hell could he identify a person such as this? "What if he or she were a terrorist?"

The pilot shrugged. "One of us ends up with our throat slit with a box cutter, the other fries when the plane hits a building."

The officer looked at the co-pilot, whose blue eyes widened. He sighed deeply. His heart tugged at him. If he were in the pain of a burn victim, would he want people pawing over him?

However, this would be the perfect disguise for someone fleeing the country. His mission was to find Augusta St. James, not A. A. Audette. He saw the duffel bag.

He rummaged through it. He checked the passport which depicted a woman named Audette. He knew no such celebrity, but he wasn't a devotee of scandal sheets or MTV, or even E!

That was his wife's hobby. He called her. "Know a celebrity named Audette?"

Her negative response made Washington that much more queasy. He thought again of staring down a video camera from Internal Affairs. It would leak. He could see it on every local network news station, possibly cable news. His face plastered on the tube. Some big-eyed reporter spouting, "Officer Washington trotted on board a private jet for hire and molested a poor, suffering burn victim."

Forget that. "Go ahead."

He deplaned and strode to his car. A feeling dogged him as he slid into the patrol car. It still bothered him when he left the airfield and watched the vintage Gulfstream go airborne through his rearview mirror.

It was late. Tired as he was, he knew he'd just made a mistake. A big one.

Officer Washington would lay odds that the patient on that jet was the suspect, Augusta St. James, flying under a fake passport as A. A. Audette. He called in, reported his faux pas to his superiors, and fretted. He was in for it. Maybe not with the press, but with the department.

Some nights you just couldn't win.

≡ ≡ ≡

Mike Morgan, en route to Crowder Field, got the bad news.

Somebody needed to alert the authorities on Alandira Island. Morgan made some calls, first to find out exactly what the officer knew, and then to set the wheels in action on Alandira. He turned his would-be super copmobile around, heading north for home. First, he'd stop by Merry Acres General to see that Georgiana was well cared for.

≡ ≡ ≡

Fifteen minutes into the flight, Augusta St. James lifted up off the gurney. "Hey, don't you guys serve beverages on these crates? You should at the rates you charge."

"Depends on service requested. Bev service isn't required for a medical transport. We don't own the plane, ma'am. I can give you a Coke from my stash." The co-pilot handed her a chilled can of soda. "Alandira is gorgeous. Where are you going to stay?"

"That"—she eyed the young woman—"is nobody's business."

"I only meant we have some experience with the island and could suggest some super hotels. Mind if I ask your name?" This was shouted back from the pilot in the cockpit.

"Well, flyboy, I could tell you"—Augusta took a long drink from the can—"but then, I'd have to kill you. Still want to know?"

Both pilot and co-pilot replied, "Pass."

"Just kidding. You know my name anyway. It's A. A. Audette. What's the ETA?"

"A little over forty minutes."

"Hallelujah. Wake me when we get there. A gal needs her beauty rest. Forget you talked to me, and there will be an additional thousand bucks apiece wired to the bank of your choice."

"No offense, ma'am, but we've heard that before," the pilot said.

The co-pilot joined in, "Then people forget their promises."

"What about me?" This came from the orderly.

"You get your cut from the clinic. Don't get greedy. Okay, what do you two suggest?"

"Banks are closed at this hour. How about we escort you to an ATM at your hotel, or, er, clinic, upon arrival."

"Fine with me. I'll first have to stop someplace and find clothes. Hey, Miss Co-Pilot, how tall are you?"

"Five-five."

"That takes care of that solution. Nighty-night."

Augusta couldn't sleep. She was too excited. She rummaged in the duffel bag for a worn paperback, *Sun and Sand*, by A. A. Audette.

The orderly snored away. Augusta said aloud to anyone listening who could hear over the engine noise, "Anybody who loves a good story ought to read this, *Sun and Sand*. An oldie, but a humdinger."

The co-pilot came back into the cabin and asked, "What's your book about?"

"It's about a gal with guts. The heroine is a middle class Greek gal who gets pregnant, leaves Tarpon Springs, Florida for New York. After some hard knocks, she ditches the kid, then hits the big time along the way and lives happily ever after."

The co-pilot asked, "What happened to the child?"

Augusta gave the woman a displeased look. "Who cares? It's the heroine's life that matters. Not many women could do what the protagonist did. Noooo, what happens in real life? Whenever some woman gets knocked up at a tender age by some silver-tongued rogue who uses then loses her, she cries and moans. She keeps the baby and ends up in a dead-end job playing single mom. This heroine acted exactly as a man would."

The co-pilot said nothing, but her expression read 'unsympathetic.' She returned to the cockpit.

Augusta started reading again. So favorably impressed was she with the author's work, she'd taken the author's name for the S&S venture with Mendez, as well as her new life, now only hours old. This author spoke to Augusta. She could relate. She'd done the same thing herself.

What really excited Augusta was the gold mine in her hands. If she could verify certain facts, she'd go from easy street to streets of gold.

Sleepy now, she put down the book.

≡ ≡ ≡

The admitting doctor insisted on keeping me overnight for observation since someone would have to check on me every few hours. Daniel's age and leg problem wouldn't stand him in good stead for the job. Nobody seemed overly concerned with the flesh wound at my shoulder. They'd treated and bandaged it, but it hurt.

Reasonably alert, I said, "Daniel, take a cab home. I'll call tomorrow when they release me." I turned to the physician. "Why can't I remember what happened after I walked into the ladies' room? It's a big blank. I walked in, and then next thing I remember, I'm here, except for some hallucination about my mother returning as an angel. Was I near death?"

"No." He smiled. "And you'll be fine, a concussion is all. Details will eventually come back. May be tomorrow, may be weeks, may be years in some cases. Rest now. Come, Mr. Duncan, I'll have one of the nurses call a cab."

Sometime later, I woke with a start.

"It's okay, it's me. I wanted to see that you were all right."

Nan D. Arnold

"Mike. Where's your cape?"

"Fortunately for your modesty's sake, I threw it over you when they took you off in the ambulance. But I picked it up at the nurses' station." In fun, he furled it around him. He looked over at the other bed, fortunately vacant, an unusual occurrence in any hospital. "You're in good hands, babe. Now, rest."

"What's that in your hand?"

"A white rose. I'll send one everyday so you know I'm thinking of you. I'll send it with a blank card so Daniel is none the wiser."

I laughed and then groaned. "Oh, my head and my shoulder hurt. I'd better hit the pain pump."

"What's so funny? I thought it was a grand romantic gesture."

"It is and I love it. I was just remembering the first BILL meeting. I asked everyone to fill out a blank card so we could determine who would host the next get-together. Nobody filled out a card. You've forever changed a blank card to a happy thought."

"You're not making a lot of sense, but that's understandable. Well, so you know, one day I'll give you a red one. When you're well. Do you remember anything Augusta said?"

"That's what's so odd. I don't remember anything after dancing with you and going to the bathroom, except Augusta was there and I don't remember luring her there as I planned. Then nothing except some vision of angels. Maybe I had a near-death experience."

"No, you weren't seriously injured."

A nurse appeared.

Mike winked at me and put on his professional demeanor. "We're finished here. If you can think of anything else to help the investigation, you have my card." He handed the nurse the rose. "Somebody handed this to me in the lobby. I don't wear roses; perhaps you could you put it in water and give it to Mrs. Duncan?"

The nurse smiled. "How thoughtful."

"Here to serve, protect, and spread joy whenever we can, ma'am."

I laughed and then endured the latest round of questions from the nurse. Mike slipped out of the room as orderlies were rolling in a new patient who would be my roommate.

≡ ≡ ≡

Two days later, at the golf villa on Carnoustie Way, my husband's and my roles were reversed. I was in the recliner. Daniel hobbled around meeting my every need. What I really wanted was conversation with Mike Morgan. Failing that, I'd like to talk to that angel again. The one I'd conjured up after Augusta conked me on the head. I might not remember everything that happened, other than what Mike and Daniel had told me, but I knew one thing. A medically measured dose of heroin couldn't have induced a happier hallucination for me than that angel who appeared following a blow to my head.

If only in my imagination, Mother had come back for me.

CHAPTER SIXTEEN

Dixie worried sick over Georgiana until a friend employed at Merry Acres Memorial called and told her Georgiana had been released.

With Gloria's help, Dixie hurried to dress for the BILL meeting being held today at Georgiana's house, really a get-well session. No more than an opportunity for the girls to pump Georgiana for details on what exactly had happened.

To think her ire over a stupid, vacant seat had resulted in Augusta's escape.

Dixie's satellite phone rang. Carlotta was calling.

It rang again. She didn't want another worry today, she had plenty already.

Gloria said, "Shall I answer it?"

Dixie waved her away and debated. At last, she picked up the phone. "Yes, Carlotta."

"I am sorry to disturb you, Mrs. Metcalf. Something bizarre has occurred."

Dixie drank in the warmth of Carlotta's island-accented English.

"What is that, darlin'?"

"My uncle called me at an ungodly hour. It seems a private jet landed in Alandira early with a passenger on board under peculiar circumstances."

"I didn't sleep well and I have an appointment," Dixie said. "I hope my mind can stay on track today. I miss having you with me and don't understand why you called."

"I will join you soon. And I'm getting to the point. The passenger's name was A. A. Audette."

"What?"

"I know, Mrs. Metcalf. That is what spooked the customs agent who, in turn, spooked the Minister of Foreign Affairs who, in turn, spooked me, so that I must spook you."

"Get on a jet and join me, girl."

"I'm packed and on the way to the airfield. We will dine together tonight. First, remember everything is under control. Don't call and pester my uncle just yet. Oh, another oddity with the person posing as A. A. Audette. The woman was dressed like a mummy. Bandaged head to foot."

"What?"

"As I said, bizarre. Customs interrogated the flight staff who said they'd been told by the attendant with her that she was a burn victim coming to a hush-hush clinic on Alandira."

"Well?"

"Not so much as a cigarette burn on her when she was fitted out with proper prison dress. She's all stony silence, don't you know. My uncle gave orders to send her to All Saint's Sanatorium. She's screaming false arrest, clamorin' for the name of the finest solicitor on the island."

"I know the woman. Contact every top-flight attorney there. Tell them if anyone assists Augusta St. James, they will incur my most vivid wrath."

"Consider it done. Also, curiously, this woman refuses to relinquish a paperback, *Sun and Sand*, which, of course, you wrote ages ago.

"Oh dear God. Can anything be done about retrieving or destroying the book?"

"We're trying."

"As if she'd let loose of it for a nanosecond."

"Now, now. Aren't you the one always admonishin' us for dark thoughts? It might be worthwhile for one of our best legal minds to work on her behalf. Interrogate her, don't you think? Find out what's she up to. Her case can be dropped in an instant for some technicality or other and referred to another lawyer."

"Excellent suggestion."

"Enjoy your visit in Merry Acres in the meanwhile. Goodbye and take heart, Mrs. Metcalf. I'll see you shortly."

Dixie hung up and called Janet Jessell. After that, Dixie staggered toward the bathroom. A glance at her Rolex spurred her on. Janet would pick her up within the hour to drive her to Georgiana's. She must go without Gloria who must stay to receive Carlotta if the visit and requisite lunch afterward took longer than a few hours.

As she applied her makeup, a feat growing more difficult what with aging eyesight and wandering concentration, she grew exasperated. "Gloria, give me a hand, dear. I can't do it today."

Dixie stared at her reflection. Angela Aurora Audette stared back. She'd chosen that name because she wanted to be guided by an angel of light. She had been lucky when she moved to Atlanta and took dancing lessons. Luckier still when she moved to the Big Apple to catch up with Philip Morgan. Along the way, she'd fallen in love with his cousin, Chester Metcalf. She'd married for all the wrong reasons, but love turned it right.

Now that book she'd written cast a chill over her. Although Dixie would pass along a large chunk of her—and Chester's—good fortune to her daughter, it would be cold comfort for what Georgiana had missed.

The woman was scarred. Dixie knew her daughter's marriage had proved less than joyful, and more tragically, her heart and spirit were riddled with recriminations that left her angry, bitter and afraid.

And now? Now, poor Georgiana would likely be stalked by Augusta, who wasn't the type to leave loose ends if she could help it.

What could Dixie do to protect her daughter? Would her failing mind hold together long enough to think of a solution? And longer still to carry out a plan?

≡ ≡ ≡

Daniel opened the door. "Greetings. Sorry, gals, you'll have to do without me. This old rooster is heading toward the laundry room, then on an errand or two."

"Bye," the women chorused.

One of the errands he referred to was a Gamblers Anonymous meeting. I was nevertheless cheered by the women trooping in, led by Missy Youngblood, who held out a bouquet of orchid sprays, freesia, and greenery.

The arrangement was pretty, of course, but couldn't match the power of the single white rose delivered each day with a blank card. I anxiously awaited a red one, the signal I could meet Mike and consummate a growing physical attraction.

"Thanks, girls. I'll see that I get my head bashed in more often."

I found a vase and arranged the flowers, listening to the women express sympathy for my mishap.

"We know we haven't paid you the kind of attention we should have, darlin', and we're sorry," Dixie said.

Remembering all the broken engagements, I stared at Dixie with an expression I hoped the woman would read as my full agreement.

Janet Jessell gushed. "Georgiana, you do more for excitement around here than anybody I know. At the first BILL meeting, the one you hosted, we heard of the Mendez murder. Then, we all heard about poor Ben at another BILL luncheon."

I smiled patiently. "Not to forget Daniel's run in, or should I say, near run over? By the way, has anybody heard from Becca? I sent her a note of condolence, which she acknowledged with one of those pre-printed cards provided by the funeral home, signed 'from the family.'"

Everyone shook their head.

Out of sight, out of mind with these women. "I'm much better. In fact, Daniel and I think it's time for me to go back to work."

Janet exclaimed, "No."

"Oh, I'm ready." I gave them all a careless smile. "Or I will be in a week or so, the doctor says." I granted them a small laugh. "Daniel and I will study for the board exam to gain our real estate licenses. This market can't stay down forever!"

The group giggled in unison as if embarrassed.

Dixie said, "You're absolutely right, Georgiana. The market will come back."

Janet said, "Dixie, ever the optimist."

"A sunny outlook doesn't cost any more than a cloudy one and pays a bigger dividend. Most times."

"That sounds too *Pollyanna* for me," I said.

Dixie looked hurt.

"I'm sorry, Dixie. I'm still a little down from that head tap. What could I expect considering the costume I selected? Marie Antoinette and head injuries go hand in hand."

Missy asked, "What happened in that ladies' room, after all?"

Now fully aware of the reason for their social call, I said truthfully, "I don't remember much." I tacked on a disingenuous, "Sorry."

Janet said, "At least tell us if it was Augusta St. James who attacked you."

Watching them salivate, I paused. "You may or may not know that there happened to be more than one Mae West present at the party. Or so I've been told. Consequently, I couldn't swear to anything, other than that someone dressed like Mae West apparently took a distinct dislike to me for some reason." I puckered my lips into an exaggerated frown. "Who knows why?"

"Hurry up and get well," Janet said. "I want to take you to lunch."

"Me, too," Missy said.

"I'd love to add my name, but I return to Georgia soon."

"Thanks for the kind invitations. We'll see. Now, I hate to rush you, and I know we'd said something about lunch, but I can't. There are some things to which I must attend of a personal nature."

"With Daniel when he returns?" Janet giggled.

"Could be. See, ladies, I'm truly now a lady of leisure." I didn't mention Daniel's other commitment, his meeting at GA.

They said their farewells and departed, allowing me a deep breath and sigh of relief.

Contentment flooded me for a moment when I re-read the handwritten get-well cards from the HELP kids Mama Smith had brought over with a basket of freshly baked muffins. One child insisted I accept his press badge for good luck and fast healing.

I'd explained to Mama Smith it would be a while before any future field trips could take place, and asked her to send my regrets to the older kids. In the meantime, I called the shelter to discuss something else.

"Hello? Hey, it's me. Georgiana. If you can spare the time, drop off one of the children who most needs help with his or her school work. Getting my tired mind off recurring visions of that attack would be a real shot in the arm."

A woman left the phone to discuss the matter and returned to say they would consider it and call back in the next day or two.

"Daniel might throw in some dance lessons, but I can't promise, so don't mention that, okay?"

I would consider working nine-to-five somewhere, but focusing on others in need provided the brightest moments, so I'd do that first.

Remembering Augusta's slur about do-gooders, I cringed. Maybe she was right. Even so, I figured the more I gave, the more I'd get back one way or another. I wasn't overly worried about Augusta coming back to hurt me either. Gussie had moved on, or so I hoped.

Besides, a certain hero was waiting for me in the wings.

≡ ≡ ≡

Daniel's cast came off within the week and our lives were altered further by headlines in the *Merry Acres Gazette* that screamed news about their former employee's misadventures in the small Caribbean island of Alandira:

"Bandaged head to foot as a burn victim, our former columnist couldn't fool local officials. St. James has been extradited to the United States."

The article went on to say Augusta had hired a hotshot defense attorney out of Miami who, so far, had enjoyed all wins in his courtroom battles. Despite his reputation, bail was denied for Augusta as a flight risk.

The real question, the reporter's article asked, was where had St. James obtained funds for such a noted mouthpiece? When the *Gazette* knew, Merry Acres readers would know. The paper cautioned readers to keep subscriptions current so as not to miss exciting details.

Even reading about Augusta gave me a mild headache.

Daniel read the news with a sanguine attitude. "At least bail was denied."

"So why am I worrying?"

He looked up from the paper. "Habit?"

"You are getting around quite well since the cast came off. That's good. I mean, just in case you must either defend, or flee."

"True."

Daniel had aged overnight. He'd lost the vim and vigor he'd gained briefly when the cast came off. Ironically, he'd sold the Vette to settle debts the following day. A pitiful sight, too. He'd stood in the driveway the longest time after the purchaser drove off. I knew he was staring after the last vestiges of youth and staring down old age. And possibly feeling death breathing down his neck, as it does when people reach a certain age. Of course, seventy was the new sixty. He might live on thirty more years.

Still, with garage clicker in hand, he'd trudged back into the bay where the Vette had normally been parked. Even over the sound of the descending garage door, I had heard him weep.

At least the act prompted his further attendance at Gamblers Anonymous meetings, to the growing dismay of card players at the club. First they grumbled that St. James was gone, and now Daniel had dropped from their diminishing ranks.

Later that afternoon, since I felt recovered enough to drive and because we'd at last satisfied our club's food and beverage minimum, I insisted we go to the Punjab Palace for a late lunch.

At the restaurant, Raj talked up the menu: Kashmiri pilafs, Punjabi tandoori dishes, hotter even than those from the southern regions of India.

Daniel drank coffee and moved lamb curry around on his plate while I feasted on a variety of spicy vegetable dishes, and chicken tandoori. It wasn't as fun as dining with Mike Morgan, who shared my tastes for the exotic, or I had to admit, previous forays with smart-mouthed Augusta.

Still, Daniel came along, so I gave him credit.

Daniel's cell phone rang. "Damn, I thought I'd switched it off. Sorry." He glanced at the caller. "This can wait. I'll turn it off now."

At home, while Daniel changed into more casual clothes for his GA meeting, I depressed the call button to learn the caller's identity so I could remind him to call whoever had called him at the restaurant.

Expecting one of the card players or golfing buddies, I stared as Caller ID indicated the name: *Rhonda*.

Crushed, I could hardly breathe, but that was a reflex action.

The sinking sensation evaporated immediately. Something worse replaced it. Apathy.

"Don't forget that cell phone call you received at the restaurant. Have a fulfilling time." I waved farewell as he climbed into our SUV. Lingering bad head or not, I was going to the HELP shelter when I had wheels. Maybe I'd rent a car from the place that picked up customers.

I called busy Mama Smith. "Let's discuss a field trip for the older kids."

"Now?"

"Now." I convinced Mama Smith I was, indeed, well enough to entertain ideas. We bandied some around and threw some of the comments the kids themselves had made into the mix. The easiest of the suggestions had been a trip to eat out at a nice place for dinner. Where? Finally, we agreed, with my verbal arm twisting, on The Athenian Garden.

Mama Smith would come, too. Never having eaten Greek food, she was curious. That meant between our SUV and Mama Smith's Toyota sedan, transportation was covered. The teenagers might not go or, if they did, they wouldn't act up as much with Mama along, a real plus.

So far, my meager charms had failed to connect with those older kids. This adventure might break the ice. I would treat everyone, Daniel's harping on expenses be damned. And we would send back take-out for the other staff at the shelter, too, to enjoy the next day for lunch.

Mama Smith would decide the night and we would go.

Then I made the call I'd been waiting to make. I called Mike.

"Hey. How ya doin'?"

"I'm better. I went for a drive with the neighbor around the Merry Acres perimeter, but admit I was dragging by the time I got back home. Your rose means a lot, but I miss seeing you."

"I know. I'm booking a suite at the Sea Side resort, water view, when you give the word. Red roses will be waiting."

"You might know Daniel is tugging at my heart strings. Pity, not love. He sold his Vette. He's given up cards, for the time being."

"Does that mean you don't want to see me anymore?"

"Nothing of the kind. I'm just sharing feelings with a good

friend."

"I take that as a compliment."

"It's meant as one. Be careful out there. I'll call you soon. Imagine I'm in your arms, with your lips on mine."

"Go on."

"Aw, Mike, that's all I can do. For now."

"What, you bashful?"

I laughed. "Bye."

≡ ≡ ≡

Finally, the night came for the HELP outing. I called Mike in case he could get away for a quick visit. He could. That prospect made me as excited as the kids who were dressed reasonably well, for teenagers. The rainbow coalition, white, black, Hispanic and a lone Asian teen entered the restaurant.

After a rousing discussion about what to order, each teen downed three soft drinks in under a minute, and we shared dolmas as appetizers, to mixed reviews, before each ordered his or her meal.

Detective Morgan walked in. I waved him over. "Want to join our merry band? I'm introducing our group to food other than American so-called food, meaning fast food." I looked at Mama Smith. "Or southern-fried everything."

Mama Smith playfully stuck out her tongue.

"Sorry. I can't, but if you have a moment, you'll save me the phone call I was going to make later."

Playing the game, I looked at Mama Smith. "That sounds mysterious." I took in the varied but attractive young faces staring at me. "I'll be right back. Don't eat all the pita chips and save some dolmas for me, please."

I followed him to the rear of the restaurant. He moved us into a vestibule leading to the restrooms. There was a payphone nearby.

I leaned into him, but he pushed me away. "Not here. Not now."

"What is it?"

"Augusta St. James is dead."

CHAPTER SEVENTEEN

Back at the table, I managed to get through dinner without raining on the kids' parade. When we left, I noticed all the cars along the street had one of those irritating advertisements stuck in the windshield. Inside mine was a single red rose.

The kids teased, but I said simply, "Now, that's advertising."

The next morning, in a few sentences, the *Gazette* detailed Augusta's death.

"Augusta St. James, detained when traveling to the islands under an assumed name for some suspected nefarious purpose, was extradited to Miami. Before her attorney could attain a trial date, she was fatally stabbed to death by another prisoner. Witnesses said the quarrel started over the return of a paperback book. No such book was discovered, however."

Daniel read the brief coverage to me over morning coffee. Our life went on. Augusta's couldn't.

Daniel informed me over lunch, "I've talked to Rhonda recently."

"I know."

His surprised expression changed to alarm. When there was no hysterics, he continued, "She's remarried."

"That's too bad," I said. "I've met someone I want to know better."

Daniel stared outside. After what seemed an eternity, he

retired to his recliner and grabbed the remote.

≡ ≡ ≡

Days after, Janet Jessell called Dixie Metcalf to report Augusta's death. Dixie fell into a black funk from which not even Carlotta could rouse her. She became irritable and the rapid failure of her memory increased her growing frustration level.

The physician at the facility gave her sedatives.

Carlotta thanked him and sat with her employer and friend.

Slightly more coherent a few days later, Dixie focused on Carlotta. "Oh hello, baby. Am I back in Georgia yet?"

Carlotta smiled, and took Dixie's hand. "Yes. Almost three weeks now."

Dixie turned her head away. "So the slide progresses."

Carlotta said softly, "It appears so."

"I can't remember much. Oh, wait. Did the widows' reunion take place? Was I there?"

"It did. You were not there this year. You'll be there next year."

"Did you go in my place as we discussed?"

"Yes. You will be happy to learn Mrs. Bernstein played us a rousing rendition of the "Merry Widow Waltz" on the steel drums. She looks fabulous. She has lost at least twenty pounds. You'll enjoy her story. She said at first she grew discouraged when her husband's agent dropped his representation for Ben's book. Becca didn't give up. She turned it into a testimonial cookbook, found another agent, and it's due out in a about a year, give or take. You know the publishing world."

Dixie smiled. "What were we talking about, darlin'?"

Carlotta wiped a tear from her eye. She stroked Dixie's forehead a moment.

Dixie grew agitated. "There was no other way. You understand, don't you, Georgiana? You forgive me, don't you?"

Carlotta, as a mercy, said, "Yes, Mother. I forgive you."

Dixie eased. "You're a good daughter. Augusta was my friend, too. We shared the same dark secret, though she didn't know that. After she told me of her past, I never enlightened her about mine. Then she stole that file. Friendship or not, I had to protect you. Call Carlotta. She has something for you, but I forget what it is." She yawned. "I'll remember it tomorrow."

"Yes, Mother, sleep now. You'll remember everything to-morrow." Carlotta went to her desk and wrapped the items in the Hermès silk scarf as they had discussed not so very long ago. She slipped them into the pouch and set the special de-livery into motion. This was one of the last things she could do for Mrs. Dixie Metcalf as she had known her.

≡ ≡ ≡

Daniel brought in a box. "It's addressed to Georgiana Dun-can. Huh? Neither postage nor a return address label is affixed to it. It was outside the front door."

I set it aside. "I'll open it later. I'll bet it's something from Missy Youngblood. What a pest. I'm happy I've resigned from the BILL."

"Now, Georgiana, it gave you such pleasure."

I looked at him as if he'd grown three heads.

"What are you studying?"

"This exam for the state board of realtors is a lot tougher than I thought it would be." I now worked four hours, two days a week, as a secretary in a realty office for a pittance. Didn't matter. I needed to learn the lingo. As Dixie Metcalf once said, the market would turn around. It might take an-other year or two, but I had a lot to learn in the meantime.

"Oh, that. I've given up on it. Who needs a new career at this stage in life? Darn"—he looked at his wrist watch—"I've got twenty minutes to make my tee time. I'll see you at din-ner, dear."

Absently, I replied, "Fine."

When the garage door opened then closed and the SUV drove away, I leaped up and ran for the telephone where I dialed the Merry Acres Police Department. "Detective Morgan, please."

When he barked his hello into the receiver, I smiled. "Are we still on for lunch?" He confirmed this in his abrupt, alpha male way, which thrilled me. "I'll see you at The Athenian Garden then."

I showered and took special care with my hair and makeup. This was silly and wrong, but, well, Daniel would agree, it took two to tango. He still had his little mind fling go-ing with Rhonda whose marriage was apparently already falling apart.

After calling a cab, dressed in a wrap-style dress of clingy navy jersey, I smiled in approval. I'd worked hard so that it fit well. I could lose another two or three pounds though as a reserve.

Still, I congratulated my success. I'd walked two miles every day at a fair clip. Daniel had excavated the exercise bike from the chaos piled in the golf cart garage and dragged it into the den where I pedaled for hours as I watched the tube with him, fantasizing about Mike. I became a regular at the club's exercise room, lifting dumbbells, and working my upper body on weight machines. Nothing short of zero gravity or surgery would get rid of the underarm flab starting to show.

Today, dressed and ready in my navy dress, I was walking out the door when I spied the mystery box. I should leave or I risked tardiness, something Mike hated. Morgan. I often called him by his last name, Morgan. A pirate's name that suited him no matter on what side of the law he trod.

"Really, Georgiana, how girlish." I stopped at the foyer mirror. "You're old enough to be his big sister." Fortunately, that wasn't how he thought of me.

The cab would be here any second. I couldn't stand it. I put down my purse, grabbed the box and tore it open. Out spilled an expensive scarf. Folded inside was something with heft. I unfurled it to reveal a worn paperback book by A. A. Audette titled, *Sun and Sand*.

"How strange."

A small wad of tissue paper fell onto the foyer table and I unwrapped it. Inside was the ruby pin Dixie Metcalf had worn at the first BILL meeting.

Three a's scripted in rubies: a.a.a.

Maybe the book held answers why Dixie would send this stuff to me. The only thing I found was a scrawl on the inside back cover: *Georgiana, darlin', you weren't dreaming.*

"Weird." Could Dixie have been the treasurer for that corporation Mendez and Augusta had set up? Was that why Augusta killed Mendez? He was replacing her with Dixie?

That didn't make sense. Dixie's handwritten message was the rambling of a fading mind. "Poor Dixie." Maybe some passage in the story was the key to this gift, or she'd absently asked someone at the assisted living place to send these to me. I'd return them, but I didn't have an address. Janet Jessell would know. I'd call her later.

Someday, when I had time, I would read the book. Come to think of it, perhaps the women at HELP would like to read it first. I'd take it by there. My heart fluttered. I'd take it after lunch with Morgan. I quickly attached the scarf that beautifully accented the stark blue dress. I could borrow this for one day. It made the outfit.

Wouldn't Dixie love that?

Further, I used the ruby pin to anchor it. The hard-to-read scripted letters created a unique design.

The cabbie honked.

I gave the cover one more glance. On it was an hour glass silhouetted against a bright orange sun. Same cover as on the paperback in Augusta's car. Yes. I must read it, but not now.

Now, I must hurry. I was late. For Morgan.

≡ ≡ ≡

At the restaurant, we greeted each other warmly. I'd recommended an allergist, and to my surprise, the detective had made an appointment and gone to see the doctor. He still sniffled some, but on the whole, looked and said he felt much better, less droopy than with other medications.

I was pleased I'd helped him, and very happy.

We'd agreed to let anticipation build further before our motel romp and this heightened the tension between us whenever we met. Only later, I knew, doubts about my sexual attractiveness would creep into my thoughts. I'd remembered some details of the night Augusta attacked me and had shared them with Mike.

And he still made dates with me. So, he must have some feeling for me.

We both ordered the specialty of the house and nibbled between small talk. I turned serious. "Is the Mendez case closed?"

He rolled an olive in his mouth, spit out the pit, chewed, and swallowed. "No, but it's turning stone cold. So, Augusta told you Susie might have killed Karl because she feared blackmail of some sort. But cause of death on Esterhause is still deemed natural causes. Without corroboration, a probe will go nowhere. Your word is just hearsay."

"Actually, more and more details about what was said in

that restroom are filtering in. Augusta said she did not kill Mendez. Nor did Augusta say Susie killed Mendez, only that she had a motive to do so. And maybe Karl. I don't buy that. Susie would know the spouse is the first person police check out. Augusta covered the opening of Dave's Dive Shop. I think she's the culprit." I bit carefully into a cherry tomato.

"I'll check with the dive shop. In my spare time." He gave a rueful laugh. "As for Mendez, my guess is Mrs. Mendez killed him. Conveniently, she was with her daughter, shopping, at the time of the murder. Rushing, she said, to pick something out to make your club deal on time. A clerk at Lulabelle's confirmed this."

He ate more salad and looked at me, allowing his brows to rise skeptically. "True? Who knows? Everybody knew Manny Mendez possessed a powerful wandering eye. Could have been a sympathetic half-truth on the clerk's part. Or good commerce by protecting a valued customer."

I said, "Blackmail money is where Augusta got the money to fly on that timeshare jet you mentioned and start over in what she called 'a tropical paradise.'"

Morgan nodded. "So she overheard two women discussing the murder weapon, you said."

"Did I say how many people Augusta overheard discussing the tire iron?" Absolute clarity about what was said might forever elude me. "What about Susie's scrapbooking party. Did that check out?"

"Mostly. Remember, Mr. Esterhause's death was ruled to be natural causes. I made inquiries on the off chance Augusta was telling you the truth, not merely providing disinformation."

"And?"

"Mrs. Esterhause held an open house kind of thing the day her husband died. It went on over several hours. That I verified with alleged attendees."

"So many women with secrets." *Like I'm different.* "What about Ben Bernstein? There's no secret there." I finished the last bite of my meal. "Is there?"

He looked at me and said nothing for a time. "Can you keep a secret?"

"Depends."

"No! Do you promise?"

"Cross my heart."

"Hope to die?" He chortled. "Bernstein drove a getaway car when he was a kid, seventeen, back in Jersey, a jewelry store heist. Maybe Augusta got wind of that. The woman was a world-class ferret. In fact, that's why she cozied up to anybody. Got close, listened to their life's tale. Learned dirt, then blackmailed them."

"What about the tire iron?"

"Never found. We dredged the pond. County divers found junk, weeds, but no tire iron." He finished his salad and called a waiter over. "Two baklavas." He looked at his watch. "No beer till later. Water for me, my nerves are jangly." He winked wickedly at me. "Greek coffee for the lady."

I blushed, hoping he was jangly in a sexually repressed way. "I don't see how that relates to Ben's heart attack."

Morgan raked his index finger across his forehead a couple of times. "Could be Augusta learned about the heist and the money, confronted him, and he dropped dead. There isn't any evidence his wife knew."

We sat silently when the dessert and drinks were served.

I carefully ate half the pastry. Then I told Morgan about the staged suicide in my garage, having grown to trust him. "Maybe Augusta slipped Ben a potassium-laced smoothie. He had atrial fibrillation. Potassium is prescribed to even the heart's rhythm, but too much, and it's lethal."

"That's curious. You know why? 'Cause an autopsy was requested, but Mrs. Bernstein refused permission. That's not unusual. We explained it was not optional. Turns out she'd served Ben banana pancakes for breakfast. His favorite, she said. Don't bananas contain potassium?"

"Not enough to do damage unless she mashed up an entire bunch in the batter."

Morgan smiled. "You like her, don't you? What if she served him banana pancakes for breakfast, knowing Augusta would meet him on the jogging trail with a smoothie, like she brought to you, only this one loaded with banana and potassium pills?"

"I don't get the connection. Why would Becca, who adored Ben, do that?"

He grinned, acknowledging my fondness for the Bernsteins. "What if Mrs. Bernstein learned about Ben's adolescent stroll on the wrong side of the law, via Augusta, or someone from his past? Fearful others would find out, tainting her reputation, or worse, her children's reputation, Mrs. B. was forced to take action. Things turned out well for her with that book and everything. Remember, this is pure conjecture."

I smiled, repeating the words he'd spoken once before. "Wildly creative thinking, though."

He said a rushed goodbye and leaned over to give me a meaningful stare. "Soon." He snatched up the other half of my baklava.

"Soon." I finished my coffee alone but elated.

That afternoon, to cut down on cab fare now that we only had one car between us, I rented a car. With my own wheels, I could drive to the HELP center. But that wasn't the real reason I rented the car. I wanted to meet Mike when and wherever.

On the drive home, I wondered if Becca could have possibly killed Ben for other reasons. Had things been as Ozzie-and-Harriet behind closed doors at the Bernstein house as appearances suggested?

Nobody better than I knew the trials and tribulations carried on behind closed doors. Maybe the public gentle Ben was a control freak at home. He had been pushing Becca hard for those recipes.

"Nah."

At home that night, as Daniel and I ate in silence, after a minor disagreement escalated into a cold war, I had further misgivings about the Bernsteins' marriage. Maybe retirement could drive a spouse to kill.

To avoid further argument, I retreated to the bedroom and read the paperback left clandestinely with the scarf and pin.

Halfway through, I made an astonishing connection.

The pin's three scripted a's could stand for triple-A bonds or A. A. Audette. The more I read, the more convinced I became that Audette was Dixie Metcalf. Dixie Metcalf, the woman who had abandoned me, was also the angel who saved my life.

Shocked, then angry, then hurt, I burst into tears.

Dixie was my mother.

How cruel fate was to bring me to Merry Acres to learn at long last who Mother was just as my mother's memory faded away.

Drying my eyes, I sought comfort. I called Mike's private number and left a message. "I'm ready for a red rose bouquet in an ocean-front room."

Mike sounded harried when he called back with details within the hour. We would meet the day after tomorrow.

≡ ≡ ≡

Naturally, I chose my undergarments with care, took particular pains with my hair and dress, trying on and taking off ten outfits before slipping on the blue silk pantsuit I'd worn to the first BILL meeting. Sunglasses completed the look.

At the rendezvous spot, I sat in my rental car and took deep breaths. The building was a coral-colored, three-story concrete block building, part of a national chain. Hibiscus hedges bordered the front. Bougainvillea climbed the side walls, loaded with pink flowers.

I went up the elevator to the second floor. The room's door wasn't locked. The night latch held the door open a crack. When I knocked, there was no answer, but I heard ocean waves even from the hallway. Maybe Mike was on the balcony.

"Hello?" I dared not use his name in case I'd misunderstood the room number.

Then, stepping inside, I saw it, the bouquet of red roses on the table near the sliding glass doors. I counted eleven. No dozen? He had one. Where was he? "Mike?" My eyes moved to the bed. One rose rested on the pillow. Beneath it, a note.

A game? My gut clenched.

With trembling hands, I opened the folded page that read.

G.

Sorry. Trust me, timing isn't right.

Meantime, I'm leaving the Merry Acres force for a better offer in Dallas.

M.

I staggered out to the balcony and drooped into a chair, staring out over the water for the longest time. Had I made an error when I talked frankly about my pity for Daniel? Mike had interpreted it the wrong way. Or, maybe he'd reconsidered. I was older, after all. How many men would prolong seduction as long as he had?

Maybe he was the noble sort.

Who better than I knew triangles had sharp points? Look where adultery had landed me after I broke up Daniel's home.

Still, my ego ached and my heart hurt, too.

Angry, I grabbed the vase and dumped the water into the bathroom sink. Foregoing the elevator this trip, lest anybody see me and point out the poor, jilted older woman with her waterless roses, I hurried down the stairwell out to the car. I removed my jacket, slung it in the back seat and rolled up the long-sleeved blouse. Hot, mad, and hurt, I pondered where to go.

Flooring it, I drove to the gravesite of Merry Montgomery.

There, ignoring thorns and barbs from the roses stabbing my fingers, I climbed through more branches and brambles tearing at my pants. It took forever to find the damned marker, but I finally did. I dumped the flowers on it.

"Enjoy, Merry."

The sun glinted on something metallic under the flowers, and it wasn't the marker.

Figuring it was probably a gum wrapper, I left.

Halfway to my car, something made me go back, thinking whatever it was might be another message from Mike. Some further explanation. Yes, I was now delusional and lovesick.

Bending down, I carefully removed the roses, noticing the marker was askew. Some metal piece was jammed at the corner and lured me to lift the marker.

When I did, I discovered the metal was gold. A wedding ring.

There was an inscription engraved on the inside band, *Forever, Karl.*

Was this Susie's wedding ring? It hadn't been here when Mike brought me here. A message? And from whom? No, just a widow leaving a farewell token to Merry Acres was my guess. I didn't know when Susie had come, but it didn't matter.

At the moment, I didn't really care. My pride, my wounded heart, and my fingers hurt. I threw the ring on the ground. That's when I noticed that beneath the marker was a shallow metal box for which the marker acted as a lid. Although small, the granite was heavy, and I grunted when I shoved the marker away for a better look.

Inside were two...four...six wedding rings, including what might be Susie's. This damn place was a shrine. Figured. Discarded wedding rings were suitable trinkets to adorn Merry Montgomery's grave, adding another layer to her growing urban myth.

I entertained the idea of tossing my own ring inside, but deferred. Better, I'd like to toss Mike's head in there.

"Time to go." I picked up Susie's ring and threw it in with the others.

This time, when I turned to follow the path back, I tripped on something under a brush pile.

Mad, I kicked at it and squawked. Whatever it was, it was hard. Now my foot hurt.

I toed away pine needles and branches to see what had attacked me.

It was a tire iron.

I grabbed my cell phone back at the car. After dialing his cell, I heard a curt message indicating the subscriber was not accepting messages. I dialed the police station.

When the precinct person answered, I said authoritatively, "Mike Morgan."

"He's left."

"When will he be back? This is important police business."

"He's not coming back."

"He's already gone?"

"Yesterday was his last day."

"Yesterday?"

"Yeah."

"Who is in charge of the Mendez murder case? I have pertinent information."

When connected, I related my discovery and general whereabouts.

Told to wait where I was, I did. Almost an hour.

After the usual name, address, occupation, I got, "You found this?"

"I haven't touched it." I stared into the cold, blue eyes of Mike Morgan's young, blond replacement. If I'd expected a gold star, I wasn't getting one. I didn't mention the wedding rings. Let junior find them. I'd worry about my fingerprints all over the marker later. And those all over Susie's ring, if it was her ring.

"What were you doing here?"

"Leaving flowers. It is a gravesite. You have heard of Meredith Montgomery, haven't you?" I barely hid my contempt, but ninety percent of my attitude was anger at Mike, and life.

"I'll be in touch." The cop lifted the metal rod with latex-gloved hands.

"Whatever." I took my aching heart, sore digits, and throbbing foot home.

There, I discovered Daniel gone. "Perfect." I made a blender full of strawberry daiquiris.

The doorbell chimed. "What now?"

Something arrived by express delivery.

I signed for it, opened a legal-sized envelope and read the first page. As usual, good news and bad. Bad news, especially for Dixie Metcalf. The message stated Dixie was dead. Good news was I was not only suddenly wealthy, but the new head honcho of the sizeable Metcalf Foundation.

More bad news. To go with my new responsibilities, I was named in a lawsuit over control of the entity. The bringer of the suit was Michael Morgan, stepson of Philip Morgan, the half-brother of Chester Metcalf.

"Michael Morgan?"

I dialed the contact number in Georgia referenced in the cover letter, and spoke with a woman named Carlotta.

"Don't fret. We'll get through this. First thing"—which sounded to me like "first ting"—"come to Widow's Rest. We must orient you and see to a proper send off for Mrs. Metcalf."

Less than enthused, I listened to the other woman who rattled off an itinerary that matched the airline ticket in the number-ten-sized envelope stapled to the legal brief.

I barely had time to grab my passport, throw a few things in a suitcase, and leave a note for Daniel before a limo picked me up and drove me way down to Broward County where an IDA commuter jet awaited. In hours, I arrived on the island of Alandira, which I'd never heard of before Augusta St. James had fled there, but soon learned was a tiny jewel for the ultra rich in the turquoise waters of the Gulf Stream, accessible only by plane or yacht.

In a beautiful courtyard, I loaned my body to a masseuse who gently kneaded away anxiety. Why had Mike come on to me?

There could be only one answer, an answer my vanity would not appreciate. He'd toyed with me to find out what I knew about Dixie and the foundation, of course. Why had he taken me to that gravesite? To read my actions, fearing I'd learned that was where he, or possibly Susie, had hidden the tire iron? I now suspected the real reason he'd aborted our little red-roses-romp was not some noble gesture but so as not to shake the better-offer boat waiting for him in Dallas.

"Better offer, ha!"

"Excuse me, miss?"

"Nothing." What was Mike doing at this hour to protect, or perhaps placate, the widow of Mr. Karl Esterhause? Mike specifically said during our musings that I had told him Augusta overheard two people talking tire irons. I never said how many women were discussing tire irons because the memory of that talk had just returned. The two people might not have been women at all; perhaps Augusta overheard Mike Morgan and Susie Esterhause.

When I mentioned this to Carlotta, also on Alandira now, the woman beamed. "How timely. Sources within the Merry Acres police force just notified me Mike Morgan's fingerprints were lifted off the tire iron found at the grave site."

"Great, I just implicated Mike Morgan in Manny Mendez's murder." I had mixed feelings.

"Here's a photo you might enjoy, under the circumstances."

It was a picture of a society event in Dallas, Texas. Mike wore a tuxedo. On his arm was a blonde who looked an awful lot like the former Mrs. Karl Esterhause.

"Thank you. I needed that," I said. "Another piña colada would be welcome, too."

Earlier, on the flight to Alandira, I'd had an epiphany. Considering I'd almost been killed in the women's room at the Barrier Isles Golf and Country Club a short time ago, I appreciated how precious life was.

The ton of money I had inherited from a lifelong-missing mom made up for some of the hurt and anger created by growing up alone. My first charitable act would be to send a check to the HELP shelter. Then I'd call Aunt Irene and send her flowers. Next, I'd buy back Daniel's Vette, or get him a new one. Maybe not a vintage model, but a Corvette.

It was time to forgive and forget. It was time to live. Would I ever reunite with Mike? No. I worried over exactly when Dixie's will had been made. The woman had suffered from a debilitating mental disease. My newfound status could disappear as rapidly as her memory, depending on which way a judge ruled.

What means could I use to hold on to what was mine?

Taking a leaf from Dixie's optimistic book, I promised myself that from this day forward, I would adhere to the rule "living well is the best revenge." Harder would be her advice to think positively.

In a better mood, mellowed by philosophy and liquor, I lay in my room on the comfortable bed and stared up at a brilliant white canopy. I felt safe in this cocoon.

I'd be called to testify about how I found the tire iron. My spin on who had originally taken me to that spot might be a bargaining chip, and an olive branch. That and agreeing to relinquish part of the estate to Mike might go a long way to keeping some, or most, of my inheritance.

≡ ≡ ≡

The last time I saw Mike was at trial.

As I suspected, when asked to testify about how I came upon Merry Montgomery's marker, I said I'd acted on a rumor about the legend of Merry Montgomery. I'd come upon it by chance, drawn there like many women in the community, looking for a place to vent frustrations from a less-than-stellar marriage.

Mike's attorney, naturally, presented a case wherein his client merely stopped to help Manny Mendez change a flat tire, thus explaining his fingerprints on the murder weapon and, that when he'd left Mr. Mendez, he'd been in perfect health. The glitch was no witnesses could corroborate this.

Susie Esterhause denied knowing anything about any tire iron when Mike's attorney suggested she'd come upon Manny and killed him after Mike had changed his tire and left. He suggested the tools were scattered about and she, wearing gloves, picked up the murder weapon and killed Manny, later planting it where it could be found to incriminate Mike Morgan, thereby clearing herself.

The prosecutor objected this was all speculation and the judge sustained his objection.

Susie vehemently denied any involvement with Manny and claimed she knew Mike socially, period. The photo of her and Mike at the Dallas soiree put rather a damper on that. Always attractive, she positively radiated as a grieving widow in black, a pretty contrast with her fair skin and blonde hair.

The jury, six men and six women, deadlocked.
A new trial was called for.
Mike could get lucky yet.
Or not.

≡ ≡ ≡

One day out of the blue, while back in Merry Acres, Augusta's tale about Daniel's part in the staged carbon monoxide suicide landed with a thud in my mind.

"Something came back to me. Augusta said she planned my demise by carbon monoxide poisoning. See, didn't I tell you that smoothie was loaded?"

Daniel fidgeted nervously.

"What's wrong? Are you late for something? Go, we can finish this chat later."

"What else do you remember that she said about that?"

"Nothing. Wait. Oh, yes. She said she caught you in a weak moment and convinced you to go along. For insurance money. I told her right then I didn't believe her. What a liar. Good one, though, gotta say." I waited for a belly laugh from Daniel. What I got was an ashen face in response. "Daniel? She was lying, wasn't she?"

"Of course."

I felt sick. I didn't need years of experience reading faces across a card table to know he'd just lied to me.

≡ ≡ ≡

Wary of Daniel, I moved to Widow's Rest on Alandira to settle the estate while Daniel stayed in the Merry Acres golf villa.

One day, Carlotta brought in a pretty confectioner's box delivered, she said, by an attractive man.

I untied the red ribbon bow and peeked inside. Baklava. "*Where* is the person who brought this?"

"Waiting for you at the island hotel bar and it's not Mike Morgan."

"Oh, he wouldn't bother, even if he could." I shrugged. "Come with me to meet the mystery man, will you? Could be some con artist."

"Of course."

Our driver waited as we two hurried along the pathway to the hotel, through the lobby, and down a series of steps to a bar set in a lush, tropical setting.

I waved the red box, and a man sitting by himself in a corner responded by lifting his hand. Carlotta and I walked to his table.

"Mrs. Duncan, is that regret in your expression?"

"No," I lied to the handsome man with piercing eyes and thinning black hair.

"I apologize for the theatrics, but a client insisted I deliver a token of his esteem personally. As I have another client on the island, the timing proved fortuitous."

Waiters dashed over upon recognizing the two most famous women on Alandira.

"Soda," I said. It was too early to drink at this time of day.

"The same," said Carlotta.

The man's eyes roamed over to Carlotta. "I'd rather discuss matters privately."

"Not possible." I rose as if to leave.

Carlotta said, "You know, I fancy a walk on the beach."

The attorney nodded. "Thank you."

When Carlotta was out of ear shot, I huffed, "Well?"

The man removed an envelope from his briefcase and handed it to me.

"I must have that back once you've read it."

"Burn after reading?"

The man's slow smile answered the question.

I recognized Mike's handwriting and almost crumpled the note, but read on.

It read:

I really did find you attractive. You weren't like the others in Merry Acres and you tugged at my heart strings, as well as other areas of my anatomy. But Susie was, well, Susie. Besides, you didn't expect a superhero to bed one woman while planning a future with another, did you?

Oh, and no hard feelings about the lawsuit. I never dreamed you were the person Dixie named in her will. I sort of got pushed into things by anxious relatives and wanted to support Susie in the manner to which she was accustomed.

Not that it matters now.

I wish I'd met you before Susie and not a day goes by I don't think of you.

As honor demanded, I returned the note. The man removed a lighter and burned it in my presence.

"Perhaps you can satisfy my curiosity, Mr.—?"

"My name is of no importance. For all practical purposes, we have never met."

"All right. I assume your client took a personal interest in me to determine what Augusta St. James might have told me germane to Mendez. He prolonged his attentions, waiting for my memory to heal after my head injury, to see if I would say something incriminating about him or Susie. Why would he have ever taken me to a place where he would have either taken Susie or hidden a murder weapon?"

"I can't say."

"Can't, or won't?"

"I don't know on the one hand, and it would be unethical to discuss anything my client may have told me in confidence on the other. I can give you a hypothetical situation. Say an honorable man, a law enforcement officer, fell in love with the wrong woman. The wrong sort of woman. He might do anything to protect her and would be in a position to do so. Including what might seem, on the surface, using others. He might also retain a subconscious desire to confess, but couldn't for fear of hurting his love interest. Do you understand?"

"I think so. So your client took me to the one place he was most vulnerable should his love interest double-cross him. Why would she do that?"

"That I don't know either but, speculating, she may have heard rumors about my client and you prolonging an...association, not believing him when he said it was for the good of everyone involved. She, perhaps, worried her status had been jeopardized."

"Hell hath no fury."

"Possibly. More likely, it was sheer luck you went to that place when you did, discovered what you did, and notified authorities when you did. My client is innocent of murder."

I remembered what Mike said about Mrs. Mendez. Looking over the courtyard, I watched happy tourists imbibe tall drinks in hollowed-out pineapples garnished with miniature umbrella frills. Part of me believed Mike was honorable.

"You are a wise woman, Mrs. Duncan. Your offer to grant my client a quarter of the Metcalf estate was prudent. I've seen people come to blows over a dollar. Of course, your pro-vision to be free of all future interference in administering the foundation was wise, too."

Not to mention my twisted testimony on his behalf. I al-most asked how the new trial was going, but thought better of it. "Goodbye. I suddenly fancy a walk on the beach, too."

"Wait." He rushed after me, handing me the red box I'd left on the table.

Briefly, I considered Daniel and Mike before my thoughts latched onto hopeful beginnings and regrettable endings. Was there a Chester out there for me? A soul mate? Perhaps, but he would be in my future. Not my past. "Thank your client, but relay my regrets. I'm on a diet. A strict one."

The lawyer bowed his head and returned to his table, the red box in his hand.

My eyes misted as I walked out along the water's edge, catching up to Carlotta.

Carlotta said nothing as we strolled along, no doubt sens-ing silence would be more healing than words.

Suddenly, we heard running steps behind us.

The lawyer, hardly winded, said. "Please, another mo-ment. May I suggest you banish a bitter memory with a sweet one?" He held out a confectioner's cup holding one baklava.

When I didn't respond, he said, "Baklava is good, but I prefer *kataifi* or *kourabiedes,* which I've enjoyed at many nup-tials, but as yet, not at my own."

"So, you're familiar with Greek pastries, and unmarried?"

"A bone of contention in my family circle, especially as I approach fifty."

"I would assume so." *Was he gay?*

"I've been busy with career matters and just never met the right woman. The right *Greek* girl."

"You're Greek?"

"Global ancestry, but the woman who holds my heart is my Greek grandmother."

"I see."

In that case, I took the confection and took a bite. "Your advice to replace a bitter memory with a sweet one is sound." I chewed slowly, looking into his eyes. Eyes as blue as the Ae-gean sea despite his dark complexion and black hair. "Bitter memories are evaporating already. As I said, I'm on a diet. Perhaps you'd like the rest of this?"

He accepted it and ate as slowly as I had, perhaps to extend the moment. "Thank you. Perhaps fate will favor us and we'll meet again when...obligations to my client are met."

I smiled and shrugged. "Who knows?"

"Until we meet again."

"Goodbye." I walked on to catch up to Carlotta again but, on a whim, turned to glimpse his hastily departing back. "Oh well."

She said, "He'll turn."

"I don't think so. Some con man. He is an attorney, after all."

"What was dat you said earlier about positive tinkin'?"

"Okay, I'll look back, but it's your fault if I turn to salt."

Global Man turned, as if he knew I'd be watching. He waved.

And I waved back.

EPILOGUE

Months later, at the hillside manor known as Widow's Retreat on the Caribbean island of Alandira, a group of women gathered.

They discussed the death of Augusta St. James. Given her compulsion for glibness, no one was much surprised at her death. One verbal jab too many and, despite her size, a stronger, angrier street warrior had handily dispatched Augusta to the great deadline in the sky.

Also on this year's agenda was a sad duty, the spreading of the ashes of their friend, known to some as A. A. Audette, to others as Dixie, to others as Mrs. Metcalf, and recently, to me, as Mother.

As a special invitee this year, I attended not as a widow, but as new owner of the estate. Everyone remarked how serene I looked. My explanation? I had found peace. Why? At last, I'd found home.

I knew many of the women. Among them was Becca Bernstein. New to the gathering this year was Lourdes Valdez, following Carlos' death in a plane crash in South America. Meredith Montgomery's curse had a long reach, apparently. Susie Esterhause couldn't make it as she was currently in Florida under a grand jury probe. Far, far away from Mike Morgan and her hometown near Dallas, where daddy was a major wheel in a minor oil company. She had big-deal lawyers working for her, however, and might make future retreats.

With a solemn nod to Carlotta, I acknowledged the time had come to begin the ceremony. She and I joined hands briefly before lifting a sterling silver urn and, taking turns, sprinkled Dixie's cremated remains out into a gentle Caribbean breeze.

The widows wept and Carlotta sobbed.

I said softly, "Don't cry." Even though tears wet my own cheeks. "She and Chester are somewhere, even now, waltz-ing."

My tears were many. Some for Dixie, the mother I never really knew, and also Morgan, my pirate, and what might have been.

I wept, too, for Daniel and what we once had. I tried never to think of his lapse during that dark period when he almost allowed me to die for financial gain. He and I grew more dis-tant with each passing day. Especially since I'd relocated to the island and signed over the Merry Acres home to him, along with the mortgage.

Merry Acres wags reported a widow, Sonja, had moved next door.

The man I was once gaga for definitely had an *a*-ending fixation. His first wife had been named Amanda, then me, then Rhonda, then possibly Augusta, and now Sonja. Rumors zinging around Merry Acres, compliments of Janet Jessell, re-ported Sonja frequently ferried casseroles to 112 Carnoustie Way. Furthermore, Sonja and Daniel tooled around Merry Acres in his new vintage blue-and-white Vette on a regular basis.

No matter. In time, I would be a member of the widow's retreat as a widow, if first as a divorcee. I thought of Mike's lawyer. At his age, he might not want children and he'd defi-nitely appeared interested. A long shot, but who knew what my future held.

In the background, "Merry Widow Waltz" played. Dixie, who had loved all dance, especially the waltz, had insisted that the song of special significance to widows be performed at every annual retreat. Only the musical style changed. This year, a string quartet performed the melody.

The wedding rings secreted in Meredith's grave stone, and never discovered by Mike's junior policeman replacement or his cohorts, were smuggled to Alandira, at my request, where I commissioned an island artist to fashion them into a wind chime. Dancing merrily on Caribbean winds, the seven rings, mine among them, played their own song.

As a tribute to Meredith Montgomery, I purchased a new

grave marker, a headstone, and had the site cleared and bordered with a low-lying fence. Who knew what wife might come to pay homage when things in her marriage went awry. Next, I gathered copies of old photos from the *Gazette*'s morgue, the library, and other sources, and commissioned her portrait, which I donated to the Barrier Isles Golf and Country Club.

Merry now graced the clubhouse above a marble ledge in the reception area. The marker remained at her final resting place, although the underlying box was empty now, so far as any of us knew. It would remain so, at least until Merry beckoned another wronged woman to Merry Acres, possibly adding another ring one day in the future.

I hoped Merry was pleased. I knew I was.

THE END

ABOUT THE AUTHOR

Nan lives with her husband, three felines, and a million characters chattering inside her head.

LaVergne, TN USA
26 March 2011
221706LV00001B/15/P